Anthony Gilbert and The Murder Room

》》》 This title is part of The Murder Room, our series dedicated to making available out-of-print or hard-to-find titles by classic crime writers.

Crime fiction has always held up a mirror to society. The Victorians were fascinated by sensational murder and the emerging science of detection; now we are obsessed with the forensic detail of violent death. And no other genre has so captivated and enthralled readers.

Vast troves of classic crime writing have for a long time been unavailable to all but the most dedicated frequenters of second-hand bookshops. The advent of digital publishing means that we are now able to bring you the backlists of a huge range of titles by classic and contemporary crime writers, some of which have been out of print for decades.

From the genteel amateur private eyes of the Golden Age and the femmes fatales of pulp fiction, to the morally ambiguous hard-boiled detectives of mid twentieth-century America and their descendants who walk our twenty-first century streets, The Murder Room has it all. **》》》**

The Murder Room
Where Criminal Minds Meet

themurderroom.com

T0351832

Anthony Gilbert (1899–1973)

Anthony Gilbert was the pen name of Lucy Beatrice Malleson. Born in London, she spent all her life there, and her affection for the city is clear from the strong sense of character and place in evidence in her work. She published 69 crime novels, 51 of which featured her best known character, Arthur Crook, a vulgar London lawyer totally (and deliberately) unlike the aristocratic detectives, such as Lord Peter Wimsey, who dominated the mystery field at the time. She also wrote more than 25 radio plays, which were broadcast in Great Britain and overseas. Her thriller *The Woman in Red* (1941) was broadcast in the United States by CBS and made into a film in 1945 under the title *My Name is Julia Ross*. She was an early member of the British Detection Club, which, along with Dorothy L. Sayers, she prevented from disintegrating during World War II. Malleson published her autobiography, *Three-a-Penny*, in 1940, and wrote numerous short stories, which were published in several anthologies and in such periodicals as *Ellery Queen's Mystery Magazine* and *The Saint*. The short story 'You Can't Hang Twice' received a Queens award in 1946. She never married, and evidence of her feminism is elegantly expressed in much of her work.

Lady-Killer (1951)

Miss Pinnegar Disappears (1952)
  aka *A Case for Mr Crook*

Footsteps Behind Me (1953)
  aka *Black Death*

Snake in the Grass (1954)
  aka *Death Won't Wait*

Is She Dead Too? (1955)
  aka *A Question of Murder*

And Death Came Too (1956)

Riddle of a Lady (1956)

Give Death a Name (1957)

Death Against the Clock (1958)

Death Takes a Wife (1959)
  aka *Death Casts a Long Shadow*

Third Crime Lucky (1959)
  aka *Prelude to Murder*

Out for the Kill (1960)

She Shall Die (1961)
  aka *After the Verdict*

Uncertain Death (1961)

No Dust in the Attic (1962)

Ring for a Noose (1963)

The Fingerprint (1964)

The Voice (1964)
  aka *Knock, Knock! Who's There?*

Passenger to Nowhere (1965)

The Looking Glass Murder (1966)

The Visitor (1967)

Night Encounter (1968)
  aka *Murder Anonymous*

Missing from Her Home (1969)

Death Wears a Mask (1970)
  aka *Mr Crook Lifts the Mask*

Murder is a Waiting Game (1972)

Tenant for the Tomb (1971)

A Nice Little Killing (1974)

Standalone Novels

The Case Against Andrew Fane (1931)

Death in Fancy Dress (1933)

The Man in Button Boots (1934)

Courtier to Death (1936)
  aka *The Dover Train Mystery*

The Clock in the Hatbox (1939)

Death at Four Corners

Anthony Gilbert

An Orion book

Copyright © Lucy Beatrice Malleson 1929

The right of Lucy Beatrice Malleson to be identified as the author of this work has been asserted in accordance with the Copyright, Designs and Patents Act 1988.

This edition published by
The Orion Publishing Group Ltd
Orion House
5 Upper St Martin's Lane
London WC2H 9EA

An Hachette UK company
A CIP catalogue record for this book is available from the British Library

ISBN 978 1 4719 1042 5

www.orionbooks.co.uk

CHAPTER I

"A deed of dreadful note."—Macbeth.

I

DOCTOR TERENCE AMBROSE was one of those unfortunate men who are compelled to do their own shopping because there is no one who will do it for them. Belonging, as he candidly acknowledged to the exasperating army of those who lose nine-tenths of their possessions and break the remainder, he showed his wisdom by burdening himself with as few belongings as possible. It would have been obvious to any woman that he classed a wife among the luxuries; his clothes betrayed that. Carrying a sandwich board he would have seemed in costume; his pockets bagged, the knees of his trousers bagged, the brims of his disreputable hats bagged; he gave the impression of having stripped a peg for a guinea. Yet in his Irish practice he was popular enough, although the men and women he brought into the world were seldom grateful; the older folk usually ascribed their cures to some herb or simple of their own or in a last resort to the parish priest, and none of them dreamed of paying his bills. On an insignificant legacy he struggled along, shabby, amused, indefatigable, being universally fleeced, aware of it but too lazy to take any defensive measures.

An unexpected collapse in his own health brought him to London to see a certain specialist in the late summer of 1927 and incidentally involved him in that most perplexing tangle known as the Four Corners mystery.

Finding himself one morning in September in a shopping neighbourhood Ambrose entered the first large store he espied and hazily demanded shirts. The very salesman perceived immediately that he was dealing with an imbecile and proceeded to load him with the throw-outs of last year's stock. Ambrose glanced with anguished perplexity from violet to plum, from plum to dove-grey, from grey to green, and was aware of sudden and overwhelming relief when someone spoke his name. Turning, he saw a tall fine-drawn man in clerical garb, with thick grey hair, extraordinarily deep-set blue eyes and a haggard expression. His own momentary silence was not due to astonishment so much as to dismay at the metamorphosis the years had wrought. He and Gervase Blount had been intimate at Balliol, whence the latter had departed to read for the Bar, while Ambrose, who had no very definite plans, found himself suddenly pitchforked into medical practice. After his return to Ireland the two men met little, though Ambrose had heard of the other's unexpected abandoning of a brilliant career in favour of Holy Orders, on the peculiar ground that mere justice alone would never solve the human problem. He was of that small army of remarkable men who believe that it is capable of solution.

"Forgot you were a cleric," murmured Ambrose tactlessly. "Got a London job these days?"

Blount shook his head; it was a fine head and his face was scholarly and handsome, despite its worn appearance. No greater sartorial contrast than these two could well be conceived. Blount had a distinguished air and a perfect tailor; Ambrose had neither.

"Up for a conference," the priest explained. "And you?"

"Some confounded bug has had the devilish impertinence to take up its residence in my blood," returned Ambrose with some heat. "And a chap called Ferguson and myself are corralling it. A case," he added with a grin, "of 'Man, know thyself.' Yes, what is it?"

The haughty young assistant had interrupted them to know what Ambrose proposed to do about the shirts.

"Well," demanded the doctor irritably, "what do you advise?"

"I really couldn't say, sir," answered the young man with a distant glance.

"Then why the devil not? If you came to me with an abscess on the liver would you expect me to ask you your opinion of it? Wouldn't you expect me to treat it? Of course you would. And aren't you here to sell shirts? And who, sir, gave you the job of selling shirts if you're so incompetent that you can't even advise me as to colour and cut?"

The assistant, shocked and alarmed by this development, hastily endeavoured to repair his blunder, but at that instant a shopwalker appeared to conciliate the offended client. Three minutes later Ambrose and the clergyman left the department, the former with a huge parcel under one arm and in the other hand a tattered paper list that frequent handling had rendered illegible.

"Why not put in a long week-end with us?" suggested his companion with some eagerness. "There are one or two people staying in the house—my member, a young chap called Scott Egerton and his wife, an interesting pair, and you must meet Pamela."

No, decided Ambrose, whatever it was that had laid that weight on his spirit it wasn't his wife. No mistaking the fellow's attitude. He worshipped the ground she walked on. That infernal bishop, probably. But it was odd that a man so violently in love should be simultaneously so wretched. His manner forbade questions. Ambrose had intended to discover how his new avocation suited him, to learn all those small but essential details that mark the great changes in men's lives, but he found himself compelled by delicacy to a sympathetic silence. Affection for his friend, however, together with an insatiable love of people and a loathing of London that was more prosperous and blatant than he hitherto remembered it, turned the scale and he said "Yes. Good scheme. What about Tuesday? A man I don't like wants me to lunch with him on Tuesday."

2

When Ambrose reached the small by-station of Little Kirbey, that links Four Corners up with civilisation, he saw no one on the sun-baked platform but a composed, slenderly built young man whose exquisite clothes were as great a contrast to Ambrose's shiftlessness as could be conceived.

There was a fresh wind blowing outside, despite

the unusual heat of the late September sun, but not a hair of the young man's head was disarrayed. The train, after the manner of unimportant country connections, was twenty minutes late, but no shadow of boredom or annoyance marred the serenity of his expression. As Ambrose tumbled out of his carriage— he was an essentially ungraceful man—and hesitated, the stranger approached, said, "Dr. Ambrose? My name's Egerton. Blount sends all due apologies, but he has unexpectedly to be in Tenbeigh to-day, and commissioned me to meet you instead," and offered his hand.

"Very good of you," said Ambrose cheerfully. "I say, half a minute. I must stop that devil of a porter. That bag's only held together with string, and he's handling it as if it were steel." He raced down the platform with one bootlace flapping, and with complete sang-froid explained the position.

"Do we ride, drive or fly?" he demanded, returning shortly to rejoin the young exquisite.

"I thought we might walk, unless you prefer the station cab. A pretty frowsty vehicle that, and the road is insufferable. You can't drive a car here, the roads weren't built for anything but buggies and gigs. But walking will give you a rare insight into the indefinable charm of the English countryside."

So the porter was left in charge of the tatterdemalion box and the oddly assorted couple set off, striking away from the road into some particularly gloomy moorland, that presently showed sparse signs of cultivation in the shape of tumbledown fences and walls. The ground made very uneven going and was thickly sown with burdock and thistle; brambles meandered incorrigibly across the narrow path the pair followed, and more than once they had to stop and beat them aside with their sticks.

"Are we saving much time by coming on this pestilential road?" asked Ambrose politely, as he disentangled his burberry from a peculiarly fierce thorn, too late, however, to save it.

Egerton glanced at the rent with expert eyes. "I can mend that for you with a bit of Dunlop repair outfit," he observed. "No, we don't save a tremendous amount in time, but the road is so unspeakably monotonous."

Ambrose preserved a discreet and unusual silence, and they pushed their way through a gap and began to climb the steep, uneven ground, turning, as the wind warned them, seaward.

"Are we far from the sea at Four Corners?" the doctor wanted to know.

"Practically on the edge. It's built a bit askew on a cliff, a particularly pleasant cliff that threatens to crumble and land us all in dissolution whenever the storm is heavy. But they say in the village that a fate protects the house. In the sixteenth century—yes, it's quite an old place—the owner, a Sir Marvell Blount, sheltered a beggar who turned out to be Christ (that's the legend), and in return the house is to be safe so long as it's in the hands of the Blounts. We're almost there now," he added five minutes later. "You can catch a glimpse of the house through those trees. That wood incidentally is also supposed to be of miraculous extraction. It flourishes and apparently provides its own soil. Nice place, isn't it? It's one of Blount's favourite walks."

They halted and stood staring out to sea. The tide was very low and the bright sunlight lit silver fires

6

on the ribbed sands. The black tower of the Penywern Lighthouse rose up sinister against the blue sky, and there was no bird nor boat in sight, not even a child walking along the edge of the sea.

"Quicksands," explained Egerton briefly, meeting his companion's inquiring glance. "If we follow this path we shall strike what's vaingloriously called the carriage road in thirty seconds; it runs round the fences of Blount's estate; this is a short cut. Mind your step."

"I don't know that I particularly appreciate those rocks," Ambrose confessed, gingerly moving a little further inland; "you keep to the cliff-edge if you like." For the sides of the cliff at this point were precipitous and grown sparsely with stunted trees and bushes covered with shrivelled black buds and straggling bramble plants.

"There's a path somewhere just here, down the side of the cliff, I believe. All right if you know your way, but a chance slip would land you among those charmingly pointed rocks. However"—his voice changed to a detestable drawl that made the older man yearn to kick him—"it's perfectly safe if you take reasonable care." He went on in front, for the path along the cliff-edge was no wider than a cattle-rut and they had to proceed in single file. Ambrose looked down unappreciatively—and stopped.

"I suppose the last chap didn't take reasonable care," he said in a dry voice, though he was sweating under his skin.

Something in his tone surprised his companion, who turned like a flash and stood staring downwards.

"What? Where?"

Ambrose pointed. "Just below that withered ash,

7

where that sort of platform hangs over the sea—result of a landslide, I should imagine. You can see him quite clearly."

Egerton, disposed to be impatient, asked, "Sure it isn't one of those blackthorns that were uprooted in last month's storms? There were several flung clean out of the earth along the coast here."

"Oh, teach your grandmother," retorted the doctor contemptuously. "I was doing this sort of thing when you were in your pram."

Egerton came closer and stood beside him, shading his eyes with his hand. "You're right," he acknowledged, "and I beg your pardon." He had a maddening knack of taking the wind out of other men's sails. "It is a man." They could both see him clearly now, a black, spread-eagled figure, lying perilously near the edge of the platform, on his face; beyond the fact that he was wearing black they could make out no details. Egerton stooped and picked up a stone; both men listened and after an endless time, very, very far away the faintest of concussions struck their ears.

"Nasty fall that," observed the young man coolly. "Further than it looks from this height. Any idea how far up we are?" He told him casually and Ambrose whistled. "If that unfortunate chap had chosen to slither a few feet either way," Egerton went on, "he'd have been with the stone by now and there'd have been no hope. As it is . . ." Thoughtfully he tested the ground under his feet. "Spongy," he remarked. "We shall have to go down, of course. Fellow may be alive. Wonder where exactly that path is."

"May not be here at all," rejoined Ambrose gloomily.

"Oh, yes, I fancy so. That platform isn't a new thing at all. There's a note in one of the old Blount records of its having been used by smugglers. I dare say there are—or were once—caves at the bottom. They cut the steps, you know. I'll find 'em in a minute."

Ambrose sighed. He was anything but prepossessed by the position; he disliked precipitous cliffs and hidden stairways and mysterious bodies. He wanted a rest and he felt that he was about to be embroiled in a complicated tangle that would probably have precisely the opposite effect. In which he was right. For the third time he looked over the cliff-side. The descent appeared to him steep and dangerous; so far as he could see from the top the platform was of a natural malformation about nine feet wide and eight feet long, jutting clear out of the side of the rock.

He was still observing it with distaste when Egerton murmured coolly, "I thought as much," and slipped unconcernedly over the edge. An instant later his face was on a level with the doctor's boots. Ambrose watched him, lithe and steady and fearless, feeling his way down that apparently impossible precipice. Like a grey fly the fellow looked, getting smaller with every movement. He sighed. It was inconceivable that any harm should befall Egerton. No rocks were impossible to him, no deserts utterly pathless. If he had guaranteed to cross the Sahara without guide or compass all his friends would have backed him to do it. Ambrose, being an average man and more than normally clumsy, thought that he would most likely miss his footing and crash to an inglorious death among the rocks.

"Look out for this tree as you come down," called Egerton calmly, his voice expressing a faint surprise that the doctor should still be on *terra firma*. "It's been hauled nearly out of the earth recently; one good rip and it would pitch overboard."

"I expect the fellow down there cannoned into it as he fell," Ambrose remarked, reluctantly following Egerton over the side.

The latter turned his head over his shoulder in a way that would have made the doctor giddy; he seemed deep in calculation.

"Shouldn't think it's likely. If he'd ricochetted against that he'd have missed the platform altogether." A moment later he had set foot on the ledge and was stamping on it vigorously with his heel.

"Funny that," he remarked. The platform itself was covered with thick coarse grass, closely matted, with wild sea-flowers, growing haphazard among the chalky stones with which the surface was strewn, in odd contrast with the top of the cliff that was innocent of either stones or flowers.

"These," observed Egerton, referring to the broken, jagged lumps of limestone lying all about his feet, "were presumably broken off by people descending; some of them are quite recent, some have been here for years. Those storms of last month would bring down a lot, I should think." He stamped again.

"Are you trying to commit suicide?" demanded Ambrose wrathfully. "I'm not a bit tired of the shadow-show yet."

"This isn't quite so simple as I'd supposed," admitted Egerton in so surprised a voice that Ambrose involuntarily chuckled. "I thought the fellow had probably slipped or been attacked by vertigo and smashed his skull. But he can't have done that."

"Why not?" Ambrose asked, gingerly straightening himself and taking his bearings.

"Because falling on to this stuff is like falling on to a pile of cushions. It's positively resilient. Look here." He drew a long pencil from his pocket and thrust it point downward through the tangle of matted grass that covered the shelf. When he withdrew it the point was glistening with dew but unsullied by earth or chalky substance. "And that's nine inches, approximately. This bed must be at least a foot deep. He couldn't fracture any bones here. Heart perhaps. But you're a pro." His gesture as he stood aside to give the other precedence was worthy of a court levee.

"Take care you don't trip!" Ambrose warned him, and at that moment caught his own foot in a tangle of bindweed and, but for Egerton's powerful grasp on his arm, would have been on the rocks. That did nothing to steady his nerves, though he found it hard to discover any trace of emotion in Egerton's handsome, immobile face. The next instant he was on his knees by the recumbent figure, and had turned it over, supporting the head.

It was clear at once that the man was past all help. "A parson, by Gad," exclaimed Ambrose, seeing the mark of the breast waistcoat and clerical collar. "What on earth was he doing here?"

"The road we followed was a right of way through Blount's property," said Egerton woodenly. "There was nothing to prevent him, though it's true the road isn't used much. Though why he came at night . . ."

"At night?"

"Yes. Look at these." He indicated the crushed blue and yellow flowers on which the body had lain.

"I'm no botanist," confessed Ambrose a shade irritably.

"And I'm not a lecturer. It's the condition of the flowers I want you to notice." The doctor looked a second time. "You see? They're all shut; and they're commonly flowers that bloom by daylight."

Ambrose took his hands out of his pockets. "You're damned clever. I see what you're driving at, of course. If the flowers were shut when he pitched down here it must have been after dark."

"Or at all events before dawn. He's no light-weight, and it's utterly impossible for the flowers to have shut after he fell on them."

Ambrose nodded and the pair were silent for a moment looking at the dead man's face. He was a tallish man, long-limbed, but woefully thin, about forty, handsome in a hawk-like fashion, with blue eyes set a shade close, thick, dark hair, rather coarse-growing, the face bronzed yet with a patchy effect as if his skin had taken the tint unevenly. He didn't look to the doctor as if he were in very good condition physically, too thin, under-nourished probably, and he would have found it easy enough to believe that vertigo was the actual cause of death. As to this, however, there was no possible doubt. In the right temple was a bullet-wound. The man had been shot clean through the head, the bullet lodging in the brain.

Without comment, Egerton rose rather abruptly and walked to the very edge of the platform, peering over in a manner that seemed to his companion suicidal.

"What on earth are you looking at—or for?" he demanded.

"His stick."

"Stick?"

"Yes. He must have had one. No man bar a maniac would attempt to take this road without a stick."

"He may not have realised how bad the road was," suggested the other feebly.

"He wouldn't have walked nearly three miles without discovering that. He'd have gone back. Unless—by George, that's right. He didn't come that way, of course."

The doctor stared at him in resentful bewilderment. "Did he fly down from the moon then?"

"Look at his trousers—and then look at your own. Well?"

"I never claimed much for my trousers," acknowledged the doctor candidly. "But I don't think they stand to lose anything by comparison. Why, I could see my face in these."

"I didn't mean that precisely. But look at the knees and the calves. Look here." He stooped and pulled a long thorn out of his own grey-flannelled knee. "If this chap took the road we did he couldn't have escaped by miraculous intervention every bramble and briar on the way. It's obvious, of course. He didn't come that way. He came by the main road and missed his path?" He frowned inquiringly.

"And laid himself neatly on his face here with a bullet in his head? You're an English politician, aren't you? I should have guessed that anyway. I'm glad you've got to convince the jury."

"Always supposing there's a jury to convince," agreed Egerton urbanely, disregarding the obvious badinage. "There's something about the chin, though, that seems helpful."

The chin was certainly distinctive, displaying two

noticeable scars of long standing, in marked contrast to the whiteness of the skin surrounding them. Egerton laid his hand for an instant over the scars, then withdrew it. The doctor, with an uneasy suspicion that he did nothing without a reason, wondered what he meant but asked no questions. Egerton rose to his feet again and, turning, stared upwards.

"It's a long fall," he murmured cryptically.

"It was a devilish long climb."

"And not much of a depression for a man of his size. Look at it." Ambrose by this time had turned the man over and let the head loll against his knee, thus leaving clear the nest left in the tangled grass by the dead man's face. "That and the stick together . . ." He mused awhile.

"The stick proves nothing," put in Ambrose doggedly. "He may have been one of those freaks who can't bear to carry a stick. After all, his boots are heavy enough."

"Yes," agreed Egerton soberly. "I'd noticed his boots, too. It's very odd."

They were clumsy boots, cheap and shabby, though hardly well-worn. The leather, through usage and exposure, had swelled into humps and depressions that must have made them extremely uncomfortable to their wearer. They were round-toed, broken-laced, very heavy.

"Odd that he should have been wearing boots without nails in them?" Ambrose hazarded.

"No. Odd that they should be so clean. Even on the carriage road they'd show splashes. This fellow's been dead—how long? Two days? Three. Right. It's been dirty weather, without being precisely stormy. I wonder how he managed it."

"There's been a certain amount of rain to wash away the mud."

"From the soles, too?" Egerton appeared unconvinced.

"It's possible," Ambrose urged. "If you can't find something more strange than that—I must confess it doesn't seem particularly odd to me that a parson should be wearing such inferior boots. Parsons are generally poor men. Gervase is an exception."

"I didn't mean it was queer that a man should own such boots. I meant it was strange that this man should be wearing some one else's."

Ambrose started violently. "Are you sure?"

"Well, look for yourself. Look at the man's hands. They're particularly finely-shaped, well-kept, fastidiously kept even; nails trim and polished."

"Well?"

"Then, unless the fellow's built out of all proportion, he couldn't conceivably wear such boots with short, broad toes. However, one glance at his naked feet will show whether they are his or not." He put out a hand then paused. "I suppose, legally, we've no right to touch him."

"Why not?"

"The police might object."

The doctor whistled. "So it is murder, is it?"

"I wouldn't say that." Egerton was nothing if not cautious, like most of his race. "But it's on the cards. Another odd point—there isn't a mark on the face, except those scars that have obviously been there for years. Yet he must have bumped on those bushes. However, I fancy the private individual isn't invited to shove his oar in in these affairs. All the same, I think I'll risk the censure of the law, and, with you as my witness that I've done nothing to contravene the workings of justice, prove my point about the boots." He went down on one knee and proceeded to unfasten one of the heavy, shapeless boots which he drew up to reveal a much-darned silk sock. "No woman put those darns in," he observed shrewdly. "The worst woman darner doesn't do work like that. A single man, or a man living apart from his wife, I should suppose." He pulled off the sock to reveal a foot, long, well-kept, slender, finely-arched, free from all contusions, callouses or corns. Ambrose realised instantly that his young companion was right. A single day of those unspeakable boots would have raised blisters on such a foot. The dead man had the limbs of a sculptor's model. A slight compression of the toes was the result of their being forcibly crushed into too short a boot; but there was no actual mark anywhere on the foot. The doctor was beginning reluctantly to switch round to Egerton's view that there was foul play somewhere, and supposed that, allowing this supposition, the original plan had been to rob the body of all marks of identification and pitch it clean over the cliff into the sea. But the fact that the crime was staged for night had led it to its partial failure. Otherwise the body would have tossed about for some time, and eventually have been swallowed up by the quicksand that was particularly treacherous there.

The left arm and hand had all this time remained hidden from them because of the manner in which Ambrose supported the body, but now he laid it gently on its back and Egerton noticed two things. One was that round the wrist was a livid blue mark; the second that the hand itself was clenched. Together they stooped over it; *rigor mortis* had set in and the doctor had the greatest difficulty in forcing the fingers apart. Lying within, apparently clutched in the death agony, was a black, bone button, rather large, showing the dragged ends of several black threads and a smooth tiny clipping of black cloth. When Egerton saw that button he let it lie in his hand for an instant, then made a gesture as if he would pitch it into the sinking sand. Then, still unaware of Ambrose's curious eyes, he slipped it into his pocket and straightened himself.

"Dirty work," he observed curtly and shuddered in momentary distaste. "Wonder what really happened. Took him off his guard perhaps."

"Then why the struggle and the button?"

"Good point. I don't know. However, we're simply guessing, always a stupid thing to do. Is there anything we've left undone? We'd better see if he's got anything in his pockets that would help us." But it was clear that all identification marks had been carefully removed. Not a letter or a card, nothing but a cheap, cotton handkerchief without marking of any kind, an imitation leather purse containing a few small coins in silver and copper, a penknife with a ring opening, an empty match-box, a small indelible pencil and some chocolate. Egerton examined the handkerchief fastidiously. It bore marks of a reddish-brown shade; he sniffed it.

"Rust," he observed. "That may be helpful." But his tone was sceptical in the extreme. "Nothing else of any use," he added tersely, sweeping the articles together and returning them to the pocket. "I see even the tags have been cut out of the clothes. We'd better go up and report this now. I think I shall turn it over to Blount. It's hardly my affair."

"If you're thinking you'll escape the publicity you

can abandon hope," Ambrose warned him, scrambling unhandily up the cliff-side. "Your picture will be in all the halfpenny dailies." He reached the top and instantly plunged inland away from that crumbling edge. His companion paused a moment longer gazing with the compassion of the young that the old find immeasurably impertinent, at the lonely black figure spread-eagled on the deserted rock.

"Seems a shame to leave the poor devil alone," he muttered; then shrugged his shoulders and turned to follow the doctor. The climb had been a stiff one and both men had reached the surface panting and dishevelled, but by some mysterious process only known to himself, within thirty seconds Egerton had regained the bandbox appearance on which his friends chaffed him so mercilessly. Even his fair hair was as smooth and scrupulously parted as always. They proceeded through a small wood that was civilised in comparison with their earlier environment, and thence through a painted gate into the long, sloping garden that was a miracle of man's perseverance. For Blount had persuaded all manner of flowers to bloom, against nature, in that deplorable soil, and from the windows the garden was a rich treasury of gold and russet and bronze.

They found Blount on the wide covered verandah with his wife and a second woman of so startling an appearance that Ambrose paused on the instant. The two were a magnificent foil the one for the other. The best expression that could be applied to Lady Blount was the out-of-date word "elegant." She was tall and foppish and dark; very perfectly-dressed, very sure of herself, cool and sophisticated and detached, the type of woman whom a man would never learn to know unless she expressly revealed herself. It was impossible, as he discovered later, to learn from her manner to her husband whether she merely liked and respected him, loved him passionately, or bitterly regretted her marriage. He wondered whether Blount himself knew, and thought most probably not. Together they would be as distinguished a pair as you could hope to meet, and yet he was pretty sure that neither was really happy. But whereas Blount would face his dissatisfaction with defiance and bitter energy, she would accept it with that slight ironical smile that lifted the corners of her perfect mouth, as though to say that in so confused a world sorrow and disappointment were concomitant with living.

Eloise Martineau was high noon to Pamela's midnight, a superb creature, golden-haired, white-skinned, magnificently built . . . with provocative lips and hands moulded on the splendid Juno-esque lines so much admired at the close of the last century, moving with a lithe yet langorous grace, beautiful to watch. Ambrose admitted to himself that he'd be terrified to find himself alone in a railway carriage with her. That feline sleepiness, under which the tawny eyes darted and watched, repelled him. Her manner was a caress in itself; she was sex incarnate; difficult to imagine that any other thought animated her mind. She was, perhaps, more to the French taste than the more restrained Saxon, but only a Saint Aloysius could have wholly ignored her. He was still watching her, half-fascinated, when Egerton's young wife, Rosemary, appeared beside him.

"Have you joined the Legion of the Damned?" she asked unconcernedly, indicating Eloise Martineau. "It's no use. She hates poor men. That's why she doesn't seriously bother with Scott. Pamela knew her on the stage, I think. Didn't you know she was on the stage when Sir Gervase met her? I thought you were supposed to be a friend of his? Yes, I know all about Ireland but there are such things as letters, aren't there? She used to be Pamela Raeburn then. Does that convey anything to you?"

"I haven't been to a theatre for generations," pleaded Ambrose.

"And probably wouldn't have seen Pamela if you had. She never got beyond the provinces. Sir Gervase met her up at Mannington when she was touring there. I think she's utterly lovely."

Ambrose drew a deep breath. This candid unconventional young woman, with her bright auburn hair and vivid personality, set him instantly at his ease.

"Tell me a bit more," he begged. "I feel like Rip Van Winkle. Who's the lady who runs the Legion?"

"Miss Martineau? Oh, she's left the stage, too. Has a millinery shop in Bond Street now." She glanced with frank distaste at her fellow-guest who was talking to Egerton with pantherine gestures of her beautiful arms (she was the type of woman who talks with her whole body); she turned her head up to him in a provocative manner, raising it a little so that the lids seemed to fall back from the sly beautiful honey-coloured eyes. Ambrose wondered how the fellow could talk to her so smoothly; he had yet to learn that Egerton's coolness and courtesy were proverbial; men who ridiculed his bandbox appearance said that his manners extended even to those lamp-posts against which he inadvertently cannoned, but his friend declared that never in all his circumspect life had he done anything so banal as collide with a lamp-post.

The conversation with Rosemary proceeded apace until the doctor was almost able to shake off the memory of that stark dreadful figure on the cliff-side; suddenly, however, someone touched his arm and turning he saw that Blount had risen at last and he and Egerton were going off to the library, a big shady room on the further side of the house.

It was Egerton who recapitulated the grim story.

Blount frowned in a perplexed way. "Deuced odd!" he commented, and the harrowed expression in his eyes deepened as if this were the last straw. "What was the fellow doing there? I know, of course, that it's a right of way, but it leads nowhere but this place. If he was coming crashing along there in the night he must have been trying to strike the road to Four Corners. But why not come up by the carriage road? It's nothing short of madness to try that path by night. I could do it because I know the way better than the palm of my hand, but there aren't many men who could say as much."

Egerton, hands in pockets, shoulders hunched under chimney-breast, said laconically, "He did come by the carriage road."

Blount stared. "Then how on earth——?"

"We don't know. And it isn't our job to find out. He must have come along the high road and tried to strike the main road to Frensham—perhaps."

That last cryptic word seemed to irritate his host. "What do you mean by perhaps?"

"I haven't yet settled, to my own satisfaction, how a man with a bullet through his brain comes along any sort of a road."

Blount drew a deep breath. "Ah-h! A bullet. What are you suggesting?"

21

"Nothing. It's not my job. Look here, I'll show you exactly where he's lying. No hope of getting him up to-night." He drew a pencil and a discarded envelope from his pocket and sketched a swift diagram. "The shelf is just there, with the Mermaids' Rocks below—but I expect you know it?"

"Quite well. But perhaps he committed suicide?"

"Perhaps," agreed Egerton gravely. "Still, in view of this, I should feel apprehensive if I were the coroner." He put his hand back into his pocket and produced the button. "Besides, why should a man on a damp unpleasant night take a long journey into a strange country, when he might as easily dispose of himself as a gentleman in his own home? However, I merely throw that out as a suggestion."

There followed a long silence; Blount gazed at the button as if hypnotised, and it seemed to Ambrose that he was sinking into one of those brooding periods of melancholy that had darkened his college life. With startling abruptness, however, he suddenly leaped to his feet and, picking up the telephone arm, gave the number of the local police station.

The conversation was a lengthy one; when at last he set the instrument aside he went across to the windows, and with a single movement hurled back the dark, heavy curtains that shrouded the room against the inclement night. Evening had ridden up the sky in a mantle of storm; an angry wind soughed in the red leaves and the spatter of rain sounded on the gravel path outside. Far to the west the thunder murmured and threatened, and even as they waited a vivid flash of lightning split the sky and the rain came pouring down, lashing against the glass, ruthlessly breaking to shreds the chrysanthemums under the windows.

"They won't dare risk a life on those cliffs to-night," observed Blount grimly. "But to-morrow. . . . You'll be in this, Egerton, as you located the corpse. And Terry. You can keep the button; it's nothing to do with me."

"Faith, that's enough for one day," reflected Ambrose gloomily, as he struggled into his deplorable dinner jacket, but there was more to come before the day closed. After dinner when the men came up from the dining-room he saw Blount subside in a far window-seat with the expression of a man who is past coherent reflection. Ambrose resisted a natural inclination to take a place near him. "Time enough to-morrow," he thought. But a moment or two later he regretted the friendly impulse. Pamela Blount was playing the "Moonlight Sonata"; it was not apposite but it was enchanting. And, suddenly, in the midst of her exquisite performance, Eloise Martineau rose like the great tawny cat she was and crossed over to her host, and began to talk in tones so low that only Blount could hear, and even he had some ado to distinguish her words. Thereafter the charm of the playing vanished so far as Ambrose was concerned. He wished he knew a little more of the precise relations of Blount and his wife. This creature, presumably, had some hold over him; so much was evident from his hard, expressionless face and her sense of ease and flickering rapier smile. She was a corrupt woman, he decided, bad enough to ruin any man for her own pleasure. He tried to piece things together. It was true that Blount was profoundly unhappy; the look on his face was terrible. Ambrose reflected. Suppose this Martineau woman had some hold over him. . . . It sounded improbable, but the doctor knew men and above all he knew Blount. He tried to imagine him in war-time, tortured, driven, half-crazed. He had seen less sensitive men go hopelessly to pieces and in sheer desperation grab at any straw that floated past. A woman like that would never loose her hold till she was beaten off. Turning his eyes away, lest his attention be noticeable, he intercepted a swift glance between Egerton and his wife. That made him more uneasy than ever, for clearly they also had noticed the couple, and what they had seen merely bore out some impression they had been harbouring. Ambrose wished it were etiquette for him to ask them outright where that trouble lay, but such a course being clearly out of the question, he could only wait in supreme discomfort until the music came to an end, and presently Pamela Blount and her corrupt companion drifted up to bed.

That evening, about an hour later, emerging from the smoking-room, he chanced upon Blount himself in the hall and rallied him on his fatigue, but after one glance his host walked straight past, almost straight through him, and there was an expression on his face that appalled his friend. It had not been there before dinner; for this was more than mere apprehension or distress or disappointment. It was a compound of desperation and hatred and fear.

When Ambrose entered his room and crossed to the window he found that the rain had passed over and the night was clear, with stars, but no moon. He stood for a long time on the balcony watching the sea; it was black and silent and full of phantom stars; the whole scene was in fact in striking contrast with the confusion and hot unrest of this sinister house. Suddenly, as he was on the eve of turning back to his room to undress he heard a noise beneath him and a

French window was opened. A faint sound announced the striking of a match and in the tiny glare he saw Blount's white, distraught face. His back was towards the sea, his face towards the room he had just left. He spoke once before the doctor retreated.

"Such scum is better dead!" he cried, and his voice matched that dreadful, livid face he had turned upon Ambrose in the hall. The latter hesitated a moment longer, irresistibly waiting to know if Lady Blount had any reply. But there was none, so he went back to his room where he remained smoking and pondering until morning.

CHAPTER II

"We want nothing but Facts, Sir; nothing but Facts."
—*Hard Times.*

I

THE body of the unknown was salvaged the next day by the local police force who, having spied out the land, brought the body to the cliff-top by a contraption of ropes affixed by the most agile of the party, who laboriously made his way down the cliff-side much as Egerton and the doctor had done the previous afternoon. Egerton, of course, was the centre of interest; all the theories that had been propounded had come from him, as had all the suggestions, though when he confronted the police he merely laid down the button, declaring that he had found it clenched in the dead man's hand, and cautiously allowed the Law to draw its own conclusions. The police, none of whom had had any experience of murder cases, were impressed and secretly excited, particularly when the police doctor from Tenbeigh confessed himself puzzled by the circumstances of the death. There were no bruises or abrasions on the body such as must have resulted had he really stumbled and pitched over the rock; nor could he find any injury to the skull.

"No reason why he should," observed Egerton laconically. "Suppose the fellow was hurled there; or shot and shoved clear over the side by someone of good muscular ability he might have missed all the bushes, and he wouldn't bruise on that cushion of grass, as we agreed last night. Nothing doing there."

The next point was to decide whether the man had taken his own life, but that theory was disposed of by the presence of the button in his clenched hand. That left only the alternative of murder, and on such a thesis the inquiry was founded. That was a very silly season as far as criminal and sensational news was concerned. The divorce of a peeress was the solitary bit of garbage an energetic press could rake up to offer as a tit-bit to the general public, and they hailed this extraordinary mystery with delight. Blount, Egerton and Ambrose were summoned to the Tenbeigh Police Station, where the body had been taken, whence they proceeded to the mortuary to fulfil the formal obligations demanded by the Law. Egerton and Ambrose had anticipated the summons; not so Blount.

"Do they think I pitched him there?" he asked curtly.

"Couldn't say, I'm sure," returned Egerton in a suave voice. "But it isn't unnatural in the circumstances, seeing that the fellow was found on your property, to ask you to view the body. It may be some chap who thought he'd like to haunt your sleep by dying in your domain. You never can tell."

As soon as the doctor's report had been received the Tenbeigh authorities got into touch with Scotland Yard, and asked for assistance that was instantly forthcoming in the shape of one James Bremner, a quick, curt, dark man who had been with Egerton in his exciting chase, against time, after Chandos' murderer. He nodded to his ex-secret service colleague, who appeared quite unsurprised at finding him there, and then they lined up and surveyed the body. It was clothed precisely as they had seen it that afternoon on the cliff, though now they could see that the tatterdemalion cuffs were tied with string, while the face seemed paler.

"I must ask you whether any of you recognise the deceased and can identify him for us," said Bremner with sharp formality. And there was a minute's silence.

Then Blount broke in impatiently, "It surely shouldn't be hard to do that. Are there so many missing clergy?"

"Four at the moment," returned Bremner drily. "One a young man who has just taken Orders; one very old with white hair and a lame foot; one aged thirty-two, fair, with brown eyes and a birth-mark on the left shoulder, and a fourth who was taken out of the Thames this morning."

"Neat work," murmured Blount admiringly. "But, of course, if this fellow meant to commit suicide——"

Bremner swept the suggestion out of sight with a gesture of his quick, impatient hands. "Can you furnish any reason why he should choose to do so on your property, grasping a button from someone else's coat in his hand?"

Blount moved with a sudden hopeless sigh. "The press could help us, no doubt. Broadcast the information that a nameless clergyman has been found, and someone will surely come forward with news of one who is missing."

"I'm afraid things aren't quite so simple as that," explained Bremner carefully. "To begin with, he may merely have said that he was going for a holiday. Possibly he was, and who's to know he's missing? If he had arranged for a room at some country inn they'd phlegmatically decide that he'd been benighted else-where or changed his plans. They wouldn't become apprehensive. If he proves to have been murdered, as we fear, there's less likelihood than ever of our obtaining help, because if you're proposing to get rid of an inconvenient corpse you don't usually notify the Yard. No, I'm afraid we've got a tougher job than that in front of us."

He glanced at Egerton who said woodenly, "Yes. We don't really know anything at all, except that the man's dead and that he was shot through the brain. We don't know who he is or what he did."

"We know his calling."

Egerton looked perplexed. "How d'you make that out?"

"His clothes, of course."

Bremner interrupted. "In a case of this kind, Sir Gervase, we don't take anything for granted. The fact the deceased is wearing clerical collar and vest proves nothing."

"If I were found lying in the gutter in a policeman's tunic, the force wouldn't arise and claim me for the Prodigal Son." Egerton amplified. "If there has been foul play this get-up may be part of the plot."

Blount passed his hand over his eyes. "I find all this extremely bewildering," he observed sharply. "But I suppose you won't say the scars on the chin are part of a disguise. They, at all events, are his own and are of long standing."

"Certainly," agreed Bremner, but there was little confidence in his voice.

"Then presumably if you broadcast a description of the fellow, accompanied by a photograph, someone —some relation or tradesman, or acquaintance—will put a name to it. Even a stranger wouldn't forget those scars."

"If he saw them he wouldn't," agreed Egerton.

"Saw them? How could he help seeing them, unless the man wore a muffler to hide them? Those weren't made by shaving last week."

"Quite. He's had 'em ten or twelve years at least. But, as you suggest yourself, he may have covered them up."

"You couldn't cover them up indoors, not permanently."

"Not with a muffler."

"Then how?"

"Doesn't it strike you there's something peculiarly incompatible about the face? Look at this." He touched the dark, strongly growing hair and the finer hairs visible on the backs of the hands. "Now look at the chin."

They all looked. Bremner appeared to know precisely what Egerton was driving at, and, suddenly remembering that gesture on the hill-side, when he laid his hand over the dead man's jaw, Ambrose understood him, too.

"Of course. It ought to be blue."

"You'd think so. This type of man usually has to shave twice if he's going out at night. And his chin is neither hard nor blue as it ought to be."

"So that normally he wore a beard?"

"Exactly. That would explain why the scars weren't visible. It's an excellent reason for a man to grow one, for you can't call those marks anything but unsightly. On the other hand, to shave the beard would be to change the fellow's appearance completely and make identification more difficult. Clearly it was done either just before or immediately after death. There's no marks of stubble here."

Bremner bent lower to examine the skin. "And no razor-slashes as you might have expected from a man unaccustomed to shave. Of course, if it were done at once after death there would naturally be no signs of blood, because the blood-stream would have ceased to operate. If we can discover his profession——"

"Something sedentary," observed Egerton. "If he'd worked in the open air he'd have been bronzed. This fellow is naturally pale."

Blount indicated the patches of sunburn on the cheeks and forehead. Egerton shook his head. "Handsome men are slightly sunburnt. All that tan came out of a bottle. Look how patchy it is where the rain's got at it. Besides, who ever shoved it on made a bad, tactical error. If the fellow had worn a beard, which seems obvious, it's equally obvious that the chin couldn't have been tanned as it would be protected from the sun. But this chap has as much of it on his chin as on his cheeks." He looked keenly at the man's hands. "Not manual work, they're far too well-kept; and not clerical work, typewriting and so forth, and not pianoforte playing; the tips of the fingers would be far more spatulate if that were the case. They're the hands of a man who's either fastidious about their appearance for their own sake, or whose hands are important in his work as a doctor's are, for instance. I think Blount's right and it will be a case of the press assisting the hounds of justice. Look here." He took up an envelope and began to sketch the dead man's face, adding, however, a beard that quite hid the scarred chin.

"A man like that shouldn't be particularly hard to

find. Do the tabs on his clothes give you any assistance?" asked Ambrose who had already forgotten Egerton's methodical examination of the body on the cliff-side.

"There are none. They've been cut out."

"Of course. I'd forgotten. Fishy that. Underclothes too?"

"They came from Willson, the big city outfitters. That doesn't tell you much either. Frightfully shabby —no links on the shirt, just loops of string."

"If the collar and vest aren't his," broke in Blount suddenly, "can you be certain that the suit is? The tabs may have been cut out to conceal all traces of the identity of their actual owner."

"That's possible," Egerton agreed. "But not, I think, probable. It's all Lombard Street to a China orange that these are his clothes. Did you notice that very slight lift of the left shoulder, far too slight to be called a deformity, yet not entirely concealed? Well, see how perfectly the suit fits that. A man grows into his clothes, you know, and he'd grown into these. They're pretty shiny anyway."

"Does the button help you?" asked Ambrose a shade timidly.

"Only thus far. That it's the button from an overcoat, which makes it likely that any struggle there was took place out of doors or in some place where coats are worn, not, for instance, in the murderer's house. I think we may safely assume that this is murder. And it couldn't have been done in a public place, because it would have attracted universal attention, so it seems likely that it was in the open air."

"There's the wrist, too. That looks rather like a rough house."

"That, of course, may be merely coincidental. The doctor's of opinion that it was administered some time, possibly a whole day, before death. It's the grip of a powerful fist, most probably a man's."

"I suppose," remarked Blount, a shade aggressively, yet with a fine hauteur, "this means you'll want to examine my property for clues or whatever else you think it may yield?"

"We shall hope not to trouble you very much, Sir Gervase," returned Bremner, courteously. "I gather that the cliff where the body was found is not far from the house?"

"A very short distance." Blount was definitely unhelpful. "I take it that my guests will be immune from annoyance? My wife, for instance, and her friends will not be approached by the police or the press?" He sounded angry, as if the bare notion of Pamela Blount being connected with so disreputable a case infuriated him.

"We can't answer for the press," retorted Bremner drily. "But no doubt Lady Blount will give her servants instructions. As for the police, we shall interfere in no way with the guests at Four Corners or, we hope, with yourself henceforward, unless there appears to be anything in the evidence to connect any of them with the affair or to suggest that they could supply information."

Blount, accompanied by Ambrose, came away immediately after that reassurance; he didn't even think it necessary to comment on Bremner's final suggestion that seemed to him absurd to the point of ill-breeding. But Egerton remained with his friend.

"Have you known Blount long?" Bremner asked thoughtfully.

"About a year. He's living in my constituency—got a parish there—ye gods, what a parish; a nice, jolly crowd of forgers and tramps and out-of-works, and a few thousand factory hands. We've had some correspondence politically, sat on the same platform and so forth."

"You know him intimately?"

"Scarcely that. I've dined at his house and he's returned the compliment, and I'm his guest here."

"You know nothing of his personal life?"

"Nothing."

Bremner considered. "H'm. That's a nuisance. I hoped you might, but I dare say your delicacy would have made the position impossible. I want to find out who this fellow is."

"Well?"

"Blount knows. I don't say definitely that he knew before he came here——"

"I should suppose not," interrupted Egerton, exceedingly drily. "That would be tantamount to accusing him of murder."

Bremner took no notice of that. "But he certainly recognised the fellow when he set eyes on him just now," he wound up hardly.

Egerton seemed unimpressed. "Think so?" It took more than a lightning flash like this to disturb Egerton's composure.

"I don't think, I'm sure," snapped Bremner, a little annoyed at the failure of his squib.

"Ah, well!" Egerton took up his hat and prepared to follow the others. "You've got a chance to earn your pay."

"I wonder whether your rotten delicacy makes you feign obtuseness or whether you really hadn't seen that," mused Bremner invitingly, but Egerton never gave his tricks away. The detective struck his hands together in a gesture of passionate impatience. "I can stand the dark if I must," he cried bitterly. "My nerves are as good as the next man's, but it infuriates me to know that next door there's a fellow with a whole boxful of matches, and he resolutely refuses to give me a light."

2

As Blount had prophesied, the first gleam of news came through the services of the press, who featured the story in all the cheap dailies, and made the utmost of the mystery. Blount, Egerton and Ambrose found their pictures in the back pages, and were besieged by press-cutting agencies for subscriptions. Photographs of the dead man, and of the same face equipped with a beard were broadcasted all over the country, and twenty-four hours after Bremner's departure for town the first clue presented itself. Shortly after ten in the morning a small voice, very refined and prim, spoke over the Yard telephone with a request for "someone connected with the Four Corners mystery." The voice was that of a lady, probably no longer young, more than a little apprehensive, doing what she conceived to be her highly unpleasant duty.

"I think I have information that may be of use to you," was all she would say over the wire, having the peculiar notion, common to her caste, that telephones are as public as 2LO, and apparently fearful of unseen vengeance. She gave an address in Bloomsbury—Miss Gell, 15 Thermiloe Square, and immediately rang off.

Bremner set out to find her at once. Thermiloe

Square proved to be a collection of smoky, flat-chested houses in the poorer purlieus of Euston. The whole atmosphere was dingy as though even the sun shrank from illuminating such grim paving-stones; trees, whose branches seldom budded, stood at stated intervals along the kerb; cheap, unwashed lace curtains concealed most of the windows; the steps were tall and chipped and ill-kept. Behind one end of the square ran a mews that was also a carriage stable; on the north side clustered innumerable cheapjack shops, where tawdry and soiled articles were exposed for barter. Cheap confectioners, tobacconists, kosher butchers, cats-meat-men, second-hand clothes shops, general stores that stocked everything from milk to paraffin —Bremner picked his way among them; the opposite side of the kerb was lined with booths in the evening, with all the naphthas flaring and the screaming of half a dozen bastard tongues smothering the air.

"Not the neighbourhood where one would live for choice," he ruminated grimly. "The fellow must have been pretty well down and out. But, then, presumably, one wouldn't tie one's cuffs with string either from choice."

In answer to his ring at No. 15, a pert, sulky looking maid opened the door, and as he stepped into the hall Miss Gell herself came out of a ground-floor sitting-room. She was very much what he had anticipated, an angular, middle-aged woman with glasses, in a long dress that rustled and swayed as she moved. A long, gold chain and a chatelaine of red satin ribbon threaded through brass rings, from which dangled a huge pair of scissors and a gold pencil, were her only ornaments. She said in her thin, restrained voice, "Will you please come in here," and showed him into a room as brown and impersonal as herself. The walls were covered with brown paper, there was a brown cloth made of plush, decorated with ball fringe, on the circular walnut table, four chairs covered in brown velvet, were set against the walls, and two arm-chairs to match stood stiffly on either side of the fireplace that was filled with orange crinkled paper and a fourpenny fern in a red pot.

Miss Gell offered him a chair, took one herself, and said flatly but a little nervously, "I should like to make it quite clear that I know nothing of the events that led up to this tragedy. I'm not even quite sure that the man who used to be my lodger and the man about whom you are inquiring are one and the same. But I have seen two photographs and they seem very like —very like, indeed. The beard makes him so noticeable."

"I think, for the moment, we may assume that your late lodger and the dead man are identical. Now— we'll begin at the very beginning. His name?"

"Mr. Charteris. Raymond Charteris."

"He has been here long?"

"He was my lodger for a little over twelve months. For some time he occupied a room on the second floor, but recently he had reverses and took a less expensive room at the top of the house."

"Was he out during the day?"

"Yes. Almost always. But there were occasions when he would stay in his room and never move from morning till night. He said he was an actor and that an accident to his throat had impaired his voice, but he was having it treated. I think that was why he was out of work so much. He was latterly in very, very poor circumstances."

"Only latterly?"

"I think he was never very prosperous, but he fluctuated. Sometimes he seemed to have plenty of money for food and clothes, and then he would be reduced to actual want. Often he would tell me, when the rent was in arrears—though never more than a week or two—that he was expecting money, shortly, and nearly always he got it. But his work—I suppose it came from his work—never lasted very long."

"Ah, well! He may have been employed at one of these suburban theatres where a play runs for a week or a fortnight and is never heard of again. Was he in debt to you at the time of his death?"

"No. Generally speaking, he contrived to pay his rent to date. And, as I say, he never allowed the account to run more than a week or two."

"Did he just rent a room here or was he a boarder?"

"He had a room. We do not really undertake to feed lodgers except for breakfast. But if they will give us notice in the morning we can always arrange for them to have lunch or dinner in the morning-room. Some of the ladies invariably dine there; they prefer it to going out alone to restaurants at night. Mr. Charteris did have dinner with us once or twice, but not more often. Even when he was at home he would not always come downstairs, and the maids won't take meals up from the basement nowadays. I used to think it was because he simply could not afford one-and-threepence, and it is quite impossible to do it for less."

"Quite," agreed Bremner sympathetically. "Now, tell me this. Was Mr. Charteris a bachelor?"

"I thought so for a long time, but quite recently he told me that he had been separated from his wife for several years, but that he had hopes of their setting up a home together in the near future."

"Did she ever come here?"

"Three or four times."

"Then you—or at all events, your maid—would know her again?"

Once more Miss Gell shook her head. "I shouldn't, nor would either of my girls. I fancy Mr. Charteris always knew when she was coming, for he would come down into the hall and open the door before the bell rang. And he always saw her out, of course."

Bremner was profoundly disappointed at the turn events were taking, but he said nothing of that, merely asking, "You can give me absolutely no clue?"

"Only this."

She dived into a deep, sateen pocket and brought out a match-box; this being opened, an incongruous object was revealed, a diamond ear-drop of exquisite workmanship, shaped to resemble a basket of flowers. Bremner bent over it in frank admiration. "A lovely piece of work," he observed, "and very valuable. This belonged to the lady?"

"Yes."

"You're sure of that? I understood you to say that you had never seen her."

"Not quite that. I caught glimpses of her on two occasions as I was moving about the house. She was tall and slight and dark, and wore a long, blue, cloth coat and sables."

"You never saw her face?"

"No. She would come in a heavy veil, as if she were anxious not to be recognised. But once when I was in the little airing-cupboard on the top floor, close to Mr. Charteris' room, his door was opened and I heard him say in a quite rough voice, 'One of those precious baubles you wear in your ears would keep me in comfort for six months.'"

Bremner paused; it seemed to him that the case savoured of blackmail. This woman whoever she might be was evidently afraid of his power over her, and probably he was using it to extort money. Those earrings could be accounted for by a lover perhaps—a lover who knew nothing of Mr. Raymond Charteris. He said aloud, "I shall have to have that jewel, of course. It will probably be of the greatest assistance. The design is unusual, and the jewels themselves valuable. You can tell me when it came into you possession?"

"On the twenty-fourth of August. This lady came to see Mr. Charteris for the third time. It was a day when I was myself indoors the whole afternoon, as were both my maids. At about three o'clock Mr. Charteris came downstairs without hat or coat and began to tap the aneroid. I was sure he was expecting his wife because he kept glancing through the coloured glass of the door. It's true that you cannot see faces through that glass, but it is quite easy to watch shadows approaching. About ten minutes past the lady arrived and they went upstairs together. I must confess that on that occasion I did feel misgivings. I had accepted Mr. Charteris' story that she was his wife and that they were proposing a reconciliation. But on that afternoon I did wonder whether his story were true. For if she were his wife I could not see why he should be so desperately poor and she so beautifully dressed. Also, I felt that she was really a little afraid of him, and, if so, why should she have come back, since he could not support her? She remained with him for about an hour, and as they came down he said, 'You'd better make up your mind. You can't have all the honour in the world. It's one or the other.' And she said in the lowest and most wretched of voices, 'I will let you know. Promise me to do nothing until you hear.' And he said, 'A week then.' Later in the day he told me that he thought he really had an offer of permanent employment almost immediately and hoped to be able to afford something better than the attic room. Of course, I said I was glad and then I had two young lady lodgers coming in that night, and I really thought no more about him, not until that evening, that is, when I chanced to see something shining almost under the edge of one of the stair-pads, and when I picked it up I found this."

"You didn't show it to Mr. Charteris?"

"No. I waited for him to speak."

"He might not have known."

"Then she should have asked if she had lost it here."

"Has she been to the house since?"

"Once. About three weeks later."

"That is to say, about the middle of September?"

"Yes."

"And shortly after that date he is found dead. Can you remember the actual date that you last saw him?"

"The nineteenth of September."

"How long was that after the lady's visit?"

"Two days, I think."

"Can you recall anything particular that took place that day which might help us to trace the story of the crime?"

"Yes. That was the night the stranger came."

"The stranger?" Bremner's eyes were intent under their thin, dark brows.

"Yes. I will tell you the whole story. But, first, about this ear-ring. You will realise that there was, of course, no thought in my mind of keeping it. But the jewel is a valuable one; it belonged, not to Mr. Charteris, but to the lady whom he claimed to be his wife. She had merely to ask for it to have it returned. It is impossible to suppose that she had not missed it. Even if she shrank from seeing me, she could have asked her husband to speak of her loss."

"You didn't offer it to her then?"

"She had only to ask for it," repeated Miss Gell with a kind of colourless obstinacy often seen among women of her type.

"She may not have realised she dropped it here."

"When a lady loses a jewel as valuable as this, she generally inquires at every possible place."

"What was your real reason?" queried Bremner curiously. "If you were sure that it was hers——"

"She might have been tempted to claim it. . . . No. She could have had it at a word. Why should she mind asking?"

"Why should she veil her face and never ring your bell or speak to you?"

"I suppose because she didn't wish to be seen or recognised."

"When she lost the ear-ring she may still have preferred anonymity to the return of the jewel."

"You mean, she would lose anything rather than let others know that she came here?"

"I don't say so, but that's one explanation."

Miss Gell bridled. "I see no reason why she should

object to its being known that she was seen at my house."

"Damn the woman for a fool!" thought Bremner irritably, and added aloud, "It wasn't the house she was anxious to conceal, Miss Gell; it was the name of the man she visited. Or so I should suppose. But had you no theory as to why she let the affair of the earring slide?"

"I suppose she was afraid I should insist on her identifying the trinket herself. Or, perhaps, she thought I should already have handed it to the police, and she may have wished to avoid them. Or, if after all it hadn't been lost here, that I might have spoken of it in the house generally, so that the news got about and people talked."

"It's pretty serious when a woman lets a jewel of that price slide rather than be identified."

"Precisely what had occurred to me. Then, when I saw the story in the papers of Mr. Charteris' mysterious death I felt that there must lie behind it some story that only the police could unravel."

"Quite," Bremner bowed slightly. "Now, to come to the last time that you saw Mr. Charteris. You say that was the nineteenth of September?"

"Yes. The day the stranger came."

"The stranger?" Bremner repeated.

"I have to call him that, because I've no idea who he was. I'll explain to you. It was all very mysterious. He didn't come and ring the bell as ordinary respectable men and women do. He skulked in behind one of my regular lodgers, who, of course, used his own latchkey."

"Ah! Could I see this gentleman?"

"He's in his office now."

"Do you know where that is?"

"It's a shipping office in St. Mary Axe."

"Do you know the name?"

"Coleman and Martine, I think."

"Thank you. And your lodger's name?"

"Willoughby—Mr. Derek Willoughby. It was rather a foggy evening, a Thursday night, and I suppose he mistook this stranger for another of my lodgers."

"He didn't give you a description of the man?"

"He said he didn't really see him, except that he was not young and seemed very much excited, though he didn't say anything. But he went very quickly up the stairs, before Mr. Willoughby could really notice his face or his suit."

"And did no one see him out?"

"Presumably Mr. Charteris would, that is, if he were not already murdered." She shuddered.

"Then no one else saw him at all?"

"No. I think the man, whoever he was, must have been afraid that if he sent his name up to Mr. Charteris he would not be admitted."

"You know nothing of Mr. Charteris' personal affairs? Nothing that would account for this man?"

"Nothing but what I have told you. As soon as I saw the papers I remembered the extraordinary visitor. It was most unfortunate that the house was empty that night."

"Empty? Except for these two, you mean?"

"Yes. One of my maids had just left me and I had not been able to replace her. The other maid had her night out on Thursdays. I, myself, had an engagement at Ravenscourt Park to a guild meeting and supper, and I was anxious not to miss these, if possible. In the

DEATH AT FOUR CORNERS

ordinary way, of course, I should not dream of leaving a lodger alone in my house, but seeing that it was Mr. Charteris, who never wanted dinner or rang his bell for anything, I felt that I might safely take the risk. I had explained the position to him earlier in the day. I thought he seemed particularly upset, his face very white and his eyes burning. I think he had had no food all day; he seemed very much excited and told me that at last his luck had turned and he expected to be able to make a change almost immediately. He also asked a great deal about a room on the floor below, just then falling vacant, and said that most probably he would wish to take it. It so happened that that night my other three guests were also out, so that Mr. Charteris was alone in the house. Mr. Willoughby, who let the stranger in, changed and went out again about half-past six. My other two lodgers were ladies who were going to the theatre and did not come back from the city that evening at all—not until half-past eleven that is to say. I had two of my rooms vacant, this large one and a small one for which I was expecting a lodger the following week. At about a quarter to seven I knocked on Mr. Charteris' door——"

Bremner interrupted to say, "The stranger was still in the house? You're sure of that?"

"Quite sure. I could hear voices. I knocked to ask if there was anything he thought he might want as I was now going out. To tell you the truth, I was a little relieved at his friend's arrival, thinking that it might soothe Mr. Charteris to have a little company. He was in the mood when he might have done something rash." Her eyes, the faded, demure eyes of a gentlewoman who has sunk to that dreary stratum of letting out rooms for a living to men and women of

45

ANTHONY GILBERT

inferior social standing, implied anything from intoxi-
cation to suicide. "He said he didn't want anything at
the moment, and asked when I expected to be back. I
said about ten o'clock or possibly a little later. My
maid would be home about eleven. I have to allow
them to be out so late as they often go to the theatres
with their friends. I thought it probable that I, personally, should remain with my friends, a local church-
warden and his wife, until half-past nine or so. I also
added that the maid was out and the house empty."

"You told him that?"

"Yes. I thought it only right to remind him——"

"Did he say anything?"

"Only that it was quite all right, and I need not
hurry back on his account."

"You are prepared to swear that it was his voice
you heard?"

Miss Gell seemed startled. "His voice? Oh, yes, I
should think so."

"I'm afraid thinking is too vague," said Bremner
keenly. "This may be a very important criminal case.
You will certainly have to give evidence on oath. Are
you prepared to swear in the witness-box that the voice
was his? It is most important to establish the very
latest time at which he was known to be alive. Would
you declare on oath——?"

Miss Gell looked shocked. "On oath? I scarcely
think I should like to do that. I was taken to a theatre
once when I was quite young, and I heard a man re-
produce exactly the voices of his companions." She began to shiver with horror. "Do you mean to suggest
that at that very moment while I waited on the other
side of the door he was already dead—murdered?"

"I'm suggesting nothing. I'm trying to prove my

46

facts so far as it's possible. Did his voice sound clear?"

"Not exactly. But I remembered that he had been a little wild in his manner all day and that that might affect his voice."

"You wouldn't say that beyond all doubt it was another man, mimicking him with intent to deceive you? No, I thought not. That's not an hypothesis, of course, but we can't afford, at this stage, to neglect the smallest opening."

"I shouldn't care to say anything on oath. Mind you, I think it was his voice, but it's impossible for me to swear to that."

"I see. And then you went out?"

"Yes. I came back about a quarter-past ten; I looked in the box as usual for letters; there were none there, but I saw a note on the table. It was in Mr. Charteris' writing—I have it here—and was very short, just saying that he had suddenly had the offer of work, and that he must leave at once to catch the night train. He enclosed a pound for his rent. He said he expected to be away not more than three days."

"May I see the letter?"

Miss Gell produced it. It was written in a rather large, masculine hand, dashing and a trifle ostentatious, and was very curt and to the point.

"I have just had the offer of a job but I must go at once if I am to have a chance. Please keep my room for the present. I shall not be away more than three days. I enclose a pound for next week's rent.—RAYMOND CHARTERIS."

"A pound?" asked Bremner thoughtfully. "Was that the amount of his rent?"

"He paid fourteen shillings and his food was extra.

But, as I say, he very seldom took any meals with us."

"Well, it's natural enough that he should enclose a pound; he probably wouldn't have the exact change."

"It seemed to me a little odd, as if he really expected to be away longer than he said."

"Why should you think that?"

"Because he'd paid me his rent the day before, so if he wanted to pay for another week, when there were already six days to run, it looked as if he expected to be away for a week or ten days at all events. It seemed to me queer at the time."

"It is queer," Bremner admitted. "Why not say he might be absent so long?"

"I can't imagine. Mr. Charteris was something of a mystery to all of us."

"Did he have any other visitors whom you can recall, anyone who might be able to help us?"

"Practically no one came here. I suppose he met them out-of-doors. His was scarcely the type of room where you would expect men to come. As I told you, at the time of his death he had been occupying the cheapest room in my house for several months."

"I'm afraid that doesn't help us at all, then. Will you finish your story of that evening? I suppose you have other specimens of his hand-writing?"

"Oh, there's no doubt that that's his."

"Quite. But I shall have to put my case to the Yard complete with proof down to the smallest detail. We take nothing for granted. We daren't, you see, when men's lives are at stake. If you have anything else——"

"I could find something, I dare say. Or he would be sure to have something in his own room, would he not? But this is his paper." The paper in question was a heavy water-marked grey sheet of parchment, with one rough edge and three brockled in gold.

"You're sure it's his?"

"Yes. I've sometimes found pieces like it torn up very small in his basket."

Bremner smiled without explaining that that was no shadow of evidence. Should the letter prove to be a forgery, which, in the light of that pound note, seemed to him extremely probable, it would be easy enough to contend that the mysterious stranger, since whose advent no one had seen Charteris alive, had used his victim's writing-pad.

"Now, please answer this very carefully—was there anyone else in the house who could possibly give information as to this man's identity, who, perhaps, overheard some snatch of conversation? There would be the man who let him in, for one."

"He has a room on the first floor; I hardly think it would be possible for him to have heard anything. No one else was in the house, except a maid who was dressing to go out."

"I think we must have her in all the same. We can't afford to neglect the smallest tittle of evidence. She is still with you?

"She admitted you a little while ago."

"And where is her room situated in comparison with Mr. Charteris'?"

"I will show you later. The maids share a large room on a kind of landing five stairs below the top floor. I had originally intended to use that for my lodgers, but I find it almost impossible to keep two maids in that one, rather small room. There is no other room on the landing."

"I see. Does any one else sleep on Mr. Charteris' floor?"

"No. There is an airing-cupboard and a very large, dark luggage loft. The walls slope right down to the floor there and quite close to the floor in Mr. Charteris' room, which is why I can charge so little for it, although the position is so central."

"I see. Now, for the maid. Her name?"

"Agnes Grant."

"How long has she been with you?"

"About twelve months."

"During most of the time that Mr. Charteris was here?"

"Yes. I think she came a week or two after he did, so that if anything has happened during that time she would doubtless remember."

"Thank you. Ah, here she comes."

Miss Gell said in her correct voice, "Agnes, this gentleman wants to ask you one or two questions about Mr. Charteris."

Bremner saw the girl's face change, grow sullen, hard, forbidding. "I don't know nothing about him," she said. "Wasn't even here when he went."

"You were in the house, though, when the stranger arrived?"

"Yes, but I didn't let him in."

"You didn't catch a glimpse of him?"

"Not one."

"Nor hear his voice?"

She glanced up, obviously startled. Bremner pressed the advantage home. "You did? Come, that may be very useful. Would you know it again?"

She stared at him in derision. "Know it again? Voice I'd heard one evening?"

"Many people find it as easy to recognise a voice or a hand as they do a face. Voices very often have most distinctive qualities. Did you hear anything the man said?"

The girl hesitated an instant longer, then exploded angrily, "I wasn't listening. It wasn't anything to me who came to see Mr. Charteris or how much they quarrelled——"

"Quarrelled?"

"Yes. Reg'lar rough house it was. They said they found a ring round his wrist, didn't they? Shouldn't be surprised if this was the fellow that done it. I was dressing to go out, and I opened me door a bit to see if I could hear the rain on the skylight, it being dark outside you couldn't rightly see—bit of a fog that night, if you recollect—and I heard voices. Reg'lar roar there was. Well, I knew how Miss Gell would feel if there was trouble in her house, so I crept up the stairs and listened a minute. I thought if things sounded ugly I could just march in and say something about Miss Gell wanting to know if Mr. Charteris would be requiring supper. I knew, of course, he wouldn't be— it's my belief half the time he didn't have anything to eat—but I knew how Miss Gell would hate to have trouble here after all these years. Well, no one was speaking for a minute when I stood by the door, and then the stranger says, 'It would be prison for you if that were known,' and Mr. Charteris 'e laughs and answers, 'It won't ever be known; you don't dare face the things people 'ud say about you if they knew the truth.' And he laughed quite excited like; then the stranger says some more that I don't hear, and Mr. Charteris answers, 'Oh, safe enough. I know that. I've got you in a cleft stick. One move to ruin me and you're ruined, too. A clergyman and all!' Well, I didn't think I was doing meself much good by standing there and I was just going away when the man says in a dreadful sort of voice, 'I'd rather see you dead, whatever the cost, and her too——' and Mr. Charteris laughs like a madman and says in a loud, fierce way, quite wild he sounded, 'And I'd rather be dead, I swear it, than go through that.' And then something more I couldn't hear, not Mr. Charteris that time, and when I was beginning to feel all of a shake, Mr. Charteris says, 'But you wouldn't get off scot-free, neither; alive or dead I'd see to that.' "

She paused and Bremner asked keenly, "And that's all you heard? You're quite sure?"

Grant hesitated, and the detective continued incisively, "You'll be put in the witness-box without a doubt. It's just as well to make your story tally on both occasions."

Still she hesitated, as if she contemplated some reckless burning of bridges. Then she tossed her dark head. "Only one more thing and that was the stranger. He said, 'I haven't got a penny for you now, or at any time.' Well, that was all I wanted to know."

"Why should that interest you?"

The girl became sullen and furtive again. "He owed me money; more'n once he'd borrowed from me to pay the rent, and when I asked him for the money he'd say he was expecting some in a day or two, but it never came. I used to watch for his letters to see if they looked like they had money in them, but you couldn't always tell. Anyway, he didn't have no letters for a week or more before he died. And I never saw the colour of my money again."

"And after that—after you'd heard that, I mean—you went away?"

"Yes. I had a date."

"You didn't say a word to any one about what had happened up there?"

"Not me. What d'you take me for?"

"You didn't think that, perhaps, Mr. Charteris was in danger?"

She stared. "Suppose he was? I'm not his guardian angel."

"He might have been hurt."

"He ought to be able to look after himself."

"And you neither saw nor heard anything further?"

"Nothing at all."

"What time was this?"

She calculated. "I went out jest after half-past six; say about twenty-past this 'ud be."

"And the stranger had come just before six?"

"That is so," interpolated Miss Gell distantly, feeling that her maid had held the field long enough.

"Then we have evidence that he is alive—I take it you will swear that it was his voice you heard? Thank you—shortly before the half-hour. Since then we have no record of him until he turns up in a remote district, stone dead, some days later. You didn't, I suppose, hear any other names mentioned during the conversation?"

"Not one. I didn't hear anything but what I told you."

Bremner was inclined to believe her evidence, that had considerably whetted his curiosity. He now turned to Miss Gell suggesting that they should climb up to the room the dead man had occupied in the hopes of discovering further clues there. The ascent was a steep one and as they mounted, side by side, Miss Gell said suddenly, "There's one more thing, very small, and probably quite unimportant. When I came back I noticed that his electric light was burning; his room overlooks the road. That didn't strike me as peculiar until I had read his letter. He may, of course, have left it on through an oversight, but, if so, it was most unusual. People who are poor themselves are usually very careful about lighting bills. But, as I say, it may be a mere triviality."

"And on the other hand it may be a most important clue. I can't say anything at present. We're working too much in the dark. I suppose the room has been put to rights since his departure?"

A flood of pink colour invaded Miss Gell's face, to settle like a rosy butterfly on the tip of her nose. "It should have been, of course; but being short-handed and having a new lodger coming in that day, it got overlooked. I should probably have had it cleaned out this morning if I hadn't just happened to see the papers."

"That's wonderful. Almost a dispensation of providence, isn't it? Is this the door?"

They had reached the top of the house by this time, and Miss Gell opened a shabby, cream-coloured door to her right, and motioned Bremner inside. The room, though not precisely small, seemed cramped and had a shabby, stale atmosphere. The ceiling paper was darkened by smoke, and in one or two places showed marks of imminent damp; the walls were covered in hideous green, and this also hung in strips in one corner where the roof lacked a tile. Being directly under the roof the ceiling sloped and so did two walls to such an extent that there was a regular tunnel to the diminutive window; the room was poorly and conventionally furnished. A bed stood in a deep recess facing the door, and was shut off from the rest of the room by a moth-eaten, red serge curtain, that was, however, drawn back now to display the bed clothes in a certain disorder from having heavy articles, possibly a human body, flung upon them. Over the bottom rail were untidily folded two towels, thin and chilly like all towels in apartments; some hooks on the wall facing the bed-head accommodated the unfortunate Charteris' wardrobe; there was no washing apparatus, for the lodger saved eighteenpence a week for "service" by using the bathroom on the first floor, when he could secure it by casual strategy or wild rushes to circumvent the other occupants. The floor was partially covered by a cheap, red jute carpet; there was a long, narrow table in the centre of the room that was at this instant scattered over nearly all its surface with torn scraps of paper that fluttered in every direction as the draught from the door caught them; under the window was a small double-shelved book-case filled with guide-books and literary achievements of a bygone age by nameless men and women, embellished with illustrations of willowy ladies, and gentlemen with short imperials and enormous collars; a cupboard, scratched and covered with a red plush cloth, faced the untidy fireplace. There were two or three chairs of the straight-back variety, standing about the room, and one with a rush seat and wooden arms near the table had been pushed back so far that it was clear the occupant must have risen in considerable perturbation and excitement; on the table, among the tattered shreds of paper, were a pen, pencil and a twopenny bottle of ink. There was no blotting-paper. The fireplace, at which Bremner glanced, held a small gas-fire, attached to which was a shilling-in-the-slot meter, and a gas-ring whereon stood a battered rusty kettle. A glance in the cupboard revealed a little battered crockery, a few cheap novels, a Shakespeare, some soiled linen, a tin of boot-polish, various articles of make-up, some grease paints, a shabby pair of dogskin gloves—all the flotsam and jetsam of an incurably untidy man. On the mantelpiece were two presentation vases, silver glass with blue flowers in low relief, a china clock set on blue china pillars, a pennyworth of paper flowers in an ornate vase, a writing-pad of cheap, white paper and one or two envelopes close by, and various bazaar atrocities on every corner of the red plush and white enamel overmantel. The pictures on the walls were negligible; the inevitable Landseer, one or two sea-views, a canvas in oils of white and yellow marguerites, a fancy head, a mere blur of pink and pale blue, a family photograph or so.

Bremner glanced keenly round the room. "Do you know what luggage he took? What had he besides that?" He indicated a shabby, distended holdall that lay at the foot of the bed, grey with accumulated dust.

Miss Gell seemed perplexed. "I don't think he had anything else. Certainly I never saw anything. That's what he brought his clothes in when he came."

"Everything he possessed? It's a small bag."

"He had some things in a brown paper parcel as well. He never did have a great number of clothes, and I think that from time to time he sold a coat or a pair of boots to pay for his rent." It was clear that she chose to disbelieve her maid's wild and indiscreet version of the case.

"And during these last few days was he indoors all the time or did he get out?"

"He went out and about, of course. Why not? In fact, he had been out on the very day of his death."

"You mean the day on which he disappeared?"

"That's what I mean, of course."

"I was wondering," Bremner explained, "what had happened to his boots."

"Wasn't he wearing them?"

"Not when he was found."

Miss Gell seemed greatly perplexed. "That seems very strange. He was so particular about his boots, always cleaned them himself—though to be sure that saved him a penny a day—kept them on trees though he was untidy enough about everything else."

Bremner nodded. "Some men are fanatics about boots."

"No, I don't think it was that, quite, because he didn't take a scrap of trouble over his shoes, the ones he wore at home, I mean. They're here."

Bremner smiled. "No man could take much trouble over such dilapidated affairs. No ill-usage could make them much worse."

"That may be the reason. But we always thought it odd. I suppose the boots were very expensive, and he knew he couldn't afford any more."

"What colour were they?"

"Oh, black. Long and narrow and beautifully kept. He'd pawned his overcoat—"

"And his hat?"

She shook her head. "I don't think so."

"Well, it isn't here."

"He'd be wearing it."

"He should, of course. I dare say that was a windy night, and a long walk—if he walked it," he added non-committally. "I think these papers are the next thing. There appear to be a great many of them."

But, although he moved over to the table and began to sift the shreds and pieces he made no effort to dovetail any of them together, or find any clue that they might contain.

"What time does your post come at night?" he asked abruptly.

"About ten minutes past nine—never later than twenty-five past if it happens to be a wet night."

"And Mr. Charteris, unfortunately, said nothing as to his plans, where he proposed to go——?"

"Nothing but what was in the letter."

"Which is precisely nothing. Perhaps these scraps may help us. You say you were home about ten?"

"Or a little after."

"Then it's reasonable to suppose that he received some urgent summons by the last post, that not only caused him to leave town immediately, but also to dispose of all this before he went. Have you a telephone in the house?"

"There's one in the back hall. Twopence is the charge."

"I don't want to 'phone at the moment. I only asked because that gives us a second string. The summons may not have come in a letter, but over the wires. There's something very odd here, though. About half an hour elapsed between the delivery of the letter and

Mr. Charteris' departure. That is the utmost time and probably it was less. He says that he is very much rushed, and yet he can pause long enough to tear up all this paper into very fine pieces, quite a long job. He'd have burned it, I suppose, but he wouldn't dare take the risk with so small a fire and grate."

"What else could he have done with it?" asked Miss Gell practically.

"He might have taken it with him in his case and disposed of it during the journey. As a matter of fact, it's very strange that he took no luggage. You wouldn't, I suppose, know whether he had actually taken any clothes with him or not?"

"He had very few to take; I never saw him in anything but the black suit he wore every day and an old Norfolk jacket."

"The one hanging on the door, I suppose? I wonder why black, Miss Gell. It's unusual."

"He told me once in an expansive mood that there were compensations about being an actor when you were unemployed, as you could still make use of some of your effects."

Bremner nodded. "Ah! That seems a good explanation. He never played in London, I think?"

"I really don't know."

Bremner let that pass, satisfied in his own mind that Charteris was one of those most unfortunate devils, the provincial actor, without hope of anything better.

"I see he's taken his stick," he observed.

"I don't think he had one. In fact, I know he hadn't. I recall hearing him say that only fools burdened themselves with surplus luggage."

"I see. You say he'd sold his coat?"

"Yes. He told me he hoped by the time the cold weather came in to be able to afford a new one."

"That explains why he isn't wearing one, then. The night was cold enough for anything. Did you by any chance enter this room shortly before his guest's arrival?"

"About half an hour earlier."

"And was there any sign of this debris then?" He waved a hand at the scattered table.

"Not a bit. I suppose he kept all those letters and things in his cupboard."

"Or in that case." There was a small despatch-case, with Charteris' initials on it, lying by itself in a corner. "He appears to have walked out of this room in the clothes he stood up in and nothing else. There are several things here that don't dovetail. I shall have to make a detailed examination of the place, of course. But, I think, you can help me a little further. I take it you know this room quite well. You say you saw it the day Mr. Charteris disappeared?"

"Yes."

"Then you'll be able to tell me if anything is missing, or if there's anything here now, some trace, perhaps, of his mysterious friend, that wasn't here in the ordinary way?"

Miss Gell looked troubled as if that were a taller order than she cared about. Her eyes brooded with severe affection on the hideous trappings of the room. She murmured in a maddening undertone, "Let—me—see. The mantelpiece—twin bronze stags, blue china mouse, vase painted with a view of Lowestoft, blue vases from Aunt Laura, clock from Uncle Hilary—he's taken a lot of letters away. He always kept his letters standing about on the mantelpiece. I expect they're there." She nodded in her turn at the untidy table.

"He had a great many letters?"

"I don't think they all came here. I know for a fact that he had had no letters for several days before he vanished. I always see them, and just now we were expecting to find his name, because he said he was anticipating a remittance."

"I see. Do you notice anything else different?"

Miss Gell turned half-round and started. "Dear me!" she said, in her pleasant, ladylike voice. "That's very strange. He's left his tie behind." On the dismal-coloured, crochet table-mat lay a dark-blue, silk tie, as shabby as the rest of Charteris' personal effects, the cotton-wool stuffing protruding from the frayed silk.

"Surely he had more than one tie," suggested Bremner gravely.

"I don't think he had. I never saw any other. But that was not what I meant. This was the tie he was wearing when I saw him shortly before I went out."

"Ah! That's very important. May I congratulate you on your observation? You will be a most helpful witness. Is there anything else?"

Miss Gell continued her conscientious investigation. "I think there was a ball of thick twine on that cupboard last time I came in here. That isn't here now. Does that help you?"

"It might. It's impossible to say. Is that all?"

Even Miss Gell, eager as she was to be of use, could discover nothing more, no matter how carefully she sought, and so Bremner courteously intimated that he would now like the room to himself for purposes of investigation.

"I shall be downstairs if you require further assistance," remarked Miss Gell a shade distantly, "and please ring the left-hand bell. The other is out of order."

CHAPTER III

"Old father antic, the law."—*King Henry VII.*

I

IN that deserted room of Raymond Charteris, Bremner came upon several puzzling but most intriguing clues. He realised that the task of fitting together the innumerable scraps of paper would be an enormous one, and after a brief scrutiny he swept them all into his despatch-case in a huge envelope, and decided to turn them over to a responsible man at the Yard who would put them together for him, thus leaving him free to pursue other possible roads of discovery. Among the papers he found a small pair of scissors, very sharp and bright, nail-scissors, presumably.

"Cut up the papers with those?" questioned Bremner dubiously. "Hardly. These papers have been largely torn, and, in any case, so small a pair would merely hack these sheets. Perhaps—by George, I wonder." He straightened himself and looked eagerly round the room, turning out the contents of the waste-paper basket and tipping them back again impatiently when he could not find what he sought. After a short time, however, he did find it—in the fireplace. Scattered like fine dust on the drab tiles, collected like a microscopic ash on the meter and the front of the fender, was a brittle substance that broke instantly under the touch, leaving the fingers smeared with blackened ash. Bremner sat back on his heels regarding it thoughtfully. Then he bent and sniffed it; it had a strange, unpleasant, singed smell; between the fingers, before it crumbled, it was like wire, with roughened, uneven ends.

"That's it," muttered Bremner. "So he was shaved here. That complicates matters a bit."

There was a good deal of it, but he recalled that the dead man had worn beard and moustache, and he knew that he was now upon the scene of the murder. For a living man would scarcely allow an intruder, however muscular, to shave him in that peremptory fashion. Something else also came to light here—two tiny, shrivelled objects, like bits of burnt linen. He stared at them in the palm of his hand for a long time before he realised that they were the tabs of the coat and trousers in which Charteris had been found. The most microscopic examination revealed no trace of the name they had originally borne; the criminal had done his work too thoroughly for that. Slipping this evidence also into an official envelope, Bremner continued his search, convinced beyond all doubt that he was now on the scene of the murder. He knew that a man must either have deeply born criminal instincts to carry through so gruesome a plot to a successful conclusion or else be in a white heat of passion, when the brain works with calculated cunning, impossible in moments of cool reason. The small scissors were easily explained by that clipped beard; he went thoroughly through the contents of the cupboard and of the drawers of the writing-table for any signs of a razor and strop, but he found nothing.

"Deuced odd," he reflected. "Even if a potential

murderer carries a revolver about with him he doesn't usually come to visit his enemy complete with razor and blades. It's scarcely conceivable that he'd planned the whole thing beforehand. It would be so much simpler to collar him unawares. Besides, a revolver shot in an empty house! I must see the constable on duty and discover if he heard anything. There are a lot of queer points about this case that I don't much like."

As he turned back from his examination his eye was caught by a long strip of paper that was practically concealed by the gas-fire; not until he was lying on his stomach did he glimpse it. It contained four words written in a feminine hand, unsigned, without beginning or end:

"To-morrow as usual. Wait."

He held the paper up to the light. It was thick, good paper, with a water-mark of a lion rampant on a shield. The handwriting was peculiar—small, strong, finely-formed, the writing of a woman of education no less than character. He put it away with the other clues in his despatch-case and began to hunt for some facsimile of the paper on which the note was written. But he could find none. Beyond the cheap writing-pad and some cream-laid notepaper, obviously bought inexpensively at some small stationer's, there was nothing of this kind in the room. He thought it probable that he would be unable to advance far in so elaborate a case until he had seen the contents of those torn sheets, though even so he imagined it unlikely that a far-seeing murderer would leave any incriminating evidence.

One more piece of knowledge he accrued before he

left the room. Under the window lay a scrap of caked mud, with a dead, limp leaf or two attached, the sort of clot that might well accumulate on a boot-heel on a bad night. He put this away too, and went down to see Miss Gell.

"Miss Gell, do you remember what sort of weather there was when you went out that night?"

"It was foggy and very cold."

"It wasn't raining?"

"Oh, no, not then. It hadn't rained all day. But when I came out after supper there was a regular downpour."

"You don't know exactly what time it began?"

"I shouldn't like to say that. I was indoors, you see."

"When your meeting was over, did you come out of doors then?"

"Oh, yes. It hadn't begun at that time."

"What time was that?"

Miss Gell calculated. "The meeting began at seven-thirty, and we sat down to supper at half-past eight. I should say I left the church about eight-fifteen."

"Then the rain may have begun any time from then onwards. But if it was fine when the stranger came, he couldn't have brought this in?" and he held out to her the fragment of damp mud.

She looked profoundly puzzled. "No, of course, he couldn't."

Bremner seemed struck by an idea. "Did you say you went up to his room on your return?"

"I did, of course, to turn off the light. Otherwise, I should have left it just as it was."

"Then, perhaps, you brought the mud in with you?"

"It was quite fine and dry again when I returned

from the station at this end. And, in any case, I cleaned my boots most thoroughly on the scraper, by the front door, and afterwards rubbed them on the mat. I hardly think I could be responsible."

"It doesn't sound reasonable," Bremner admitted. "Did you go right round the room?"

"No. I stood in the doorway and looked at the room a minute and then I switched off the light."

"Then it's clear that some one else entered the room after the rain began, some one who couldn't have been the stranger." (But there was nothing, of course, to show that he hadn't been the stranger's accomplice.) "Are you quite sure, beyond all doubt, that your maid or some one else in the house did not enter the room later?"

"Absolutely. My maid had not returned when I came back, and nor had any of my lodgers. As soon as I had switched off the light in Mr. Charteris' room I locked the door and took the key away with me. Seeing so many papers on the table I assumed that it would be wise to admit no one until it became necessary to clean the room, and, if Mr. Charteris really intended to be back within three days, I could ask him to dispose of his own papers before I sent a girl up there. Gentlemen, I find, are very queer about their papers, and I make it a rule never to touch them unless they are actually destroyed and put in the basket."

"Very wise of you, I'm sure. Now, I want you to keep that room locked, to allow no one to enter it, and not to enter it yourself until you hear from the Yard again. This is a very peculiar case and will take some time to sift. And, now, I want to see your back entrance."

Miss Gell stared. "The back?"

"Yes. There is a back door, of course."

"Oh, yes. But I hardly see——"

"We can afford to take no risks, Miss Gell. All these premises, of course, were open to any one inside the house on the night that Mr. Charteris disappeared?"

"Of course."

"I take it that your maid had a key that would let her in again?"

"Of course." Miss Gell looked perplexed.

"That was merely by the way. It occurred to me. It probably hasn't the slightest connection with the affair. Now, supposing this mysterious visitor, decided, for fear of being seen, to escape via the back entrance, how could he do it?"

Miss Gell led him down four steps between a pair of dusty, Prussian blue serge curtains, and down a short passage, where, although it was not yet mid-day, a blue and yellow gas-jet flared to the discoloured ceiling. A row of hooks and an impromptu umbrella stand were obstacles in the way, and the economy of the mistress of the house was obvious by a glance at the linoleum that had been made up of a great number of scraps and squares neatly nailed together. Facing the foot of these stairs was a painted, wooden door that led to the coal-cellar; this door, however, was locked, a necessary precaution, Miss Gell explained, with the modern servant.

"And it was locked on the day of Mr. Charteris' disappearance?"

"It is always locked. I carry the key about with me."

That appeared a barren source of evidence, and Bremner let it pass. This part of the house consisted of a large sitting-room—the room where meals were served to the lodgers approximating to the usual apartment sitting-room, and offering nothing in the way of information; beyond this was the kitchen— a large rather untidy room littered with boards and saucepans and rolling-pins; beyond the kitchen door the linoleum ceased and the bare stone, rough and uneven, was uncovered. The scullery, at the end of a short passage through the kitchen, was large and gaunt, with walls washed a dull red, the usual sink, boards, rack and larder in one corner. The back door of the house opened out of this scullery, and beyond this stood two dustbins with lids precariously balanced on piles of malodorous garbage. The door into the garden stood at right angles to the coal cellar and was on the opposite side of the house. It was towards this door that Bremner turned.

"No basement," he thought acutely, opening the door and looking over the prisoned square of garden where no flowers ever blew, and where the grass was tall and straggling, and weedy. "Is this door used much?" he inquired of Miss Gell.

"There are two sheds, as you will see, just in the yard here. One is a shed for gardening tools, and is never used; the other is the servants' W.C. Otherwise, I should suppose that this door is never opened, and, in fact, I should have been glad to have it barred up. But in the circumstances that's impossible."

Bremner noticed that the handle turned easily and the door opened without creaking. "Is the garden ever used by any one?"

"Only the neighbours' cats." Miss Gell essayed a wintry smile. "They're terrible, particularly at night. There is, unfortunately, a dairy not very far distant and the cats come regularly——"

Quite ruthlessly he detached her from her cats. "Quite. What I really meant was—is it used by yourself or your lodgers or your maids?"

"Certainly not by myself or my lodgers, and I have never seen a maid there. It is really only a gravel square, though the grass has grown alarmingly during this wet spring and summer. It is really scarcely worth my while to have it put in good order as it would so quickly grow again."

Bremner agreed. "I should like to see it all the same. This is a corner house. Does the garden lead anywhere?"

"I have never been into it," returned Miss Gell primly. Bremner went past her out of the door, past the potting-shed, and up three ill-kept steps into the weed-grown garden. This was by no means large and was bordered by dusty, flowerless, lauristinus bushes and everlastings, all tainted by the peculiar grime of London that is compounded of fog and soot and dust.

"Some one's been here, pretty recently," was his shrewd comment, as he stood surveying that wild square with its coarse grasses, its withered clover patches, its vigorous growth of plantain and trefoil. For through that tangle a track had been carved by a body pushing resolutely towards the further end of the garden. Bremner endeavoured with the aid of powerful lenses to deduce something from the footprints, but the wet grass gave no clue. It was so matted that the steps had not penetrated to the damp, stony ground beneath, and he was forced to give up hopes in that direction. Following the track, though careful to avoid stepping in the first-comer's trail, he was not surprised to find himself facing a mossy, oozing wall, wherein was set a narrow wooden gate, so much washed out in colour that it was hard at first to realise that it had once been green. The latch was very stiff and rusty, but cobwebs and bindweed, that had grown over the frame, had been ruthlessly broken down. From the fact that they had not yet begun to form again it was clear to the detective that that gate had been opened within a very few days. It opened now with a soft growl of annoyance, and immediately revealed a vista of new possibilities. It led into a narrow lane that had once been a short-cut to the station, but was now blocked up because of extensive building operations in connection with a dairy. The lane was very muddy and grown with coarse grass, and almost touching him, as he turned to the right, was a second door set in a wall. This door also opened with some resistance. Bremner smiled. Then he commenced to walk along the back of the gardens of all Thermiloe Square. Each was furnished with a back gate, an inestimable boon to secretive servants who were anxious to meet lovers without being spied upon. Leave that gate on the latch and a man might linger for hours in a misty garden without fear of discovery. The outer door, he found out when he opened it, was set in a gloomy wall that ran to meet another at right angles and jointly formed a cul-de-sac. On the other side of the road, with its side windows facing those of No. 15, was another tall, gloomy house, ornate with dirty stucco, but here the tradesmen's entrance was in the front, to the right of the main door. Thus, reflected Bremner, keenly, a man emerging from the wooden door set in the cul-de-sac (that was called

with illogical humour Thornton Avenue) would probably be unobserved. Beyond the side of the house
labelled 13 was a short stretch of brick wall, and
then some tatterdemalion stables that had been con-
verted into second-rate garages leased at low rates.
The cars of such a neighbourhood would be poor
enough; there were six lock-up sheds, and above these
the space was used as a kind of warehouse. A very
dirty, slovenly youth was lounging near the garages,
spitting languidly on the pavement and idly glancing
through a day-old paper, mid-day (racing) edition.
Him Bremner approached.

"Know anything about these garages?" he asked.

The boy looked more bored than ever. "Don't
b'long to me," he mumbled.

"Oh? I thought, as you were hanging about here,
you might be connected with them."

The boy looked up, cocking an insolent eyebrow.
"Oh, reelly! Ain't bought the street, 'ave yer?"

Bremner laughed. "I wanted some information
about a possible vacant lock-up," he said. "You don't
know who owns them?"

"Carters." The boy jerked his head backwards.

"Does he hang about the premises?"

"Try the foreman."

A stalwart rubicund man in the early forties appeared from an open door. The boy jerked his head
a second time and resumed his occupation of staring
at the soiled news-sheet.

"Yes, sir?" asked the man, civilly enough.

"I was merely asking about the garages. You don't
happen to know where I could find the proprietor?"

"Well, sir, they belong to Carters. This is their
warehouse above here; we're shifting some goods at

the moment. Most times there's no one here at all."

"Really? You don't happen to know if there's a vacant garage?"

The foreman shook his head slowly. "Reelly couldn't say, sir. Shouldn't think so. Generally snapped up here; houses are so old, y'see, there's no chance of building private garages. But if you was to apply to Mr. Cleek, Mr. Geoffrey Cleek, in Bishopsgate, 'e'd know."

"Thank you very much. You're not generally on the premises then?"

"Not us. Only came down yesterday; shan't be here after to-morrow. Thank you, sir."

Bremner came back through the wooden gate into the garden and here, almost by chance it seemed, he found something that fitted in perfectly with the explanation that he was beginning to evolve. A sudden ray of sunlight, wan and transitory, smote that smut-laden garden; it kindled the weeds to a momentary beauty, struck a faint illumination from the dusty leaves of the laurels, and lingered for an instant about the stunted bough of the slender, barren cherry-tree. It struck a spark also from something small and bright that lay quite close to Bremner's foot on the damp earth, something that must have lain there some days because it was sunk almost level with the ground; Bremner scooped it up and let it lie in the palm of his hand. A ring, narrow, cheap, of inferior workmanship, such as may be bought from an hundred suburban jewellers for fifty shillings, a gold ring set with one small diamond, and on the inside a monogram, worn faint by contact with the finger it had once adorned. Bremner could with difficulty make out that tangle of letters in the uncertain London light, but he thought they were a P and an R intertwined, a rather garish design of lettering, with many curls and flourishes, arrogant yet flashy, and on the other side a very wanly defined 1918. Walking slowly back across that rough tangle of grass spears he tried to piece it together with the rest of the evidence. There was nothing, of course, to show that it had part or lot with this particular tragedy. It might be some legacy of war that had dropped there unnoticed, perhaps forgotten, or even have been flung there by one who had been betrayed and cast aside. Bremner thrust out of sight the temptation to weave tragic romance out of a cheap ring and revised his conclusions. Second thoughts showed that, though the presence of the bauble in that place might be mere coincidence, it clearly could not have lain there long or the constant rains and storms of English climatic conditions would have driven it underground before now; or else some jackdaw, the Autolycus of the bird world, would have espied it and carried it away. It might, of course, have belonged to one of the servants, or some distracted girl lodger who had hurled it there. Nevertheless, it seemed to him strange that so tawdry a trifle should be kept for more than eight years and should then be discarded. It was in any case useless to follow up these idle conjectures at this stage, and he said nothing of the matter, merely taking curt leave of Miss Gell in her hall and coming down the dilapidated steps into the smoky, mid-day sunshine. There were two or three people he must see before he could verify any of his suspicions; first, there was Willoughby, who worked in St. Mary Axe. Then he must discover the constable who had been on duty on the foggy night of the nineteenth when Raymond Charteris had disappeared, and if possible, the postman. Bremner did not hope that the man would remember whether he had actually left any letters at the house that evening, but he might conceivably recall whether the fog had delayed him very much. Postmen do remember such things.

Willoughby proved to be a narrow-chested, rather nervous young man with scrupulously parted hair, pale eyes, an indeterminate moustache and a manner that set him for ever in the rank of those whose earning powers are limited to six pounds a week. He was clearly ill-at-ease at having been summoned, and the sight of Bremner, alert and efficient, brought him no relief.

"I want you to tell me anything you know about Mr. Raymond Charteris," said the detective briskly.

"Mr. Charteris?" The young man looked unnerved. "But—I say—he's dead."

"I know. We're rather anxious to know as much as possible of what took place on the evening before his death."

Willoughby said instantly, very pale and apprehensive, "I didn't see him—I swear it."

"Quite. But I believe you, inadvertently, admitted a stranger who has not yet been identified, and who may conceivably have something to do with his decease."

"I couldn't help that; not my fault. Feller comes up behind you on a foggy night, says, 'Oh, thanks; save my key' and goes on upstairs. Well, put it to you, man to man, couldn't shut the door in his face, what?"

"You didn't recognise him?"

"Recognise him? Never saw his face. How sh'd I?"

"You heard his voice?"

"Just that minute."

"Think you'd know it again?"

The clerk was frankly incredulous. "Know a voice I'd heard just like that in a fog? Not much."

"If you hadn't any idea who it was, and you didn't know the voice, weren't you taking rather a risk by letting him into the house at all?"

"No. Might ha' been one of the fellers who live upstairs."

"And you wouldn't recognise him?"

"Feller can't know every other feller that lives in his house," explained Willoughby earnestly. "Always changing, those chaps. Broke, I suppose."

"I see. Then I'm afraid you can't help me much there. Now, did you know Mr. Charteris at all?"

"Well, I've seen him on the stairs."

"You didn't have anything to do with him, didn't know him personally, never went to his room or invited him to yours, never went out with him——?"

Willoughby got in a word. "Never spoke to him at all. Understand he was an actor out of a job. Commonest type known. About twenty thousand of them, a pal tells me, going round the provinces and the London offices just now. Not my line at all."

"You never saw him with a friend who might conceivably help us? Or met any visitor on the way to his room?"

"Never. Dessay shouldn't have noticed if I had."

It was so obvious that this young man would be of no assistance that Bremner let him go back to his work. From a telephone booth he rang up a man at the head office of the Bloomsbury Postal District, and asked him to ascertain the name of the man who delivered at Thermiloe Square on the night of the nineteenth, and if possible to detain him against his (Bremner's) return. Then he sent a similar message to the police station, asking here for the constable on duty at the time in question. That done he decided to solve the mystery of the ear-ring. That there was some very deep puzzle behind the body Egerton and the doctor had discovered on the hillside was obvious. The tube took him from the city to the West End of London. Bremner had had a good deal of experience in jewel robberies of late years, and although he could not definitely claim knowledge of its designer, he could, at any rate, narrow the field down to half a dozen. The trinket was exquisitely wrought, and must have been ordered by a man with a deep pocket. Bremner having made out his list of "possibles" proceeded to put this to the test. Turning into the jeweller he thought the most likely to have supplied the ear-drop, he asked for the manager. To him he explained that a valuable trinket had been found and given into the custody of the police; officialdom had reason to believe that it had been stolen, and was therefore anxious to obtain its true history in order to compare this with the story told by the man who was seeking to recover it from them. After some hesitation, the manager said, quite clearly, that the work had not been executed by his firm, and Bremner walked fifty yards down the street and over the road into the second shop. Here he met with similar denials, but although he had not located the actual craftsmen he was at all events put on their track. An elderly man in a grey suit, with semitic ancestors and a charming manner, suggested, after examining the ear-drop most minutely, that it was beyond doubt the work of either Messrs. Trent and Willard or Messrs. Nettle and

Beard, but probably the former. Both these names were on Bremner's list, Trent's being fifth and Nettle and Beard third. He went to the former first, as being nearer, but, here again he was foiled. In no way dispirited, since he knew from experience that murderers are not found so easily as caterpillars in springtime, he took a taxi to Messrs. Nettle and Beard, and here the work was instantly recognised.

"Oh, yes, sir," said the manager. "We remember that very well. And I shouldn't be surprised if you're right about it being stolen. We made it to a special order four years ago; it was a wedding present—do you wish to know the name of the gentleman who ordered it?"

"I'm afraid I must press for that. It's most important. Of course, we will treat the information as confidential, so far as we can, but it may have to come out."

"It was Sir Gervase Blount, a clergyman. I dare say you know the name. Quite a lot of people are talking about him because of this book of his. He was particularly anxious that we should use very fine stones. You will have recognised their quality, of course. I believe I'm right in saying, Mr. Bremner, that it is mainly through you that Mr. Neville Pierson is at present serving seven years?"

Bremner grinned. "And I believe I'm right in saying that he diddled you out of a nice little sum before we got near enough to put salt on his tail."

The manager smiled ruefully. "Quite right. I hope we've been able to assist you in this matter?"

"Yes. I think—in fact, yes. They're a handsome present, you know, even for a wealthy man."

"I think the bridegroom was in the frame of mind when nothing would seem excessive."

"No doubt," agreed Bremner in a tone that suggested he had lost interest in the matter. "Thank you for the information. It's what we suspected. At the same time, until we have made our final move, perhaps you'd be good enough to say nothing of this conversation. A hint in the right quarter and all our work is thrown away."

He came out of the shop frowning deeply. "What did that fellow mean by saying he wouldn't be surprised to hear that it had been stolen? What more does he know? And how do I find that out?

A message to the local police station informed him that the constable who had been on duty in Thermiloe Square that night was now at the Yard and available for examination. Bremner decided to polish him off next, and returned instantly to Bloomsbury.

The man in question, whose name was Mayhew, was a tall brisk man, with a tanned face and an attractive manner, an intelligent witness, Bremner decided, with a fistful of personal ambition.

"You were on duty at Thermiloe Square on the nineteenth?"

"Yes, sir. Evening duty, that is."

"Quite. Do you remember anything special about that night?"

"It was the night of that bad fog."

"Did you notice any one coming or going at No. 15?"

"I saw the lady come out just before seven, but I didn't think much o' that, of course."

"Did you notice any one in particular before that?"

"No, sir. Can't say as I did. At these lodging-houses there's always some one going or coming."

"Did you see any one go in after that?"

"No, sir. But I saw a gentleman come out."

"What time was this?"

"Twenty to nine, sir."

"You're sure?"

"Quite. He came across and asked me the time."

"The fog was at its thickest then, wasn't it?"

"That's right, sir?"

"Then how could you see your watch?"

"Illuminated dial, sir."

"But I suppose you couldn't see his face?"

"Well, nothing to speak of. Anyway, he'd pulled a derby hat right over his eyes to keep out the fog, I suppose; has a nasty habit of getting into your eyes, fog has, and he'd turned up his coat collar, I think, because there was hardly any face for me to see. I wasn't surprised. Fog can be mortal cold."

"Did he ask you anything besides the time?"

"Oh, yes, sir. He said he wanted to get to Victoria Station. He had to catch a north-going train that evening. He'd had a message and he had to go in a great hurry. His train went at nine twenty-five, and it was most important he shouldn't miss it."

"You're sure he said north?"

"Quite, sir. He said it twice, most emphatic."

"In order that you shouldn't make any mistake when you reported the conversation," reflected Bremner grimly. "Can you give me no sort of personal description then?"

Mayhew slowly shook his head. "Wouldn't be fair, sir. Couldn't see him hardly."

"What did he wear?"

"Something dark. That's all I could make out. Anyway, the fog was so black that you couldn't see no more than his head and shoulders, and not them any too clearly."

"Gloves—stick—carry a bag?"

"No, to all those, sir."

"How can you answer if you couldn't see him?"

"He said more'n once how cold it was, and slapped his hands together. I'd have known if he'd been wearing gloves, and he couldn't have had a stick or bag or he couldn't have swung both hands. And he didn't stoop and put anything down either."

"You couldn't see his throat?"

"No, sir. Only that he'd turned up the coat collar."

"Then, of course, you wouldn't catch a glimpse of his collar or shirt?"

"Afraid not, sir. Coat was turned right up over the chin. Well, no wonder with a fog on like that."

"What about his voice?"

"It sounded hoarse, sir, like as he had a bad cold."

"Or as if he were trying to imitate some one else," meditated Bremner. "Did you see if he wore glasses?"

"Well, you couldn't see much with his hat like that, but I should say not, certainly not. There was a lamp quite near, you see."

"You're prepared to go into the witness-box and swear he came out of No. 15?"

"Yes."

"Of course, several people may have come out of that house at that time. . . ."

"Beg pardon, sir, they couldn't."

"Why not?"

"Because they wasn't in there. He said something straight away about the house being empty. And I happened to look up, and, bless my soul, there was a light blazing in the top room; a queer little square window it had, very small because of the sloping walls. I know those rooms; I've slept in others like them. Well, I said, 'House empty, sir? Then haven't you gone and left your light on?' and he sort of stammered and exclaimed, 'So I have. And I haven't time to go back now.' "

"This was twenty minutes to nine, you said. And his train didn't go till twenty-past—and he had no luggage. It wouldn't have taken him long."

"No, sir. But he said some one would be home soon."

"Then he went towards Victoria?"

"Yes, sir."

"Without saying another word?"

"Nothing to matter, sir."

"How can you tell whether it matters or not? You'll never pull down a big job, Mayhew, if you're as casual as that. Did you never hear of the twisted hairpin that hanged Mme. Martine? Or the nail in the window-sash that led to the discovery of the murder of Beryl Wilcox? The Yard is like God— there is no last or first. Everything's important—terrifically important. It's in casual conversation that a man will betray himself. He'll have planned all the things that are to cover his tracks and at the twelfth hour in an excess of zeal he'll blurt out some commonplace that condemns him. Didn't it strike you as odd that he was going to Victoria to catch a north-bound train? When he was on top of Euston, too! Didn't think about it, I suppose. That's the most important thing you've told me to date. What else did this fellow say?"

Mayhew, considerably crestfallen, yet intelligent enough to know that he had been taught something uncommonly useful to his career and keen enough to benefit by it, considered a moment.

"He said what a shame it was the fog had come; it might make his train late; and didn't I find it was a thankless job; and was mine a long beat and when did I come off duty? Things like that, sir."

"Was all this after you'd pointed out about the light?"

"Yes, sir."

"So that he could have gone back to his house, two or three times over, climbed the stairs and extinguished the light during the time he spoke to you?"

"He certainly could."

"So his time wasn't so precious as he wanted you to believe?" Of course, he added inwardly, he didn't go back because he couldn't. He wasn't Raymond Charteris, so he hadn't a key.

"Doesn't seem like it, sir," assented Mayhew.

"And after that he went to—er—Victoria?"

"Yes."

"And you saw nothing more of him?"

"No, sir."

"Did you see which way he went?"

"To the right, sir. That's the way to the buses and trains to Victoria Station."

"Quite. And you?"

"Went on with my beat."

"In the opposite direction?"

"That's right."

"How far does your beat extend?"

"Round to Mayburn Square on the north, and to the High Road on the south."

"So that when you're in Mayburn Square you can't see the house he came out of—No. 15?"

"No, sir."

"Mayburn Square is pretty long, isn't it? It would take you at least a quarter of an hour to get there and back in sight of the house, even if you walked briskly all the time. Could you do it in fifteen minutes?"

"I always allow twenty, sir. And, then, if some one stops to ask you the time or anything, or if you stop yourself, as of course you do, p'r'aps for several minutes, that delays you still more."

"Exactly. Did you meet any one that night?"

"An old lady, I remember, sir. She'd lost her tippet. A little grey one, she told me, just a little grey one with a head and a tail. A kit fox she called it. It looks, she says, like a long grey cat. D'you s'pose any one who sees it'll think it's a cat and will try and shoo it off? Rare upset she was. As if any one could ha' seen a bit of grey fur on the ground in all that fog. Wanted to know where she could go and inquire for it, and gave me her address in case I found it anywhere, and she'd pay something to have it back. Must ha' kept me there talking a quarter of an hour. I couldn't shake her off."

"And all that time the house was unguarded?"

"Well—, you might put it like that, sir."

"And any one might have come in or out?"

"They didn't, sir." Mayhew's voice was triumphant.

"How do you know?"

"Because, when I came back the light was still up in that room, but not in any other room in the house."

"That isn't any proof. Suppose, for the sake of argument, there had been some one else in that room when the man came and spoke to you: suppose a crime had been committed there, and he had left a confederate upstairs, what was there to prevent his going round the corner, telephoning him to leave the house as he saw you turn into Mayburn Square, leaving the light burning? Was there any sign of a car in the road?"

"Not one. No one but a lunatic would have taken a car out on such a night."

"But the fog dropped quite suddenly. At ten o'clock it was fairly clear again, except for the rain."

"Well, sir, I was patrolling up and down here all the evening and I didn't see any car."

Bremner nodded shortly and dismissed him. His next examination was of the postman, a short, swart man, clean-shaved, walking with a slight limp.

"You remember the foggy night last week? Put you out much?"

"Should think it did. Finished me rounds hour and a 'arf late."

"What time do you generally deliver at Thermiloe Square?"

" 'Bout ten-past nine."

"Do you remember at all what time you delivered your letters on that night?"

"After ten."

"You're sure?"

"Quite. Some young feller come along behind me, and stops me as I'm coming out o' the gate of No. 19. 'Anything for fifteen?' he says. 'What name?' I arsks. 'Marsh,' 'e says. Well, I looks. There's orfen letters for Marsh, addressed by his own type machine. Writes stories 'e does, and back they comes like 'oming pigeons hevery week. Well, this night, it so 'appens, 'e 'adn't got one. Nothing, I says, and 'e looks a bit thoughtful-like and asks again, 'I s'pose you're sure?' I says a bit angry because I'm cold and wet, and all sooty with that dratted fog, 'Well, look fer yerself if yer like. There ain't nothing for No. 15 at all.' So 'e sighs, and says, 'Right you are,' and goes on in to No. 15, and I goes past."

"You don't remember if there were any lights up in the house at the time?"

"There were lights in the 'all and the dining-room."

"You're very sure. How can you remember?"

"I was thinking o' that young Marsh and 'is miserable face goin' away when 'e found I 'adn't a letter for 'im. And as I passed 'is 'ouse I looked up and saw them lights burning, and I thought, 'You young cub, you don't know when you're well off, you don't. 'Ow'd you like my job, tramping through all this slush and fog'—though the fog was lifting then as a matter of fact; still it was wet and gloomy enough—'leaving other folkses letters, I thinks. You jest try it. Wish to Gawd it was me be'ind them snug curtains sitting by a fire wiv a sausage on me knee.' Oh, I can swear to that, sir."

"Good. You may have to. And the time as well?"

"That's right. This young spark says, ' 'Ow late you are,' as if I was Gawd A'mighty and sent the fog apurpose to annoy 'im. I snaps, 'Yes, after ten, ain't it?' and 'e says, 'Quarter-past, I should say.' Good enough?"

"Excellent."

When he had dismissed the postman Bremner looked at the watch on his wrist and did lightning calculations. His inquiries and investigations had taken a good deal of time, and it was obvious that his next step must be to go down to Four Corners and interview Blount. It was manifestly impossible, however, to do so this evening, since trains to that remote spot were infrequent, and it was hardly likely that there was anything to be gained by making so uncomfortable a journey to-night, even if he could have contrived it by an ingenious succession of cross-country connections. He went, therefore, to headquarters to report developments, and when he left some time later went back to his own rooms where he sat at his window, hands locked round his knees, and went carefully in his mind over all he had learned about the case, trying to dovetail the various scraps of evidence or information, to make a coherent whole.

The principals in the affair were three—the dead man, the woman who had visited him, and the stranger who had probably murdered him. It was particularly unfortunate that so little was known about Charteris himself. He had been an actor, he had been unemployed for some time and was not above borrowing the earnings of a servant girl to pay his rent. Exactly how far the dead man's relations with that girl had gone Bremner felt it unnecessary to inquire, although in the light of her fierce 'If there was any money going I meant to have some of it' set up an ugly suspicion in his mind. At all events, he had made no suggestion regarding repayment of the loans, although he had told his landlady that his luck had turned and he expected better times, almost immediately, sufficiently sincere in that declaration to make preparations for changing his room. That fact prejudiced Bremner strongly against the man, though he endeavoured to disregard it. At all events here the tangle lay. Charteris, desperately poor, none too scrupulous about the way he laid hands on ready money, is suddenly visited by a nameless lady—a lady who comes by appointment, is shrouded heavily in a veil, and who is so much terrified of recognition that when she loses a valuable diamond trinket she prefers to cut her loss rather than take any risks. To claim the jewel without giving any clue as to her identity would be a difficult job, and she makes the best of a thoroughly bad case. There is always the chance that the jewel was not lost there. Presumably she inquires at Scotland Yard, giving a detailed account of her movements during the day, but mentioning nothing of her visit to the Bloomsbury boarding-house. Supposing the jewel is found in the neighbourhood she will have some yarn ready for her husband to explain its presence there, and not being a fool will probably be able to substantiate it. These circumstances, taken with the jeweller's evidence, convinced Bremner that the lady in question was none other than Pamela Blount. It is perfectly clear, Bremner continued, reasoning just under his breath, that Charteris is threatening her; he wants money and has some hold over her, presumably knowledge of her past that she is anxious to keep from her husband. The fact that she was an actress before her marriage makes things look black for the pair of them. The actual fact at issue isn't of much consequence at the moment. But either she turns in desperation to her husband for help, and he was the mysterious stranger who invaded Charteris' room on the night of his disappearance, and probable death, or else he learned the truth through another channel. Either way he's implicated, I imagine; though I can't be certain till I hear his version of the affair. The conversation overheard by that slut lends colour to the first hypothesis. The word "prison"—I suppose you know this is a criminal offence—smells of blackmail. And Charteris' reply, that he wouldn't dare bring an action because of the position in which he personally would find himself, bolsters up that story. Of course, if the fact at issue is some incident in Pamela Blount's past, it's reasonable to suppose that Blount himself would be prepared to pay heavily for its suppression. By coming at all to see Charteris he played utterly into the fellow's hands, and Charteris was probably wise enough to realise that. If he had the remotest glimmer of intelligence it must be obvious to him that whereas, before, he had only a woman from whom to extort money, a woman, moreover, with nothing to draw upon but a limited allowance, by dragging Blount into the case, either through his wife or by some other means, he now has a wealthy man whose position and calling are such that he'll go to almost any lengths to prevent mud being pitched at him through his wife.

Bremner also had heard that the man was devoted to his dark, beautiful, enigmatic bride; given these circumstances, the bride, the villain and the opportunity, what presumably followed was comprehensible enough. Blount must have had sufficient experience of the world to recognise that once a blackmailer sets his claws into a man he is like a vampire, never letting him rest until he has sucked him utterly dry. To yield, to give him money, meant to deliver himself for ever into the hands of the tormentor. To refuse his demands very likely meant that he would put his threats into action. These actors were queer fish; though Charteris was broke to-day, he probably knew a number of men among whom a story connected with Lady Blount's past would quickly circulate. Blount himself was known to be ec-

centric—that word so dearly loved of the press!—
and this very dissimilarity from the majority of his
clerical brethren had given him a prominence that his
personal appearance and striking manner had greatly
emphasised. No doubt any gossip about the couple
would be readily taken up. There was little, if any
doubt in Bremner's mind, that the strange visitor had
actually been Blount himself. He was sure that the
man had recognised the body, and there had been an
odd, strangled triumph in his eyes as he looked on his
defeated enemy. No question but that he hated him,
and that hate warred with the man's realisation of the
duty he owed to his cloth.

Coming back to that fatal night there remained the
fact that the intruder, whom for the purposes of argument, Bremner decided for the moment to assume was
Blount, had known that the house was empty and that
no one would return before ten at the earliest. That
left him a clear field. No doubt all manner of argument
had been employed. The ominous blue ring, encircling
Charteris' wrist told its own story of rough usage. The
struggle might have been protracted, but Blount must
have gone prepared for any measures, for when he
recognised that nothing else would save the position
and the wife to whom his whole heart was given, he
drew the revolver and shot the blackguard through the
head. The house was a corner one and the walls thick,
so it was conceivable that no noise had been heard outside. Moreover, a fog so dense as the one that night
had been would effectually diminish if it did not altogether drown even so sharp and piercing a reverbera-
tion, and it might have seemed to passers-by, of whom
in such circumstances there would naturally be few,

no more than the snapping of a wooden lath. In any case English people are reticent and slow to interfere in another man's business. A momentary pause, a hesitating, a slight feeling of discomfort, and then the shrugged shoulders, that imply that an Englishman's house is his castle, and the suspicion, at all times faint, would be stifled and its owner move on, convinced that all he had heard was a bursting tyre or a man cracking a whip to intimidate a disobedient dog.

Then, with the body crumpled in front of him, much remained to be accomplished. The house had been empty since some minutes before seven; it had been a quarter to nine when the man descended the steps and spoke to Mayhew. During those two hours much might be done; Bremner knew that at such moments as these, when a man is in a white-heat of passion, or when instinct warns him that his own life is in peril, he will display a caution and a cunning of which he is normally quite incapable. With the body of his enemy before him Blount found himself working against time to obliterate all signs of the murder. The first consideration was clearly to dispose of the body and to dispose of it in such a manner that it was unlikely to be found for a long period, if, indeed, it should ever be discovered at all. Had the murder been committed by some other means, by a blow on the head for instance, the mere disposal of the body in some attitude or position that would suggest an accident would be sufficient and far safer than to make that hazardous journey down to Four Corners by night, as must clearly have been done. No doubt, Bremner reflected, Blount had considered the alternative of leaving the revolver at the dead man's side to suggest felo de se, but the danger was too great. The revolver would probably be traced and the whole story that the murderer was so anxious to conceal would fill the penny press. Therefore, the only solution was the total disappearance of the body, with sufficient clues left on the scene of the crime to allay temporarily, at all events, the alarm that might otherwise be roused. A letter purporting to come from Charteris, laid conspicuously on the hall-table, should serve to deceive Miss Gell, who, when her erstwhile lodger did not reappear, would presumably re-let his room and store his baggage, such as it was.

That the letter was a forgery seemed to Bremner certain; no man, actually travelling, would leave his sole handbag in his rooms. No man would leave at ten o'clock at night without taking any luggage. So far the matter seemed clear. The real puzzle lay in the actual disappearance of the corpse. In order, further, to carry out the story of the letter, Blount must have concealed part of his face and made a point of chatting for a few moments to a policeman to give the impression that the house was now empty, and that Raymond Charteris had actually set out for the north. Then he could have returned via the back entrance, that doubtless he had already inspected; or, choosing a time when the policeman was out of sight, have let himself in again with Charteris' key by the front way. The next difficulty was the removal of the body from the upper room to the desolate hillside at Four Corners where it was found. This was a more baffling problem. It began to seem probable that that ring was connected with the case. The monogram "P.R." might easily stand for Pamela Raymond and the year 1918. Bremner paused and jotted a code note on to a pad at his elbow. He had the wise man's shrinking from committing himself

in writing to anything that any one else could decipher.
That done he went on with his musings.

Even a man with a beard and moustache must shave
and he recalled Miss Gell's description of Charteris as
a man with a neat, dark beard and foreign-looking
moustache, so it was reasonable to suppose that a razor
and soap would be forthcoming. Blount, wishful to
provide against all contingencies, was taking every precaution against the body being recognised, if, by some
ill-chance, it were discovered. To shave off the hair
and reveal the sinister scars, to clothe the body in a
priestly collar and vest, to add the appalling boots,
would be to disguise it effectually. The discovery of
those scars must have come as a blow, for they were
sufficiently distinctive to attract attention anywhere.
It became, therefore, the more important, that the
hiding-place should be secure. His brain working
rapidly, the murderer went hastily through the dead
man's letters seeking any that might have a bearing on
the intolerable situation that had arisen. Time had
been too short to burn them, but they were shredded
very finely, no doubt in the hope that a fastidious landlady would dispose of them all via the waste-paper
basket before awkward questions were asked. These
papers were at the moment of his cogitation being
carefully sifted and made intelligible by trained men at
the Yard. In the morning Bremner proposed to go
across and see the result. There was no doubt that the
shaving process had actually taken place at the flat;
those burnt cinders told their own tale, and if support
were needed, there was the presence of that tie to
corroborate his suspicions. Nevertheless, Bremner was
a little perplexed, wondering why a man who had
planned to cover his tracks so magnificently should have

blundered here, when, by opening the window, he might have tossed the evidence into the air. He came to the conclusion, however, that Blount must have feared lest the ashes should fall on the balcony that jutted out immediately beneath the window, and these being noticed, uncomfortable questions be asked.

Next came the point of the boots. Whence had a man of education obtained such deplorable specimens? Bremner thought hard. Obviously these had not been part of the original scheme; in fact, he was inclined to think that the actual murder was unpremeditated. Some instinct of self-preservation had probably decided the man to take a revolver with him on his visit. Most likely it was in the blood-heat of an instant of uncontrollable fury that he had fired. At this juncture Bremner added a second coded note to the writing-pad. The shaving of the face might be an inspiration, though there was still the difficulty of the razor to be solved. For if Blount had taken the razor with him the crime must have been carefully planned. For the instant he let that pass until he had cross-examined the man and heard his own story. He came back to that problem of the boots. Clearly there must have been something that made them noticeable, thus rendering it imperative for the murderer to remove them, lest they betray the identity of the victim. It was reasonable to suppose that their cut would make them distinctive. A man with such beautifully kept feet no doubt had his boots made to measure at some expensive shop, and these could easily be traced. As he ascertained later, this was true, although the proving of the suspicion did not actually at that stage help the case forward. At all events, they must be disposed of, but they must not be left in the dead man's rooms lest they arouse suspicion in the minds of any who might make a search for him. For a murderer with so much forethought, would, Bremner argued, make allowance for all such eventualities. There would, of course, be no alternative boots on the premises, except those in which Blount himself stood, and these would be as revealing as Charteris' own. Where, then, could a man in desperation obtain a pair that could never be traced at all? It was some time before he found even a possible answer to that question. He recalled the fact that Blount's name was invariably connected with work in aid of the destitute and unemployed, particularly ex-service men, and he knew that the fellow was secretary and treasurer of a small fund designed for their assistance. This organisation had its offices in Aldwych, and here Blount was often to be found, since he understood better than most the gruff silence, the apparent suspicion and bitterness with which the British working man will so often veil his gratitude. Bremner had a sneaking suspicion that those frequent journeys to London had done nothing to ameliorate the position between Blount and his bishop, who believed that north-country vicars should expend their activities among their own flocks, and not be connected with half a dozen extraneous labours. Of course, as secretary and treasurer, Blount would be in possession of keys not merely to the office, but to the cupboards in which stores for the assistance of these waifs of society were kept. The clothes, that were sent from all parts of England, were separated and put away in orderly rows in the room in Teddington Street, Aldwych. It would, therefore, be the work of a few instants only for a man who was completely at home in that office to extract from the requisite cupboard a pair of dilapidated boots, re-lock cupboard and offices and return in stealth considerably aided by the weather conditions, to the car he would have left at the kerb-side. Had it been noticed during that brief absence its presence there would excite no comment. A passer-by or policeman would merely note that there was a man in the seat next to the driver, for it would be simple enough to prop the corpse upright and wedge it into position with a couple of motor cushions. On such a night, and in such weather, it was improbable that the car had even been noticed. Teddington Street was a turning out of Aldwych proper and it was ten chances to one against a constable patrolling it at that particular time. He would not, of course, exchange the boots there, but would wait until he reached some secluded spot where he could be certain of privacy. As for Charteris' own boots these might be anywhere on the road from London to Tenbeigh; search for them would be futile enough. If they were ever to come to light it would be by the merest chance, and Bremner did not bank on that.

Fantastic as the notion at first appeared further reflection convinced Bremner that he had stumbled on the correct solution. As for the altered collar that was most probably done on the spot; it would take Blount no time at all. The vest was a more difficult matter, but in view of the discarded tie that might also have been put on the body at Thermiloe Square. It was even possible that Blount had stripped off his own, and that would explain the turned-up coat collar to hide the absence of the clerical vest. Then, the disguise, barring the boots, reasonably complete, the murderer was faced with the problem of getting the corpse out of the house. In accomplishing this, he had two distinct factors in his favour. The first and most striking was the empty house; the second was the fog. It must be supposed that he had driven up in a car, and this he might well have concealed, either by chance or design, in the cul-de-sac running up the side of No. 15. His next task would be to drag or carry the body down the stairs. Charteris was by no means a tall man; and as Ambrose had testified he was far too light, by reason of malnutrition, for his actual height. Blount on the other hand had muscles of steel—so much Bremner had gathered on the sole occasion of their meeting when, by virtue of his acquaintance with Scott Egerton, the pair had shaken hands. It would, therefore, be a difficult but not an insuperable task for such a man to carry the body down the stairs, or even drag it, since they were carpeted and would make little enough sound, to take it through the garden and out of the garden door into the waiting car. The fact that there was no basement would immeasurably assist him. All this was, of course, supposition of a rather elaborate kind, but Bremner hardly thought he would dare descend the front steps in full sight of the street. A casual passer-by might choose that precise instant to pause to kindle a match; the constable might just then return. But the side of the house was ideally safe. The warehouse was closed and dark; no one in his senses would be taking a car out on that night of fog. No windows from No. 13 overlooked that side of the street. The further wall was blank and high; behind it lay the untilled waste ground of the railway community. There would be no one about at such a time. There was, moreover, the sinister fact of the ring. It was not impossible, always-supposing that it had any connection with the case, for Charteris to have hurled his own ring into the garden, but Bremner regarded it as highly improbable. In the first place, his room overlooked the street and in order to reach the back of the house he must ingratiate himself with one of the other lodgers, and, from all accounts, he was a man of mystery to every one of them. The only other way would be to walk through the deserted garden, and Bremner was sure that Miss Gell or her servants would have noticed him and commented on his presence there. On the other hand a man carried in a more or less horizontal position is quite liable to lose small articles from his pockets, as they will roll out and probably be unnoticed. Supposing the ring to be in a waistcoat pocket, the jolting of the body, for even Blount would find the task an awkward one, might easily cause it to be jerked on to the earth where mere chance had revealed it to the detective.

There was, of course, the risk about those unbolted doors. Blount would be bound to leave those and trust that they would remain unnoticed as very probably they would. At this stage Bremner recalled the odd, reddish stains on the dead man's handkerchief and realised that these were rust. That seemed to him to clinch matters. Blount, anxious to avoid the slightest suspicion, had wiped his fingers on the victim's handkerchief in the belief that this would never come to light or, conversely, if it did, that no question about such stains would ever be raised.

The body once in the car the rest was easy. There are not a great number of places where it is safe to hide a murdered man; but the sea is the most secure. Unexpected storms will sweep over ditches, uncovering the horror that earth and leaves have been heaped to hide; poets may stray over lonely countrysides and discover in some thicket the hideous thing that was once a man; but the sea tells no secrets. It was a hundred to one that the treacherous sands in that spot would draw the body into themselves, leaving no trace to show where, for a brief instant, it had lain. But, even if the corpse were ultimately washed ashore, the verdict must surely be, after so long a lapse of time, "Found shot" with nothing to show whether the wound were self-inflicted or not. And, of all the safe spots on the coast where no search would conceivably be made, surely the best was that wild and lonely cliff-side hedged about with deep, ice-black pools fringed with rocks, where the sands were too dangerous for the most foolhardy to explore, and even the sea-birds eschewed the sides of the precipice? During his short stay at Tenbeigh, the nearest town of any pretensions to Four Corners, Bremner had learned that there was a passable motoring road, carved out by some dead and gone Blount, that wound among the lower reaches of the coast, passing at no great distance from the place where the body was found; this was, indeed, the road to which Egerton had referred, and that ran directly round Blount's estate. To halt the car at that spot, to carry the body fifty yards and then to pitch it overboard is no great matter for a man of good physique. Bremner wondered if he had stayed there long listening in vain for the splash that would record the final yielding of the body to the sea. The nights there were dark and sinister enough, and all that time from a little after ten until dawn, a light, maddening rain had fallen. A new thought struck him. He had no proof that down in Thebeshire it had actually rained throughout the night; he must first learn from the natives what sort of weather there had been. But in any case the wind would have whistled in that solitary watcher's ears with eerie screams, as he waited, between pitch-black sea and lowering sky, sick with doubt and numb with apprehension. The picture was a grim one. Bremner thrust it out of sight and stood up, preparatory to going to bed. There was plenty of work to be done to-morrow. His last waking thought was of what Blount (or whoever the actual murderer might prove to be) must have felt when he discovered the button missing from his coat.

2

The next morning was fine and clear. Bremner rose early and walked through St. James' Park to the Yard. His first task was to find out what the experts had been able to make of the papers he had given them; his second, to telephone Somerset House (in accordance with the first coded note on his paper), and his third, to inquire, either in person or through some trustworthy messenger, whether any one had heard the sound of a revolver shot on that particular night.

At the Yard he asked for the man who was engaged with the letters, a small, alert fellow, called Peterson.

"Not particularly satisfactory, sir," said the latter dubiously. "It's a bit queer altogether. These are bits of any number of letters, a couple of paragraphs, in most cases so mutilated you can't make much of 'em, and hardly ever anything to get hold of definitely. There's one thing, they're all female hand-writing. Strange, isn't it? A crowd of women all writing to one man, and suddenly he's murdered and little scraps of all their letters are torn to atoms and left in his room."

"Are there no names?" asked Bremner in keen disappointment. "Nothing that will help us?"

"Oh, any number, but they're pet-names mostly. Rosie, Joy, Enid. . . . Leaves any number of lose ends, doesn't it? Fellow may have been blackmailing any one of 'em and an irate husband put in an appearance, put the fellow out of his senses, and destroyed the papers so that no other wretched woman should be involved."

"Very pretty," agreed Bremner austerely, "but that doesn't explain why the body was found on Sir Gervase Blount's property."

"Unless he was one of the injured husbands, what? There's something else, though. Something interesting. A distinctive hand-writing, too." He handed Bremner a long slip, scrupulously placed and pasted, though it had originally been torn into several scraps:

". . . . s . . ner . . . an . . t . him kn . .
I . . s eve . . . . ife."

"This is what I make of it: 'I would'—then some threat or other—'sooner than let him know I was ever your wife.' That gives us a motive—what?"

It also backed up a theory Bremner had already improvised and upon which he hoped to found a case.

"Anything more in this writing?" he asked.

"Only one. Look at this."

The second sheet of paper resembled the first. Bremner took it and read:—

". . . . ill yo . . . . . event you . . . llin . . . he . . . th."

"H'm. 'Kill you to prevent you telling the truth?' I fancy so. A threat or mere bluff? Can't tell at present, of course. We don't even know its context. It may run, 'He will kill you to prevent your telling the truth to the world.' Or perhaps, 'I will kill you to prevent your telling the truth to him.' Impossible to guess till we've more information. Meanwhile——" he opened the case he carried and drew out the long slip of paper he had found in Charteris' room.

"You're an expert," he observed. "What d'you make of that?"

Peterson took the slip and compared it keenly with the other pair. "Identical hand-writing," he pronounced. "Know whose this is?"

"I have my suspicions, but I can't verify 'em for a few hours more. Anything else?"

"One more odd thing. Among those letters were some torn scraps of a white envelope on which a word or two had been written. Here they are; you can see some of the letters. Here's 'FO' and then the paper's torn savagely; and here's another 'COR' and this one that roughly approximates to it 'NER.' Convey anything to you?"

Bremner stared and before he could speak Peterson went on, "Of course I hunted for the rest of the address but I found nothing but a slip with 'THE' on it. What I want to know is where's rest of that envelope and what do those words mean? Why should it have been savaged right across the middle of an address?"

Bremner was smiling in a peculiar way. "I think I can tell you that," he murmured. "As you say, these two scraps 'COR' and 'NER' do roughly dovetail. Very roughly, it's true, but then the paper's been torn there and it's slightly frayed, though it is only cream-laid paper. The 'THE' fits in too. It's part of an address I think I know. 'Four Corners, Thebeshire.' Very pretty, that. I'll take the whole bag o' tricks along to the chief."

The chief nodded brusquely as he appeared, and said. "Well, what developments?"

Tersely, Bremner outlined the case. "These letters confirm a private suspicion of mine. I've an inquiry put through to Somerset House—I ought to get an answer any minute—asking for a copy of Blount's marriage certificate. I think we may take it that the veiled lady is Blount's wife. I haven't been down to Four Corners again, but there's no question he did recognise the fellow, and there wasn't a scrap of sympathy or compassion about him, as you might expect for some poor devil who's been shot and thrown overboard. And he isn't the callous type either. There's personal feeling in this. Moreover, there's a certain tension down at that house. All the guests feel it. I'm going down there on the twelve-twenty. It's the only passable train of the day. All the others necessitate changes and lengthy waits for connections. It's occurred to me, what with all this talk of wives and this ring——"

"D'you say you found that in the garden?"

"Yes. You'll notice it's a small ring, too small for a man to wear. Therefore, supposing he keeps it at all, he'd probably have it in some pocket." He outlined rapidly his suspicions in such an event. "Of course," he wound up, "I shall have to show this trinket to Lady Blount and watch her face. But I've a notion all this will fit together like a jigsaw puzzle. Now, to go back to my theory. Suppose, when they were both on the stage, Lady Blount married Charteris. This is clearly meant to be an engagement ring. From inquiries it appears that she comes of a good, but very impoverished, family and that she went on the stage because there was quite literally nothing else she could do. She doesn't seem to have achieved anything very brilliant there. I should say from what I've seen of her, which candidly isn't much, that she's too thin-skinned ever to get very far. Then in 1924 she marries Sir Gervase Blount. I want that certificate from Somerset House to see, precisely, how she describes herself, whether as Pamela Heath, her family name, or as Pamela Charteris, widow. She may have thought this fellow dead—he's a bit of a swine I should say, judging from his voluminous female correspondence—and suddenly he discovers her and threatens to tell her husband unless she gets him money. I fancy in this case it's money. Sometimes it's passion. But here, I don't think there's any doubt it's gain. That there's some peculiar link between them that doesn't exist in the case of the other ladies is pretty clear. None of the others come to the house, and even she is heavily veiled. You get the position? It's very pretty. Blount has made a name for himself, quite apart from the name his ancestors bequeathed him, and that's pretty fine on its own account. His views are noted and commented on, and very often adopted by large numbers of people. He isn't in the position of the ordinary vicar or curate who doesn't exist outside his own parish. Blount's name is a household word since he brought out that book. And suppose he's suddenly faced with the fact that his marriage *non est*. It would be a scandal, of course. I'm not thinking of the scurrilous minded few who'd pitch mud; he can afford to disregard them. But he can't afford to disregard the attitude of the average man and woman towards his wife—or the lady whom he has hitherto believed to be his wife. And when the true story of Raymond Charteris is known—incidentally we don't know it ourselves yet, but Lady Blount's position would hardly be an enviable one. It isn't surprising that she does all she can to shut his mouth, or that she has that close-lipped look that means she isn't giving anything away. The fact that Charteris is alive is bound to affect their relationship; eventually either she tells her husband or he is informed, possibly by Charteris, who wants to raise money and realises that she is no use. She's nothing of her own, while he's a wealthy man. That's pure theory so far, but I can test it pretty well when I'm down at Four Corners. I've also got to discover what Blount was doing, on his own showing, on the night of the murder. If we can prove an alibi he's out of it, and then we've got to find some one else. This chap must have had hosts of enemies."

Shortly afterwards a messenger arrived with a copy of the marriage certificate of Pamela Heath, spinster, to Sir Gervase Blount, bachelor, the marriage being celebrated at St. George's Church, Parkington, Lancs., on the 24th May, 1924.

Bremner looked a little dashed. "Possibly it was not a wedding, but an unfortunate incident of which she hoped to keep her husband in ignorance," suggested the chief drily. "Such things are not unknown."

Bremner, who cherished a secret lust after the higher paths of psychology, choked down a desire to say that such a course was practically impossible to Pamela Blount. Instead he took the copy of the certificate, put it with the strips he had taken from Peterson, and the ring and the ear-drop, and departed. It was still quite early and he had time to make his inquiries in person in Thermiloe Square. This was not a very long task, since the sound could not be expected to have reached very far on such a night, considering the location of Charteris' room. Moreover, had anyone actually heard the sound or even believed that he had heard it, he would almost certainly have come forward by now. And so he was neither surprised nor disappointed when all his efforts to gain information from this quarter proved abortive, and he decided to abandon speculation until he had seen Blount and his wife and heard their evidence.

CHAPTER IV

"Tell me the cause: I know there is a woman in't."
—JOHN FLETCHER.

I

THE thirty-six hours that had elapsed since Bremner's departure from Four Corners had been a period of extreme embarrassment to the party gathered under its roof. Ambrose, indeed, said in his casual way, "Like us to clear out, Gervase?" to which Blount replied, "Sorry. I'm afraid that isn't possible. These policemen will be back soon enough asking questions, and as you were one of the couple who found the corpse you're implicated up to the hilt."

Ambrose, recognising instantly that he had received a confidence and understanding, as Bremner and Egerton had already done, that the lives of his most intimate friend and this dead unknown had at some time touched and intertwined to the hurt of both, said lazily, "D'you suppose they'll evolve one of their damned intelligent theories that I pitched the body there? Or would that drag Egerton into it, too, as an accomplice? Not even a fictional detective—and they're as crazy as hens—could suspect Egerton of anything illegal."

The only person who appeared completely at ease during that period was Eloise Martineau, who turned up to time on all occasions, exquisitely gowned, without a hair out of place, calm, radiant, with an air of exultation that the others found rather disgusting, though none of them except the candid Rosemary gave any indication of their feelings. As for Pamela Blount, it would have been impossible for any one to guess what was passing through her mind just then. The name of the dead man and such facts as had been ascertained about him, had already been broadcasted by the press, though no mention had as yet been made of the earring. Pamela moved through her small world with the same self-possession, the same perfect and remote poise, the same serene fastidiousness, that invariably distinguished her. But Ambrose, by chance, was forced to realise that of all their party this affair had struck none other so deeply to the heart.

On the evening of that first day, before Bremner had tossed his bombshell into their midst, Ambrose was wandering thoughtfully up and down the garden cogitating and wondering whether any power on earth could make Blount open his heart to his friend. The September twilight had come down suddenly like a curtain over the luminous sky; already the leaves were falling in soft fugitive showers and somewhere out of the dim branches a robin sang. That sweet and poignant melancholy, that haunts travellers in lands where no robin has ever been heard, and that sings remembrance irrevocably into the heart, struck the impressionable listener to a sudden, anguished pity; he realised that before the thread of suspicion, now lying in Bremner's fingers, had been wound into the ball of fulfilment they would have reached the heart of tragedy for two, at all events, of the players in the drama. And remembering them he fell unexpectedly to thinking of the dead man, whether he, too, were mourned, whether (with a guilty twinge) Pamela Blount were at that moment thinking of him or whether this elaborate theory he had built up on a chance revelation of Blount's was merely solid as ocean foam. Thus pondering he turned and observed the dark house towering up into the misty sky; lights shone at some of the windows, but the general impression was one of darkness; very powerful and sinister it seemed to him, with its twin towers standing permanent and immovable against their opaque background. And then another light was switched on, a window was opened and Pamela Blount stared out over the heads of the trees into the black distance. Only one glance did the watcher get of her face; one glance was enough. Then he turned swiftly away, flushed and embarrassed, as if he had been deliberately spying. A terrible expression to see on any human face had been printed in that instant on hers; dumb agony, heartbreak, an awful fear that would not allow itself speech. The mask had been lifted. Did even Blount guess what lay beneath? Ambrose remembered certain dreadful nights when his mother had lain dying of cancer—the screams, the smothered moans. They had been appalling to hear but less so than this silence. The face, like the face of a dead woman, the dark eyes burning as if with fever, the lips so closely set that they were scarcely visible, was stamped on his imagination. Was this then the answer to his question? Did Pamela Blount wear that look of intolerable anguish because Raymond Charteris lay in the mortuary at Tenbeigh? He blundered into a side-path and into Egerton's arms. Egerton extricated himself with his customary grace. Ambrose didn't apologise, but there was that in his face that warned the younger man that he had received a shock. He turned and they paced up and down the path in silence until a gong, reverberating from the hall, broke through the peace of the evening and sent the tranquil shadows flying for safety into the darker beds and walks.

Bremner came down next day. The impassive butler said, "I think Sir Gervase is engaged at the moment. Will you wait here, sir?"

The hall at Four Corners was large and square; one wall was practically filled by a shabby but extremely comfortable chesterfield. There was a square table set against the opposite wall and on this was a box for outgoing letters. While he waited a woman with a long pink face and the brooding air of a sheep came slowly down the stairs and put half a dozen letters, sealed and stamped, into the box. Bremner detained her an instant.

"I wonder whether you could tell me if Lady Blount is in? It may be necessary to have some purely formal evidence from her. I am from Scotland Yard," he added, seeing a look of bewilderment pass over that stupid, placid face.

"Her ladyship's upstairs," said the woman after a pause. "She's been writing letters. Did you want to see her now?"

Bremner shook his head. "Not at the moment. I'm waiting to see Sir Gervase. Thanks very much." He looked at the ground to intimate that he had no further use for her. His chief desire was for her to disappear before the butler returned, so that he could compare the writing on those envelopes with the writing on the slips of paper in his possession. Fortunately Blount was detaining the man and as the maid vanished Bremner started to his feet, a lightly-moving, swift, neat-fingered man, small-boned, bronzed of feature, alert, efficient, and for an instant halted at the table. One glance was enough to identify that peculiarly characteristic writing. There was no need even to produce his own evidence; quite clearly one hand had written them all. He resumed his seat, and an instant later Sanders appeared, saying, "Sir Gervase will see you now, sir." And showed him into the large, austere library, its walls lined with books, two oil-paintings of dead and gone Blounts over the mantel, and a sword brought by an earlier ancestor still from the battle of Edgehill, strung above the low door.

Blount, a ceremonialist to his finger-tips, who would have courteously offered the devil a seat even though he had come to denude him of all his possessions, indicated a chair.

"What can I do to help you?" he asked, and no one without inside knowledge would have guessed that he was in the position of a man crossing an abyss on a single plank that bent and swayed under every step.

"You know who the man really is, of course?"

"I have read the newspaper reports."

"He's an actor named Charteris—at all events that's the name he used on the stage. It's quite likely it isn't his real one. But it's the name by which he appears to be known everywhere. All his letters were addressed Charteris. Our chief difficulty is that we know so very little of his past. No one has so far come forward with relevant information."

"I hardly see how I am concerned with this," Blount observed fastidiously.

"I must ask you to identify this as Lady Blount's property." The detective opened his hand that had been lying closed on the table, and the ear-ring fell on to the green leather surface of the writing-desk.

Blount stared at it, seemed incredulous, then picked it up and stared afresh.

"May I ask how this came into your possession?"

"It was dropped some weeks ago just outside Charteris' room in Bloomsbury by a lady who had been in the habit of visiting him. It has been identified by the makers as one of a pair ordered by yourself four years ago."

Blount looked puzzled, but behind his perplexity was something resembling relief. "It is undoubtedly the pattern of Lady Blount's ear-rings, though I was promised that it should not be copied. But I'm afraid the jewellers have broken their bargain with me. Lady Blount was wearing her pair only two nights ago."

"Perhaps you would send for them. This is going to be an important detail in the evidence."

Blount was very pale with a controlled, inward rage, but unless he was a consummate actor his surprise was genuine. When a servant answered the bell he said coldly, "Is Rogers downstairs?"

"Yes, sir. She's just left her ladyship."

"Send her to me."

Rogers, her long face wearing an expression of alarm, came an instant later.

"Ask her ladyship if she will allow me to have the case containing the diamond ear-rings for five minutes, please. Mr. Bremner wishes to see them."

There was a long minute of silence while they waited for the woman's return. Neither attempted to speak. Bremner remained coolly neutral; he had seen such magnificent acting before, though his sympathies as a private individual (since professionally he was allowed none) were all with this dignified, self-contained man whose happiness was being rocked in the balance and would, in any event, probably crash into the abyss before this case was completed. Then Rogers returned with a small morocco box in her hand. Blount took it and waited till the woman had gone, snapped it open. In their velvet bed the twin ornaments sparkled and caught the light, reflecting it and flinging it back in coloured prisms.

"You see?" said Blount, distantly polite. "I'm afraid the one in your possession has been made to some other order. I will at once take up matter with the makers who have been guilty of breach of contract, it being distinctly understood that they should make no other ear-drops to this precise pattern." (A typical gesture of the Blounts, this, as Bremner recognised. Not only must their wives have the best, but they must have the monopoly of it.)

For the moment, however, he paid no attention to that. Without moving he asked, "May I examine the pair you have? Thank you." He bent over all three without, however, taking the pair from their velvet bed. Suddenly he looked up.

"Sir Gervase, have you a photograph of Lady Blount before her marriage?"

Here at all events he got under his hearer's skin. Blount was literally transfixed with amazement, but that swiftly gave place to a furious anger. His face was dark-red.

"A photograph before——?"

"Yes."

Blount's voice was low but outraged. "This seems to me the most unwarranted impertinence——"

Bremner might have been an automaton. "I'm afraid it's bound to appear like that to you, and I regret intensely the necessity for pressing the question."

The other made no attempt to stir. "I'm not at all sure I can lay my hands on such a thing."

"I see. Then no doubt I can get the information I require from Lady Blount's friends before her marriage."

Blount held his eyes steadily. "And that information is——?"

"A photograph of Lady Blount before her marriage."

His host knew when he was beaten; and although he could not at this moment conceive what his unwelcome visitor was hinting he had no intention of letting the hounds of scandal loose beyond his own doors, so long as it was possible to keep them leashed there, and he recognised that both he and his wife were too deeply involved in this affair to feign indifference. Going to a desk in the corner of the room he unlocked it and handed Bremner a cabinet photograph, in furious silence. But his expression said clearly enough, "What cads you fellows are!"

Bremner appreciated the position and wished with all his heart either that some other man had been entrusted with the case or that Scott Egerton had not chosen this precise time to be a guest under Blount's roof. He took the photograph, glanced at it and instantly handed it back.

"Thank you. I see that before her marriage Lady Blount did not wear ear-rings."

Blount laid the pasteboard face downwards on the table. "Was that what you wanted to know? And does it affect the matter?"

"I think it may. Presumably when you ordered these," he tapped the velvet case, "you had them fitted for unpierced ears."

"Certainly I did."

"And since then the ears have been pierced?"

"Yes."

"When was that?"

"Quite recently."

"You can suggest no approximate date?"

"I should say about six weeks ago. Lady Blount became apprehensive lest she should lose one of the drops. I fancy there was a narrow escape when she was visiting a short time ago. That, as you will understand, would have been inconvenient." No one but a Blount, reflected Bremner, would have chosen precisely that word.

"And so the fittings were changed?"

"They were."

"So much is evident from the trinkets themselves. But if you will look you'll see there's a slight disparity between these." He bent over the pair in the case and pointed out a trifling discrepancy. "It would be unnoticeable when they were worn, or indeed at any time, to anyone not looking for a distinguishing mark. But the difference, such as it is, is accounted for by the fact that one has been changed from the screw to the pin while the other was made originally with a pin for pierced ears and needed no such alteration. Now, you say these were made rather more than three years ago."

"Yes."

"During that time, to your knowledge, has a duplicate drop been made?"

Blount smiled grimly. "A duplicate in circumstances like these is quite a considerable affair. You may be sure Scotland Yard would have heard something of them if one had been lost."

"Could you tell me whether Lady Blount has worn

them with any frequency during the past six weeks or two months?"

"They are not jewels that are suitable for all occasions. My work has kept me busy of late and immediately afterwards I came down here where such occasions are practically nil. It was in response to a mere whim of mine that my wife wore them at all a night or two ago."

"So that it's possible during that time for one to have been lost and a duplicate supplied. I imagine that the makers would expedite the work as much as possible for so important an order."

"You suggest that Lady Blount having lost one of the ear-rings gave instructions to the jewellers to replace it in record time?" Blount's voice was level and forbidding.

"It seems the only explanation. But, of course, Lady Blount will be able to verify that."

Blount started violently. "I had hoped you would find no reason to drag her into this sordid affair."

"I'm afraid she's in it already. Her evidence is bound to be asked for. This ear-ring alone——"

Blount put his hands in his pockets and strode fiercely up and down the room. There was irresolution and thwarted rage in every step he took. It was clear to Bremner that his one desire was to keep Pamela Blount out of the witness-box, and that not for his own sake but for hers. Coming to a sudden halt at Bremner's elbow he said abruptly, "It's quite out of the question that what you suggest is the fact. Lady Blount could not have repeated the order for the ear-rings. I may say what is, of course, obvious to you that stones of this quality and made up into so intricate a pattern, and so magnificently mounted are a very costly affair. The price would be quite out of the question——" He paused in obvious distaste. No doubt, he reflected, this fellow knew as well as most people that Pamela had come to him without a penny. He paid her a very generous allowance, but the most generous conceivable could hardly have covered in a single quarter the cost of the duplicate ear-drop. And Pamela was not economical. She spent her money as she had it, mortgaged it up to the hilt. It was extremely unlikely that she could have saved sufficient to cover the expense, while his pass-book showed that she hadn't drawn a cheque on their joint account. But it was intolerable to have to put a point like that clearly to a total stranger, even if he did chance to be Scott Egerton's friend and ex-Secret Service companion.

Bremner, however, understood him well enough. "It's conceivable, since the duplicate has probably only been in existence a matter of months—weeks actually —that the bill has not yet been settled," he suggested.

"But not conceivable that the makers should not have sent it in to me," countered Blount drily.

"Might it not be addressed to Lady Blount?" murmured Bremner and saw instantly that he had enraged his man.

"No," snapped Blount.

"Then perhaps it's been put away with some circulars and mislaid or overlooked; or the postal authorities may have lost it in transit. One can find plenty of reasons why it shouldn't have reached you." Plenty of reasons—yes. But one didn't give voice to them all if one had any kind of wisdom and was face to face with a man of the temper of Gervase Blount. Nevertheless, both men saw the same suspicion in his companion's mind. What if Pamela, half-crazed with terror, had concealed or deliberately destroyed the bill?

Bremner asked, "You have a locked letter-box?"

Blount's eyes were like flint. "And what does that imply?"

"That if you have a locked box and yourself keep the key, it does seem strange that the account should not have reached you. In any case you would be aware whether any letter from Messrs. Nettle and Beard had been received; but if a servant sorts the letters then it is quite easy to believe that one has been set aside with advertisements and circulars, and accidentally destroyed."

"That may be correct," Blount agreed. "No, I don't sort the letters myself."

The detective was struck with a new thought. "Is it possible that they would enclose the bill with the parcel, which would presumably be addressed to Lady Blount?"

"It's quite probable. But in that case——" he paused sharply, and the long, sensitive fingers closed over the rounded edge of the writing table. Bremner could finish that sentence for him and knew why he had stopped. "In that case she would have brought it to me," that was how the sentence would have tailed off, and he had hesitated because, if Bremner's suspicions were true, that was precisely what she wouldn't have done.

"Perhaps you'll let me telephone these people and ask them for the exact date they returned the earrings," he went on. Better to telephone them now than later when Pamela Blount, still under the influence of that fear, had denied what afterwards would be so simply proved. "Even if Lady Blount remembers the precise day on which she gave the order it's unlikely that she'll also recall the day on which they came back, and we have to have things perfect to the smallest detail."

Blount, realising that in no event could he stop Bremner making the inquiry, and feeling a certain security in having it made from his own house, agreed, and Bremner put the trunk call through. He was quite certain in his own mind that he had discovered the truth, for this would account for the manager's cryptic saying that probably the jewel had been stolen. Whilst waiting for the telephone bell to ring he proceeded with his cross-examination.

"Sir Gervase, do you own a revolver of any kind?"

"A small Browning. I bought it shortly after marriage when it became necessary occasionally for me to leave my wife for several days at a time. She would spend whole weeks here and the remoteness of the place and its accessibility to any stray tramp or burglar in the neighbourhood made it wise to have some sort of protection."

"And you keep this—where?"

"In my desk over there, in one of the drawers."

"Loaded?"

"Yes."

"Fully?"

Blount frowned. "So far as I can remember. Or—wait. I had occasion at the end of last year to shoot a dog that had been badly mauled in a trap. Whether I slipped in the sixth cartridge or not, afterwards, I'm not prepared to swear. But you shall examine the gun for yourself."

It didn't, Bremner decided gloomily, help him much, the number of the cartridges, for if he had shot Charteris he would certainly fill up the empty chamber on his return. Nevertheless, if he had been interrupted or had overlooked the matter this explanation of the shot dog covered the missing bullet.

Blount had crossed to the cupboard for the second time and now jerked open a drawer. There was a moment's silence. Bremner was watching, had in fact risen silently and stood a couple of feet distant. He had no intention of being the witness of Blount's suicide, and experience had taught him that it is impossible to be too watchful on such occasions as these.

Blount, however, one hand thoughtfully holding his chin, was staring at an empty drawer. He turned suddenly to find the other at his elbow and recognising the meaning of his presence there he coloured slightly and said, "I've never kept it anywhere else. And no one else has a key. It's odd. Can I have put it away somewhere and forgotten?" He appeared genuinely perplexed.

"You're quite sure no one else has a key?"

"Absolutely."

"When did you last see the weapon?"

Blount became vague. "Oh, probably not since I shot Gyp. I've had no reason to look for it."

"Then it may have been missing for some time?"

"There's nothing to show that it hasn't, of course. But what's the motive?"

"That I can't tell you. Have you, perhaps, at any time left the key where it might be taken?"

"It's on my ring. I always carry that about with me."

"Still, there are times—at night, for instance—when it could be removed without your knowledge."

"I'm an extremely light sleeper and should certainly hear any one who came near me in the night."

"You invariably sleep with it in your room?"

"Invariably."

"Well, suppose it was taken when you were in your bath, say? You don't carry it to the bathroom, I suppose?" Bremner put the question in desperate earnest. He was beginning to feel highly uncomfortable about the whole affair.

"I don't, of course, but that's rather a fantastic supposition."

"Fantastic, if you please, but the only alternative."

"Alternative? Ah, I understand you. To my having deliberately removed the thing myself. That's your telephone call, I think." He hesitated, as if he thought it conceivable that Bremner might prefer to be alone, but the detective motioned to him to remain as he lifted the receiver.

"Is that Nettle and Beard? . . . I want to speak to Mr. Beard, please. . . . Bremner of Scotland Yard. Is that Mr. Beard? . . . Good-afternoon. You'll remember my calling yesterday and asking you to identify a diamond ear-drop? You told me that was made to the order of Sir Gervase Blount. I now understand that a duplicate was made by you to replace the one in my possession, quite recently. Can you supply me with the actual dates?"

He waited while the reference was turned up. He was aware of Blount in the room behind him, a stark, tragic figure, invested with extraordinary dignity. It was possible at this moment to believe him capable not only of the murder but of the whole elaborate designing of the plot. A man so fanatically devoted to his wife as Blount had shown himself to be during this interview was scarcely normal on this point. Here the voice recommenced speaking at the other end of the wire as Mr. Beard said, "The order was given by Lady Blount in person on the twenty-fourth August. I was on the premises and saw her. She wanted the new ear-drop in a great hurry, and the order was executed with the greatest possible despatch. But the work necessitated the sending of an expert to Holland to match certain diamonds, and it wasn't sent to Lady Blount in the north until the fourteenth September."

"And this ear-ring was made for pierced ears?"

"Yes. And the other ring was changed. Anything else we can do for you?"

There was not at the moment, though Bremner reserved to himself the right to follow up that conversation later in person, when he would be relieved from the disability of Blount's presence. Hanging up the receiver he turned to put a final question.

"You are perfectly certain"—he spoke with great emphasis— "that there is not a single soul who could possibly get at the contents of that desk?" He was thinking of Pamela and Blount knew it.

"Not a soul," he returned very curtly.

"And you're absolutely sure you never took it up north with you?" The detective's tone was slightly scornful; he could not for the life of him actually believe in Blount's attitude of perplexity.

"Never. I got it especially for our protection on this estate. In Mannington we have the usual burglar-alarms and we don't consider we need weapons there. In any case, it would be unbecoming. But there have been several acts of violence and one actual murder in this neighbourhood, and it would be difficult to get hold of the police in a crisis."

Either the man was a brilliant actor or he was transparently sincere, Bremner decided, torn between admiration and pity. "Perhaps we may come back to this point later," he went on courteously. "May I take it that you were aware of the correspondence between Mr. Charteris and Lady Blount?"

The dark blood surged into Blount's pale face. For a moment he was beyond speech. Then he said in a voice so charged with feeling that even Bremner experienced a stab of apprehension. "I was."

"From the outset?"

"Had that been the case there would have been no correspondence."

"You mean that since you recognised its existence you took steps to put an end to it?"

Blount, holding himself rigidly under control, answered icily, "I didn't consider Mr. Charteris a fit person to be in communication with my wife."

"And you told him so?"

"I did."

"In person?"

"It's hardly safe when you're dealing with scum of that kind to put anything on paper."

"And you saw him—where?"

"At his lodging in Bloomsbury."

"I believe I'm right in saying that his object in communicating with Lady Blount and in forcing meetings between them was to levy blackmail?"

"That was his intention."

"In which he was not successful?"

"I believe my wife gave him a small sum to tide him

over a particularly unfortunate contingency. Had I been aware of the position I should certainly have vetoed that."

"But he anticipated that you would yield where she, perhaps, would not." He meant and conveyed *could not*, for surely Pamela Blount was in no position to pay blackmail without her husband acting as her banker. Blount made no move to correct him.

"I don't know what he anticipated, but you may take my word he never got a penny from me."

"Perhaps, Sir Gervase—I'm sorry to seem importunate, but this is the crux of the situation—you would tell me exactly what were your relations with this man and when you last saw him, and what took place at that meeting?"

Blount seemed to be coolly considering exactly what would be relevant to his evidence and what he might conveniently discard. That the story was a painful one was self-evident. Bremner began it on his own account.

"You've known this man for a long time?"

"I met him precisely once in my life."

"And that was quite recently?"

"Very recently."

"Can you remember the exact date?"

"The 20th of September."

"The day on which he disappeared."

"That is so."

"You had hitherto been in correspondence with him?"

"No. But so soon as I realised that he was causing annoyance to my wife I asked for her confidence, and in the circumstances it appeared necessary to see the fellow."

"And the time of your visit?"

"The late afternoon."

"You can't put it nearer than that?"

"I should say about six-thirty."

"Ah! Mr. Charteris was expecting you?"

"Certainly not."

"You were sure of finding him in?"

"If he had been out I proposed to wait for his return."

"You sent up your name?"

"No. I went straight up to his room."

"You were given instructions by the servant who admitted you perhaps? . . . Since this was your first visit you would hardly know where to find him."

"No servant admitted me. I followed one of the inmates into the house. It was most important that I should see Mr. Charteris and settle the matter once and for all. My wife had told me the location of his room."

"And you went straight in?"

"I did. And found him at home."

"Will you tell me what transpired after that?"

"I told him that his—his———"

"Threats?"

"Threats to my wife must cease at once or I would take steps to prevent them for the future."

"Meaning that you would have him committed for blackmail?"

A spasm passed over the rigid face. "Hardly. He was far too old a hand at that game ever to be caught so easily. He had written down nothing that could be construed into blackmail. His letters, that I have seen and destroyed, are on the face of them mere invitations, candid replies, perfectly innocuous. Only those aware of his reputation and manner of living could have seen beneath the surface."

"Then when you ordered him to put an end to the correspondence, what weapon had you in your turn?"

Blount was silent. He was uncertain how much this fellow from the Yard had nosed out. He would have liked to deny all knowledge of the affair, but quite apart from the ineffectiveness of such a policy he felt himself unable to perjure his word even for Pamela's sake. The debt, such as it was, had been contracted. Now it had to be paid.

"And the steps to which you referred?" urged Bremner.

Blount said slowly, "I would have kept this secret if I could. He had made himself liable for a term of imprisonment for an offence of which no one except myself and Lady Blount was aware. I warned him that if his persecution of her continued I would take the evidence I possessed direct to the Yard and have him arrested."

"And that evidence was? I'm afraid you'll have to lay all your cards on the table. It's going to be very important to establish the true position. This offence, for instance."

"He had signed Lady Blount's name to a cheque for two hundred pounds. The signature was obtained by the old method of tracing."

Bremner looked puzzled. "Your account was in the joint names of yourself and Lady Blount?" he asked, frowning.

"Certainly." How the fellow's eyes could spit fire. An unpleasant enemy, Bremner reflected. He was perplexed again, since this new information opened fresh possibilities. For if Pamela Blount could have drawn upon her husband's capital why had she not satisfied Charteris demands in that way rather than allow her husband to hear of the affair? He decided to let that slide until he saw the lady herself.

"Then in her correspondence with Charteris, Lady Blount had signed her letters?" he observed sharply.

Blount opened his mouth, hesitated, as if he suspected a trap and finally replied, "I never saw a letter of hers addressed to him."

"Obviously she must have done so or he could not have obtained the tracing. Unless he had letters of hers of an earlier date?" (But it would have to be since marriage in order to get the complete signature.)

Blount was as aloof as a piece of statuary. "As to that I have nothing to say."

"Did Charteris admit the affair of the cheque when tackled?"

"Unaffectedly. Was positively brazen about it, saying that I shouldn't prosecute as I wished to keep my wife's name out of the affair."

"Lady Blount knew about the cheque?"

"She informed me of it."

"Thank you. And then?"

"The argument became violent. He demanded money with menaces, and I refused him a halfpenny. Had he lived to annoy my wife further, I should certainly have been as good as my word and put the affair in the hands of the police, not merely for personal security, but simply as a citizen. The man was dangerous."

"Ah!" Bremner was non-commital. "Can you account for the bruising of the wrist?"

Again the painful colour came into the thin face. "Probably," he admitted. "It would have given me the greatest pleasure to strangle him on the spot."

"And in the struggle—you weren't by any chance trying to take anything from him by force?"

"Take anything? Certainly not."

"Letters, for instance?" persisted Bremner.

"I was not."

"Then in the struggle did he tear a button from your coat?"

"A button? Oh, the one that was clutched in his hand. No, of course not. I wasn't wearing a coat."

"You're quite sure?" Bremner sounded sceptical. "It was a foggy night and extremely cold and damp."

Blount interrupted him. "I don't mean that I had come out without one, but Charteris' room was extremely warm and I remember flinging it across a chair. Our conversation was not likely to be a short one——"

"And during that time no one entered the room?"

"I fancy not."

"So the button could not have been yours?"

Blount's control was stretched like a tense elastic. He said with a passionate striving after reasonableness, "It could not. But you're at liberty to question my man." He rang the bell as he spoke.

"Send Paull to me." And when a short, dark man entered the library, "Bring me my coat, Paull. The black one I wear every day, in which I went up to town on the twentieth."

Mystified but submissive the man retired, and when he returned with the garment Blount motioned to him to remain by the door, while he himself crossed to the window and looked out. Bremner took up the coat; it was an ordinary clerical overcoat, extremely well cut and having the air of a garment worn by a man who understands how to carry his clothes. Minutely, with the aid of a glass Blount examined the three buttons. The first was a little loose, and had clearly not been sewn on for some time. The third was in similar condition, but the second was stitched firm and close. Bremner looked again; then he drew a sharp, small penknife from his coat pocket and very carefully cut a thread or two, gently working the button lose. After a moment it was clear that this button had only been stitched on recently. Further examination under the glass showed him something else, that a small portion of the material of the coat had been removed with the button.

"A pretty good wrench would be needed to account for that," he reflected shrewdly, and then turned to the man.

"Just sewn this button on, haven't you?"

"Yes, sir."

"Remember when?"

Blount turned from the window where he was standing with his hands clasped behind him to say with a shadow of a smile, "This is all routine, Paull. Be as concise as you can," and turned back again.

"It was when Sir Gervase came back from town in the third week of September, sir. I noticed at once that the button was missing and put on a spare one."

That scrap of evidence seemed to Bremner very sinister indeed. "Do you often have occasion to stitch on Sir Gervase's buttons?"

"No, sir. Often as not he doesn't shut his coat up. Buttons don't get much of a strain on them, you see."

"It isn't possible, I take it, that the button was missing before Sir Gervase went up to town?"

The man stiffened with icy pride. "Quite impossible, sir."

"And I suppose it's asking too much of you to say whether this"—he opened his hand—"is the actual button in question?"

Paull came forward and without touching the button nodded an affirmative. "I'd known that anywhere, sir. You see, there's a bit nicked out of the rim. Time and again I've wished that button would lose itself. Sir Gervase said it was well enough as it was, but it always got on my nerves. When I saw it had gone at last, I thought what a good thing it was that button and not one of the others."

"Ah! Thank you. That's very useful." He dismissed the man. Blount came back from the window. He spoke before the other had an opportunity.

"That clinches it, doesn't it?" he asked, and now he was smiling. His was the coolness of the man who believes that wisdom lies in apprehending the uttermost and who realises that now nothing worse can touch him. Bremner was frowning. "Think well, Sir Gervase. When you'd got your coat on again there wasn't any repetition of discord? He didn't at the last moment try to intimidate you, perhaps try to detain you——?"

Blount shook his head impatiently. "Won't wash. I was in a white heat myself and simply caught up my coat and left him. I didn't put it on till I was on the steps, and realised that the fog hadn't abated and that it was absurdly cold."

"What time was this?"

"About seven-thirty, I think."

"And then? I take it you met no one on your way out?"

"I understood the landlady to say that the house was empty. At all events, I let myself out."

"And when you left the house?"

"I went down to the offices of the Christian Peace Organisation. I've been doing rather a heavy task of work for them recently and was behindhand with my work. It seemed to me an excellent opportunity to catch up. I didn't propose to go down to Four Corners that evening, and the unsettling day——" He broke off and began again. "I thought I should be wise to buckle down to work and keep my thoughts off my own personal affairs."

Bremner hesitated. Then he said slowly, "You don't, I suppose, feel inclined to lay all your cards on the table. It would help us a great deal if we knew the precise nature of the hold that Charteris had over Lady Blount, and that made it possible for him to suggest blackmail."

When Blount answered him his voice was almost languid. "I haven't any intention of raking up the ashes of that unfortunate story. If the Yard can achieve it that's their affair, but now this fellow's dead I fancy there's no one except my wife and myself who could enlighten you, and I can safely say that neither of us proposes to do that."

But even as he spoke a tremor of apprehension crossed his face and Bremner, whose job it was to read other men's expressions, realised that he was racked by a genuine fear lest some person should turn up who knew all the unhappy history, and who would be more willing than himself to blaze it abroad for the benefit of the newspapers. It was a pity, the detective thought, to maintain that attitude of rigid reticence, since a man had been since last night at work hunting up the dead actor's record, who would probably unearth the miserable incident in which Pamela Blount had figured. That there had been an engagement seemed clear from the ring found in the garden. How much further the affair had gone he could only guess and even so without any great clarity.

He abandoned that line and returned to the attack. "These offices of yours, Sir Gervase—where are they?"

"In Plum Tree Court."

"And they were open on that evening?"

"I have a pass-key. All the office keys are on the premises."

"There was no one else there at the time?"

"No one."

"Not a porter or a messenger?"

"They all leave shortly after six. During times of stress we have all of us frequently stayed till ten o'clock, six days a week, but this work of mine of which I was speaking is something specialised, something that must be done by myself. I can't even employ a stenographer. I find it necessary to write everything out by hand. Dictating irks me unconscionably."

"You can't produce any one who can vouch for your being at the office at that time? If you can establish an alibi it will clear the court a good deal."

"I'm afraid I can't. No one's likely to be about in such a district on a foggy night. It isn't a place where I should normally be found myself."

"You didn't speak to a policeman? Or take a taxi?"

"No taxi would be found in a fog like that."

"It cleared just before ten, didn't it?"

"I believe so. But this was a little before eight when it was still very thick."

"Quite so. And later?"

"I worked until shortly after eleven. In fact, I got through a great deal of reading. I had a knotty point to elucidate, purely technical, and, of course, no concern of this affair. But it kept me busy and when I had done reading I drafted part of a chapter, and then was surprised to find it was eleven-fifteen."

"'You left the office then?"

"Yes."

"There's no caretaker or cleaner on the premises?"

"There is no caretaker. I believe a cleaner—or several cleaners—take up duty early in the mornings and scrub the place out, but no one would be there at eleven at night."

"And from Plum Tree Court?"

"I walked to a small flat that I rented before my marriage and that I still keep on as being more convenient than a club, because it's situated quite close to this office. It's a very modest affair, a couple of rooms and a bath. I spent the night there. The next morning I had breakfast at a neighbouring A.B.C. that opens at seven-thirty and afterwards caught the eight fifty-five to Eversfield, where I had to change for Little Kirbey. You may recall that the fog of the previous night came down again just before eleven, and I missed my connection by minutes and had to wait until nearly three o'clock for the next. The trains to Little Kirbey, particularly in such weather, are few and far between."

"Couldn't you have come to Tenbeigh and motored over?"

"That did occur to me. But if the fog was as dense there no motor could have got through. And in any case it's death to any car to run much on those villainous roads."

"Did you, perhaps, telegraph or telephone to your house saying you were delayed?"

"No, as a matter of fact I didn't. I didn't consider

133

it necessary. I had given no particular time for my return, saying that I might be engaged longer than I anticipated. Had I spent another night in town I should have telegraphed, of course."

Another slender hope gone, thought Bremner dejectedly. "And during those hours of waiting?" he asked.

"I spent most of the time in the cathedral. It's the third oldest in the country."

Bremner let a glint of relief show in his face. "You went into the chancel, of course, to see that marvellous stained glass behind the high altar?"

"The chancel? No, not that day. I'd often been there before."

"You didn't?"

"I didn't. I was very tired and I simply sat in one of the aisles and admired some amazing lace-work on the ceiling of St. Paul's chapel. In any case, I doubt if I should have attempted the chancel that afternoon. The town was crowded with tourists who swarmed into the cathedral to escape the fog. Some notable was coming down to unveil a new war memorial in the Market Place at three o'clock, and it appeared to be an affair of great excitement to the whole neighbourhood. I'm afraid all this is very little use to you. I realise, of course, what you're aiming at. Had I gone into the chancel I should have signed my name at the gate, and that would have been proof of my presence there. Afterwards I made my way down to the Market Place and had some tea and toast in lieu of lunch at a small shop, a pastry cook's. I don't recall the name but it stands about ten doors from the cathedral and is painted buff and strawberry colour, and here, too, the crowd was enormous. Three people shared my table, a man and two girls, all very conversational. I doubt if they so much as realised there was any one else in their world. I stayed about ten minutes, and when I came out the fog had lifted considerably, and I made my way down to the station. I caught the two forty-nine that came in at three twenty-three, on account of the fog. It was very full for three stations, and I had to stand in a third-class smoker; the firsts were full of trippers, but at Telverton a great many of them alighted, and I managed to get a first with two other men. I shouldn't know either of them again; indeed, I didn't really see their faces. They were deep in a cross-word puzzle, and I question if they so much as glanced at me. They got out after about twenty minutes, and I had the carriage to myself for the rest of the journey. It isn't a long run from Eversfield, and by this time the fog had practically cleared. The train was due at three-twenty and actually arrived just before four. I took the station fly up to the house. Cars, as I've said, are ruined on those roads. I've never attempted to take mine down there."

"Keep it at Mannington, I suppose," suggested Bremner carelessly.

"As a matter of fact, it's in the garage adjoining Plum Tree Court at the moment. I find it useful. And in any case, I motored down from the north in it. It's quite an insignificant affair."

"It comes to this," Bremner warned him gravely, "that you're the last person who admits to seeing Charteris alive, that you're on your own showing on bad terms with him, and that during the critical hours after his disappearance you can't prove a single alibi. Didn't you turn into a shop or anything when you left Thermiloe Square?"

"I stopped for coffee and a brace of ham sandwiches at a place called Farmer's. It's one of those establishments where men range themselves along the counters and eat standing up, generally in a hurry. I very much doubt if I should be known again. I'm not an habitué. Also I wear lay attire, as you probably realise, when I'm off duty, so there's nothing to distinguish me."

The more Bremner considered the position the less he liked it. He could see no loophole anywhere. Blount's story was conceivable, but, he thought, improbable. Certainly his experience had shown him that it is possible for a man to spend considerably more than thirty-six hours without meeting any acquaintance who will be able later to furnish him with an alibi, but these circumstances made him feel distinctly sceptical. He doubted also whether there was a shadow of a hope of discovering any one who would recognise the man. For, after all, who were these possible people? Owners of cafés and tea-shops that he had frequented admittedly at hours when they were crowded, and without even the distinctive badge of his profession that might have strengthened memory. Moreover, that affair of the button distressed him a good deal more than he cared to show; for a man who in a frenzy tears a button from the coat of an assailant must, on its own showing, have little time left for anything else if, when the body is discovered, the button is discovered in his hand. If it had been torn off and Blount had left him alive and hearty, as he averred, was it reasonable to imagine that when he was attacked by a second enemy he would, in the hour of death, clutch that button in his hand? Bremner was certain that the frail case would fall to the ground at a touch, even though he sought out every possible witness who might support the suspect. There was in addition the mystery about the revolver and the ludicrous explanation Blount had given of its disappearance—an explanation, in fact, that was no explanation at all. He confessed himself puzzled and seemed ready to leave it at that.

Dismissing those considerations from his memory for the instant, Bremner said, "I should like to see Lady Blount for a few minutes."

Pamela's husband hesitated and faltered badly. "I —if she is still in——"

"I understood from her maid when I arrived that she was writing letters."

"I'll inquire for you." He rang the bell and the servant who answered it agreed that her ladyship was in her room. It was here that Bremner saw her. She still preserved that miraculous look of detachment as though all this bother and tragedy were no concern of hers at all.

Bremner opened fire without delay. "Lady Blount, I gather that at the end of August you lost one of your diamond ear-rings, and commissioned Messrs. Nettle and Beard to match the second in order to complete the pair?"

"Yes," said Pamela Blount, without any change of expression or any lift of her voice. Of course, reflected the other, she'd been warned by that request of her husband's concerning the trinkets half an hour ago.

"I think I'm right in saying that Sir Gervase at that time knew nothing of your loss?"

"Nothing."

"Although the jewel was a very valuable one."

"Nothing," repeated Lady Blount.

"In fact, you dropped the first immediately outside

the room occupied by Mr. Charteris in Thermiloe Square."

Lady Blount nodded reflectively, as if this was just what she had anticipated.

"You didn't care to approach the Yard about the matter?"

She looked faintly surprised. "The Yard? Oh, no. That was quite out of the question. I was particularly anxious that no publicity should be given to my visits to Mr. Charteris. You will recognise the necessity for that, of course." She was as cool, as elegant, as remote as if she had been making negligent conversation in some one else's dull drawing-room.

"I think I'm right in saying that at that time Sir Gervase knew nothing of these visits?"

"Quite right."

"But later you decided to tell him?"

"He was informed, and asked me to leave the matter to his judgment."

"Which you did?"

Her exquisite eyebrows lifted ever so slightly. "Certainly."

"You knew that on the day in question—the 20th of September—he proposed to see Mr. Charteris?"

"He told me he meant to do that if he could find him at home."

"Ah! Mr. Charteris had just forged your name to a cheque for two hundred pounds?"

"He had."

"And had drawn the amount?"

"I believe so."

Of course, reflected Bremner, he must have drawn it. Otherwise the cheque would never have come into Blount's hands. He made a mental note to discover what had happened to the money. "What date was this?"

"The day before he travelled up to town. That would be the 19th of September."

"Thank you. Now, Lady Blount, perhaps you can tell me where your husband's revolver is at this moment."

Like the unnamed soldier who drew his bow at a venture and smote King Ahab in the joints of his harness, Bremner saw this bolt of his suddenly flash home. In an instant Pamela Blount had changed. He guessed that before his arrival she had steeled herself to answer almost any question he could put, no matter how intimate, but she had never allowed for this. He followed up the advantage swiftly. "It's of the greatest importance," he urged, "that I should have an answer to that question. On it may hang much of the case against the murderer of Mr. Charteris. Sir Gervase tells me that he normally keeps it in a locked desk that is inaccessible to any one else. It is now missing, and the first thing that a coroner's jury will want to know will be whether the bullet found in the murdered man's brain corresponds with the bullets that fit that revolver. If you can throw any light on the mystery you may very considerably help Sir Gervase's case."

"Help him?" Now she was white as death, eyes black in her pinched face. "Do you mean there is any question of danger to him?"

"His position is serious," said Bremner unhesitatingly. "A jury could make out a good case both as to motive and circumstantial evidence. If it can be shown that on the night of the murder the revolver was not in his possession or was in some place unknown to him, it would very materially clear the ground."

He had been watching her face, but now he turned away just as Ambrose had done on that night in the garden. She made no pretence now of hiding her anguish, but she did not instantly reply. Bremner wondered whether that swift and calculating brain were fencing for some story sufficiently credible to put the police off the track.

"You mean," turning to him with simple candour, "that if it could be shown that on the night of Mr. Charteris' death my husband did not even know where the weapon was he would be automatically exonerated?"

Bremner could not quite agree to that; for it was possible for Blount to own a second revolver, though even he considered this supposition fantastic; or he and his wife might be together in this. You couldn't tell.

So that all he would say was, "It would strengthen his case certainly."

"I can assure you of that," she answered in that deathly quiet tone that was so much more alarming than passion would be. "In fact, I can tell you where it is now. It's here." She turned to a Jacobean bureau which she unlocked; from a secret drawer she took a small Browning revolver and silently passed it to the detective. Bremner snapped open the breach. There was one cartridge missing!

"May I ask when you concealed this?"

"On the morning of the twentieth, very early."

"The day on which your husband went up to town? But I gather from him that no one else can get at the contents of his desk, and that he carries the key about with him at all times."

"I took it while he was dressing. He never knew I had returned it before he could miss it." An essential dignity in voice and bearing robbed the words of the sense of shoddiness that must normally have accompanied so sorry a confession. To pick a man's pockets! And Pamela Blount of all women.

"And abstracted the revolver? Why?"

"I thought it safer."

"You knew he would be seeing Mr. Charteris?"

"I did."

"Had he said anything about travelling up armed?" She hesitated. "Not precisely. But—"

"You thought it extremely probable that he might be tempted to do Mr. Charteris some injury?"

"Most likely it would never have occurred to him to take the revolver. But I dared run no risk."

"Come, come, Lady Blount, he must have threatened pretty desperately for you to take so much trouble to get hold of it. That day was his first to Charteris?"

"Yes."

"He'd only just heard that he was threatening you with blackmail?"

"He had."

"And was naturally in a mood of considerable violence. What time did you take the revolver from his desk?"

She considered an instant, her fine, dark brows drawn together in fastidious disdain. "Between eight and half-past on the morning of the twentieth."

"Of course you were alone when you took it? No one saw you going or coming?"

"I hardly think so. Personally I neither saw nor heard any one."

"And no one saw you put it away?"

Again those fine eyebrows registered distaste. "Certainly not."

Bremner seemed disappointed, as indeed he was. For this was not evidence at all. No one could corroborate Lady Blount's statement as to the actual time when the revolver was locked into the Jacobean bureau. It might have been secreted there after Blount's return. Who knew? In any event, the cartridges were identical, and there was nothing to show that this was not the weapon that had done Charteris to death.

He made a last attempt to get the hang of the position. "Lady Blount, it would greatly facilitate us if you could tell us the exact position between yourself and Mr. Charteris at the time of his death. It might help us to unearth some of his past history. At present we're working in the dark."

He thought he had never seen so poignant an expression pass like a shadow over any face. Then she said, "Did you ask my husband that?"

"Yes."

"And he answered——?"

"He had nothing to say."

"Nor have I."

Bremner's expression did not change. "I'm sorry. It would have saved our time. Can you remember the exact hour Sir Gervase returned on that evening?"

"It was quite late, just about tea-time, I think. We had expected him for lunch."

"He telephoned perhaps? No? Ah, a pity. He told you that he had seen Mr. Charteris? Anything else?"

"Merely that we shouldn't be troubled with him again."

"And you understood by that?"

"That the matter was satisfactorily settled."

"He gave you no details of his interview?"

"I asked for none. I was content."

He felt compelled to believe her. Yet the result of his conversation was quite negative. On the whole it darkened the case against Blount. For how could any man be utterly sure that matters were satisfactorily settled and the rogue's mouth forever closed unless the fellow were dead? There are no other men who cannot tell tales an they will, and opportunity is kind.

Further cross-examination merely elicited a recital of the story Blount had already told as to his vexatious delays and inconveniences. More and more did Bremner feel convinced that the revolver had been locked in the drawer after Blount's return, and that Pamela Blount knew it. She spoke like an automaton that has never been known to break down or to utter a false cadence. Everything, in fact, ran just a little too smoothly to please the detective. He would have preferred some natural hesitation, a little groping after memory. Pamela was word perfect as a parrot might be or a machine. There was nothing human about bearing or voice.

He tried one last question. "At this moment, then, your husband knows nothing of the revolver's whereabouts?"

"Nothing."

He was forced for the moment to leave it at that.

As a forlorn hope he next tested the servants with the truth of Blount's story. They all agreed, so far as they had heard it, in every detail, and left Bremner wondering how it was that the domestic staff should have been given the explanation with such minuteness. Why, indeed, unless it seemed probable that they might be asked to repeat it later? He could find no alternative answer.

CHAPTER V

"Some circumstantial evidence is very great—as when you find a trout in the milk."—THOREAU.

I

REALISING that the suspected man must be given the benefit of every doubt, and that he must not overlook the smallest loophole, Bremner set to work immediately on his return to town to test Blount's story, and to try and find for him some alibi which could clear him of the ugly imputation of murder. First of all, he attempted to establish the fact of his presence at Plum Tree Court on the night in question. For if it could be shown that he was at the C.P.O. office at ten-thirty it was impossible for him to be concerned in the murder. Bremner calculated that he must have left the house in Thermiloe Square at a few minutes before ten at the latest, in order to avoid Miss Gell. The distance to Four Corners by road was a lengthy one, and would take, on such a night and considering the state of the roads, probably between five and six hours. Then if his suspicion should prove to be founded there had been the preliminary business of fitting up the man with boots and collar. So that it must be some time after four before he would arrive at his destination; it would take some further time to dispose of the body, and then would follow the mad drive back under the lightening sky, haunted by the fear of pursuers, as amateur murderers always are, terrified of recognition each time the car rounded a corner. Altogether it seemed obvious that he could not have reached London earlier than nine o'clock, and even then there was much to be done before he could set out for Four Corners. He would have to stable the car (Bremner made a note to inquire whether the garage consisted of private lock-ups, that would afford no evidence, or was merely one large, open shelter, accessible to every one, in which case probably some employee would have seen him) : he must then go across to his flat to leave there some definite proof that he had occupied the room overnight, pack himself a suit-case; and it was manifestly impossible for him to do all these things and catch the eight fifty-five. He had, therefore, not started from Charing Cross at all, but had caught the Victoria through train, at twelve-nineteen, which would enable him to catch the connection to Little Kirbey from Eversfield. This, Bremner reflected, was the line the prosecution would take, if need arose.

He went first to the offices of the C.P.O. in Plum Tree Court. These were small and rather inconvenient, but quiet. Posing as a plain-clothes detective from the Yard, detailed for an unimportant piece of duty, Bremner explained painstakingly to each tenant in turn that he had on a certain night in the preceding week seen a man loitering suspiciously in the yard adjoining the chambers, and it was believed that he had actually succeeded in getting on to the premises. He wished to know whether in any particular office signs of the intruder had been found or whether anything were missing. In every case he received a reply in the negative. Then he would add casually, "You weren't on the premises yourself, of course? Well, hardly, at that hour. Must have been close on eleven." The result of those investigations had been no more unsatisfactory than he had expected. He had endeavoured to learn both from the porter and from the very diminutive staff at the C.P.O. whether any traces had been found in the waste-paper basket or on the desk, whether a book had been out of place, any triviality that might help to bolster up Blount's version. But to every question his companions had shaken grave, considering heads. Nothing had been disturbed, not so much as a penholder. No trace had been seen of scattered MS. No drawer or cupboard appeared to have been forced. Bremner, remembering the flawless neatness of the study at Four Corners, withdrew discomfited and decided next to visit the garage. As he left the offices, however, he saw in the distance a strolling policeman. Crossing the road he walked along, slowly scanning each name-plate as he passed, and as he and the constable drew abreast he approached him, and said, "Can you tell me where are the offices of the C.P.O.?"

"Just along there," returned the policeman indulgently, as if to intimate that these leagues didn't hurt him and presumably amused their founders. "Ground floor, No. 32."

"Oh! I passed there just now, can't say I noticed them. A small organisation, isn't it?"

"Couldn't say, sir. One of these 'ere freak things that have sprung up since the war. Too much talk about the war, if you ask me. If you 'ave to fight"— he had himself fought for two years before being invalided out—"well, you 'ave to fight. Like copping a burglar; 'e may be armed—you don't know, but it don't 'elp to stop and sing about it. Jest get on with the job and don't talk no more about it. Jest the same with war. These blokes that wants to write books about it—can't get 'em no'ow."

"They work pretty hard though, don't they?—the C.P.O. people, I mean? I was expecting a man from there to come and have dinner with me the other day, and he telephoned at half-past ten that he was still at his office."

"What, here? It's mostly shut down by six."

"Well, he said he was 'phoning from his room here, and he'd been so busy he couldn't get away. The twentieth it was. Perhaps you weren't on duty that night."

The policeman hesitated in obvious calculations. "Oh, yes, I was, sir."

"Then how do you explain it?"

The constable winked discreetly. "Lots o' gentlemen finds it useful to be busy at the office from time to time, married gents particular. But stands to reason if there'd bin a light in one o' these offices after ten o'clock I'd ha' gone to find out why. Tain't as if they was ordinary houses, they're offices, if you get what I mean. I'd have knocked 'em up—asked. I was on night-duty here all that week. Well, I didn't knock 'em up, didn't ask. Stands to reason then, doesn't it, there wasn't no one there." His logic was as simple as that.

Bremner thanked him and went into the entrance of the block of business chambers. He lingered in a dark corridor for five minutes to give the policeman time to get out of sight, and then emerged, thinking furiously. The man's suggestions could hardly be taken as evidence; Bremner had ascertained that the room in which Blount normally worked faced the street, but there was a library at the back where he might have sat and made notes, without using the front room at all. There was no way of proving this except by asking the man point-blank, and in any case he could be relied on to say that he sat in the library. As, indeed, he might well have done. On the whole, Bremner felt he had drawn a blank.

He next visited the garage, where he presented himself as a man anxious to rent a lock-up. He was told that at the moment there were none vacant. But he could garage the car in the large garage if he pleased. Bremner didn't please. He wanted a lock-up, he said. "I know a man who garages here," he explained. "Sir Gervase Blount. Hasn't he a lock-up?"

"Yes, sir. But then he's had it for a long time. Doesn't use it much neither, because he mostly lives in the north."

"Surely he's in town now, though. I had an appointment with him only a day or two ago."

"His car's here. Can't say more than that. He may have used it lately—well, what I mean is he brought it down about twelve days ago or p'raps a bit more. But I don't know when he uses it or even if it's there now. With a lock-up, you see, you can get at your car night or day. That's why we started some when we had a chance to buy a bit more ground. The garage closes at eleven, so if you want to stable your car after that you must go somewhere else."

"Still," urged Bremner, "the lock-ups adjoin the garage. If a man stabled his car about nine or ten in the morning you'd see him, wouldn't you? As a matter of fact, I'm particularly anxious to get hold of Sir Gervase in a rattling hurry, and no one seems to know precisely where he is. I thought, perhaps, you or your assistants might have seen him lately."

The proprietor shook his bald head. "Not likely, sir. Suppose he came in about nine or ten *as* you say, why me and my mate mightn't be knocking around. Most likely repairing in the shed at the back. He may 'ave bin in and out 'alf a dozen times the last week, but we mightn't catch a glimpse of him."

"I see. That's rather unfortunate. Well, I'm sorry you can't lease me a lock-up. I'm afraid the garage wouldn't be any use to me. I often motor very late at night—can't sleep. And I want some place where I can turn her in just as it suits me. I've heard of a flat close by, just the sort of thing I want, but I must have the car handy."

"Sorry I can't help you," said the proprietor who appeared to be a kind man. "Don't know of any lock-ups anywhere very close. Whereabouts was this flat o' yours?"

Bremner hastily invented an address, adding vague directions. The other thought a moment, then said, "Don't know of any place just there. If you like to leave your name we could let you know if one of these should fall vacant——" Bremner left the name of Arthur Wintle of Chiswick and came away.

So far he had substantiated none of Blount's story. He took a taxi to the insignificant flat that the priest occupied on his rare nights in town, in the hope of finding a porter or, perhaps, a charwoman who could tell him something useful. The flats themselves were obviously for poor professional men who could not afford the expense of a club; the porter was small and shabby; the brickwork was chipped and needed repairing; paint, varnish and hall linoleum all told a tale of poverty. Bremner wondered why Blount, who was fastidious to the point of foppishness, should have selected anything so penurious, until he remembered his peculiar views on the subject of money. Himself a comparatively wealthy man he held views very much allied to socialism, and his personal expenditure was incredibly low. Even his car was kept more for use than pleasure, and was, as he had said, a pretty insignificant affair. His only extravagance, indeed, was books, a point that Bremner recognised the instant he set foot inside his rooms.

The porter, who resembled a black-and-tan terrier, with a tired stoop, was civil and mournfully interested.

"Can you tell me which is Sir Gervase Blount's flat?" Bremner asked.

"Sir Gervase? Oh, this one here on the ground floor. But 'e ain't in."

"Not in? You're sure?"

"Oh, yes. Ain't bin 'ere for a long time."

"That's very strange. He wrote to me—look here. This is his letter." He drew from his pocket a letter that he had written before starting, a letter beginning, "My dear Swaine," and signed "G. B." "See what he says. 'I can't understand how we missed last week, but I shall certainly be up next week.' I was meant to meet him last Thursday. He was staying in town then. But somehow we slipped one another and I didn't realise then that he was putting up here or I could have come straight along."

" 'E wasn't 'ere sir. Take my davey 'e wasn't."

"But he must have been. He said he was. Perhaps you missed him. What time do you knock off?"

"Ten o'clock—an' two hours too late at that."

"And what time do you come on duty?"

"Eight, sharp."

"Then if he came out of his room any time after that you'd be sure to see him."

The porter shook a grizzled head; his expression was one of sarcastic amusement. "I got other things to do that time o' day than jest sit around and see the gentlemen walk out of their flats. If 'e come out so early why I might be anywhere, swelp me bob."

"Well, I think I recall his telling me that he didn't as a rule breakfast here, as he had no attendance. He made arrangements to get food outside."

"Dessay that's right, sir. 'E don't 'ave no one to look arter 'im. Sort of idea 'e's got, I think. But it stands to reason if 'e was 'ere last week some would ha' seen him."

"That sounds all right," Bremner agreed. "Who else could have done so?"

"There's the charwoman, Mrs. Waley, and 'er sister, Miss Brand. They live in the basement, and do for the tenants. They call 'em service flats, ye see. That means they empties yer basin and yer waste-paper basket and draws the quilt over yer bed."

"Then if he had been here one of them would have done his room?"

"Well, 'e's a bit odd, won't 'ave no one messing around. Says 'e can look after 'imself. All 'e ever does is to put out 'is waste-paper basket to be cleaned up. Plainest basket I ever see," he wound up dejectedly. "Not worth the trouble o' pinching it."

"Well," said Bremner energetically, "it doesn't really matter whether he was here last week or not. The fact remains that I missed him, and you say he isn't here now?"

"Don't s'pose 'e'll be up now for a bit."

"Oh? And why not?"

"Ain't yer read the papers? Ain't yer seen about this 'ere body they've found close up by 'is 'ouse? 'Orrible mangled it was, jest under 'is study winder they say. And 'ow did it get there? Yes, sir, you may well ask. Everybody's askin'. 'Orrible sight for a man when 'e pops up 'is blind to see that garshly, grinning face all among the daisies."

"There aren't any daisies at this time of the year in Thebeshire. And I fancy the body was found on the side of a cliff. Anyway, I don't see why that should prevent his coming up to town. Is there any way of getting into his flat? I should like to leave a note for him. I have his letter here, and from it I'm certain he'll be up to-night, even if he was delayed yesterday. Has any one a pass-key?"

"The caretaker, sir. She lives on the premises. I don't meself, just comes in about eight in the morning. But Mrs. Waley or Miss Brand, they'd be sure to 'ave one. If you was to ask 'em. Or I'll ask 'em meself," he added with alacrity, foreseeing a possible half-crown in Bremner's attitude.

Bremner, however, dissuaded him. "That's all right. I see there's a bell here. I'll just press that. Thanks." Silver changed hands as a door slammed down in the basement and there was the sound of hurried but impatient feet on the stairs. Behind Bremner's back the porter made strange signs to the new-comer, indicating that, with tact, a tip was forthcoming. The woman who answered the summons was thin and worn, and limped a little from an accident she had had five years ago when acting as lady's-maid in a house in Earl's Court. She was glad now to live with her widowed sister and her two children.

153

"Yes, sir?"

"I've come a long distance to see Sir Gervase Blount, but the porter tells me he isn't here, after all. His letter distinctly states that he will be here to-night, but unfortunately I can't wait. I have to go north this afternoon. I want to come in and leave a note for him. It's extremely important. I understand you have a pass-key."

Miss Brand (Mrs. Waley was out shopping) impressed by the visitor's brisk manner of assurance, produced the skeleton key and opened a door to the left of the hall.

"This is Sir Gervase Blount's flat. We didn't know he was coming up to-night, but then he never lets us know."

"He was up here the other day, surely?"

"I don't think so, sir. None of us saw him if he was."

"He might come at a time when you weren't naturally about. Do you often see him;"

"I never seen him but once, and my sister, she was saying the other day he's hardly been here at all since he was married. I've only bin here meself the last two years."

"I see." He entered the flat and glanced swiftly round him. "Convenient little places for a shake-down. What lies on the other side of that door?"

"That's a bedroom, sir. And a bathroom. Some of them has a kitchen as well, because there's ladies likes to do their own cooking o' nights. But this ain't one of 'em. There's jest a bathroom the other side of the bedroom, and, of course, a gas-ring in 'ere for cocoa or the like."

"You never came into his flat, did you?"

"No, sir. Funny 'abit of 'is."

"I dare say you're right. Are there any flats going in this building just now?"

"There'll be one in the New Year, I believe, or p'raps it was March. Gentleman on the second floor. But it's built just the same as this."

"Ah! I don't think he'd mind my glancing into his room to see the size, etc. What's the outlook?"

It was fortunate that at this juncture the caretaker's bell rang again. "I shall be all right," Bremner assured her quickly. "I'm only going to scribble a note. You'll be sure he gets it when he comes in?"

The instant the door had closed behind her he laid upon the desk a half-written letter he had prepared earlier in the day, and set his fountain pen beside it. Then he began his rapid effectual search. The flat was certainly a very modest affair; there was a gas-ring in the sitting-room and a gas-fire with a small ring in the bedroom, so that it was possible to do a little cooking, if required. Both rooms were very simply furnished, but there was a fine austerity about the whole atmosphere that accorded well with Bremner's impressions of the man.

He commenced his search in the bedroom. On Blount's own showing he had spent only one night there, and Bremner wanted to discover some obvious trace of his presence, recently. But there was nothing to betray the fact that any one had slept there for a month. The bed had that cold dejected appearance of all beds that are seldom used. There was a layer of dust on everything; that seemed to Bremner fairly conclusive; a man of Blount's disposition would not allow the dust to lie on the mirror in that fashion. He passed into the bathroom, where he found a second mirror as dusty as the first. However, the window, both here and in the bedroom, and as he subsequently discovered in the sitting-room also, was open. This might have been a point in Blount's favour had not the detective known that it was a foible of his never to close windows. Returning to the bedroom he began to look carefully for something, opening the corner drawers, and then, less optimistically, the larger drawers of the dressing-table, sifting through the clothes-basket for soiled linen, even opening the wardrobe and peering under the bed, and at last coming through the communicating door into the sitting-room. Here the table was covered with papers weighed down into several piles. Bremner glanced at some of the dates, but none of these were recent. That was not evidence in one direction or the other, since there was nothing to show that Blount would have letters sent to this address. Moreover, he had specifically stated that he had done nothing but sleep here. Dust in this room was equally plentiful, but the detective reflected that the windows opened on to a stone yard where dust and grit would accummulate. The chair was an ordinary swivel desk chair; cigarettes lay on the table-top; one or two books were scattered round the room; a dead match lay in the grate.

"For the gas-fire presumably. Was it cold enough on Monday? Ah, yes, a fog and afterwards rain. Didn't he say he made himself some cocoa?" He crossed to a corner cupboard that he opened to assure himself that the cocoa and crockery really existed. He found both, together with a cheap kettle, two plates and a spoon. The cup was stained a brownish colour at the bottom, but there was no dust on the outside.

"Been washed recently but not dried," he reflected. "That bears out his statement that he was here. But he may have looked in during the fog in the afternoon. He had plenty of time. This murder looks to me as if it had been pretty carefully planned, but not by an expert. Egerton says the fellow's clumsy, but he's pretty far-seeing. An amateur wouldn't think of things like sticks and boots." He shut the cupboard and continued a meticulous examination of the flat. He had once secured the arrest of a brutal murderer by the discovery of a bodkin concealed in the thick pile of the carpet. The waste-paper basket was empty, and Miss Brand had assured him that neither she nor her sister had seen it for some time. So clearly he had not used it on the important Monday night. Drawers, desks and papers he examined without success, and then stooping he swept the long, shabby, green curtains off the floor. And here, for the first time was something of importance. Screwed up and pitched into a corner of the room behind one of the curtains was a scrap of paper; the writing on this smudged and blotted but still perfectly legible. With growing mystification Bremner read:—

"I have been offered a job
                        job
                        job
            offered a job in the north
                              north
                              north
                              north
but I must go
            go. . . ."

The detective stared. The fragments of writing seemed fantastic and meaningless. Why should certain words be written more than once? "Job" three times for instance and "north" four? He pondered; then he noticed something else; the word "job" had a slightly different appearance each time. The "j" began with a distinct tail, but the third "j" was little more than a single stroke. The same was true of the word "north." The "t" had at first a cross and a curl, but the final formation of the letter was a black harsh line readable only because of its context. The wording, too, appeared familiar, and light broke suddenly over his face. This was the original draft of the letter found on Miss Gell's hall-table! So it was here that it had been written. Bremner stooped to examine the blotting-paper, but the writer had known how to avoid clues. There was no imprint of any such wording to be found; in any case the smudged appearance of the letters told their own tale. He wondered what had happened to the rest of the paper from which this scrap had been torn. In vain did he search for a sheet of thin, white paper corresponding to the fragment in his hand. Then he hoped that, perhaps, he would find some trace of papers having been burned in this or some other room, but again he was unsuccessful. He was, therefore, forced to the conclusion that Blount, exhausted, at a very high pitch of nervous intensity, had in a moment of aberration crumpled this scrap and tossed it away from him, and forgotten it when he carefully collected the rest of the trial letters. That moment of carelessness was likely to cost him his life, and once again Bremner longed to know the actual story lying behind the crime. Probably the usual tale of uncontrolled passion reaping its harvest years later.

Rough on Blount, he thought, for Charteris was scarcely the type to spare a wounded opponent. The room yielded one other important clue in the shape of a yellow box of writing-paper, still containing several sheets. Bremner knew them instantly; they were precisely similar to the one on which the letter was written.

"That rather clinches it," he murmured, shutting the drawer again.

The flat had nothing more to give him in the way of information. For the second time he raised the question of the waste-paper basket with Mrs. Waley and her sister, but both swore that they had had nothing to do with it for several days, so that any destroyed papers deposited there on Monday, the twentieth, must be there still. Bremner left his letter completed, neatly folded and addressed in the centre of the table, and came out feeling a little sick at the turn events were taking. Near the district station he came suddenly upon Scott Egerton, whom he greeted without any sensation of surprise. It was one of that young man's natural gifts to turn up just when the situation became imminent. Egerton explained that he had travelled up to see a man called Smythe on business concerning the constituency. He proposed to take the afternoon train down, leaving his car for repairs at a London garage (characteristically he drove a car down at Four Corners where no one else could) and calling for it on his return a few days hence.

"Found what you wanted, James?" he asked casually, as the latter put three pennies in an automatic machine and drew out a green ticket.

"No," returned Bremner shortly, who was sufficiently intimate with his companion to realise that all such metaphors as "grave" and "sphinx" were inadequate where Egerton's silence was concerned.

"What was that?"

"A handkerchief."

"Had he none?"

"Plenty. But not a soiled one. And no collar either. Nothing at all——"

"Probably took 'em on to Four Corners with him," suggested Egerton sensibly. "Don't suppose he'd leave them there to moulder. Two points, if I may. Did you find any water in Charteris' room?"

Bremner scowled. "What the devil——?"

"You didn't? I thought not. Then was there a tap outside on the landing?"

"There was not." Bremner seemed hopelessly at sea. "Anything else?" he added ironically.

"Wasn't it rather a small pair of scissors?" returned Egerton unperturbed, and without waiting for a reply he vanished in a downward lift.

2

On his arrival at the Yard to report progress Bremner straightway compared the fragment of writing he had found in Blount's flat with the letter discovered by Miss Gell on her return on the night of the twentieth. The comparison was instructive. The first "j" on the draft differed materially from the finished article, which, when set next to writing that was indubitably Charteris' own, and that had been supplied by his late landlady, proved to be identical. Similarly the last "north" on the draft was in an excellent imitation of Charteris' hand-writing, whereas, the first would have been discernible to any one at all accustomed to that writing as a forgery.

That point cleared up, Bremner was informed that another part of his perplexity had by this time been answered. The man who had been employed on the task of turning up the dead man's previous record had done it with marked ability and success. The typewritten report lay on the chief's table when Bremner walked into the room.

"This will interest you," the chief observed, flipping it across.

Bremner read it intently. The man who called himself Raymond Charteris had been traced back to Liverpool in the year 1912, at which time he was twenty-three years old. He was reported to be an actor without many prospects; occasional clippings mentioned his name, but not with any especial enthusiasm. He had acted in Liverpool itself, and had toured with second and third companies for several years. In 1915 he had managed to get a commission as second-lieutenant in a Liverpool regiment, and in the late autumn of 1916 had been cashiered for conduct unbecoming of an officer and a gentleman. What precisely that conduct was the authorities were disinclined to state, on the ground that it could have had no relation to his death.

Bremner looked up at this point, to say, "Bit thin, what? He may have injured some fellow-officer who's been waiting all this time to pay off old scores."

"Possible," agreed the chief, "but fantastic. As a matter of fact, and in strict confidence, I've a friend at court who 'hints' that it was something fishy connected with money, not a woman or anything that would live for fourteen years in a man's memory."

After his dismissal Charteris appeared to have posed as a wounded soldier who had been demobilised as unfit; he obtained work at a munitions factory during 1917, and remained there for the duration of the war. In the spring of 1918 he married Miss Pamela Heath, whom he had known during their stage days, and who had miraculously reappeared at the factory at the beginning of that year. After the Armistice there was a long gap, and in 1922 he was again to be found touring the provinces. A list was given of the various third-rate shows in which he had figured, and in 1925 he was traced back to London. He had been employed very little during the past two years, and chiefly at work that had no connection with the stage. Clerical work at low pay he had obtained now and again; he had attempted to sell maps of London to commercial enterprises; he had travelled for a certain suspicious insurance company that had unexpectedly wound up its affairs and decamped. That was all.

"Not a very savoury record," Bremner commented. "But it puts Blount in a worse hole than ever. You remember that Charteris referred to Lady Blount as 'my wife,' said they'd been separated for years, but that they hoped to set up together again shortly. There's no mention of a divorce, I see."

"I'm having special inquiries made. There's no question that the lady who married Charteris and the lady who now calls herself the wife of Sir Gervase Blount are one and the same. I fancy, in any case, that Lady Blount must have believed her husband to be dead. I see they were married at a church in Leicestershire. Now, if she had divorced the rascal it's practically incredible that Blount should have married her. His church views on the subject are well known. He adopts the Catholic aspect, and even if he had married a woman who had divorced her husband he would certainly have felt himself unable to retain office. One might suppose that she married in the belief that she was a widow, were it not that she expressly describes herself as 'spinster.' So we are left with the alternative that she hadn't mentioned Charteris' name, not, that is, until it became inevitable. I don't see that the evidence we have leads to any other conclusion. Now she's discovered that she's committed bigamy—because I dare say she did genuinely believe her first husband to be dead—and she's doing her level best, with his help, to avoid a scandal."

"H'm. Sounds reasonable enough. But I must confess I shouldn't like to be in Blount's shoes now. I'd imagined something less drastic than marriage where the lady and Charteris were concerned. But since the marriage actually took place it's clear that nothing short of death could right the position. Blount, particularly with his views, could hardly continue living with a woman whom he knew to be some one else's wife."

"Have you got any forrader with the evidence?"

Bremner enlightened him. "I can't get a scrap of information to back up a single incident in his story. And this bit of paper seems conclusive. Of course, Lady Blount would be standing in with him in this. That goes without saying. I'm afraid the yarn about the revolver is very thin indeed. Sneaking her husband's keys when he was in his bath, and removing the thing and locking it in her own room. Not very likely, I'm afraid."

"There's the button, too. Yes, an ugly case as you say. And our next step?" He glanced inquiringly at his junior who nodded grimly.

"I must go down to Eversfield and test Blount's

story there, too. If we can discover a soul who can swear to his being on the platform or in the cathedral between twelve-thirty and one-thirty, it may even yet be possible to over-ride the rest of the evidence. Because he couldn't have got down to Four Corners, disposed of the body, returned the car to the garage, faked an alibi in his flat and caught the eight fifty-five. I've been working it out, and the very earliest he'd get back to town would be some time after nine. I'll go down there now, and be back to-night."

At Eversfield, however, he did not anticipate meeting with any notable success, any more than he had already done at Farmer's, the London restaurant where Blount had supped according to his own story on the night in question. The man was not sufficiently well known to attract much attention on so crowded an afternoon. Bremner drew a blank both at the tea-shop and the cathedral, and returned to the station where he engaged the station master in desultory talk. After all, he reflected, Blount had changed at Eversfield every time he had gone to Four Corners, and there was a ten minutes' pause between the connections, so possibly his face would be comparatively familiar. For Eversfield is a small suburb of Addersbury and strangers are few and far between, and likely to be noticed.

"That was a nasty fog you had the other day down here," he observed amiably.

"Yes, sir. Blacker in London, though, they tell me."

"It was. Smashed a lot of people's plans, mine included."

"And ourn, sir. That was the day the Duke of G—— was coming down to unveil the war memorial. Rare bad luck that, sir. The weather was so unpleasant and him not so young he didn't come at all, but sent his aide-de-camp. The people was rarely put out about that; many of 'em had come over from Addersbury, a good seven mile away, just to see 'im, and they wasn't over-pleased at getting a bit of a boy with a pink face, he couldn't even grow a moustache on, and yellow hair, and a stammer you could hear all over Eversfield, like Kent's old cow when she's wheezing of a Sunday."

"Ah! That probably accounts for the crush. I thought something must be on."

"Was you here that afternoon, sir?"

"Yes. I was going to meet a man, but I never found him. I pushed my way through batches of people; dare say I missed him altogether, if he ever turned up. He swears he did——"

"Folks 'ull swear a mort o' things, sir, in rain and fogs."

Bremner appeared to be considering. "I suppose you wouldn't remember him? He's Sir Gervase Blount, the man who owns Four Corners."

"Blount? Don't recall the name, sir. But I did 'ear some one was living in the place agin. Sort of madman I thought he must be, taking a wife to a haunted house like that."

"Oh, nonsense. It's a very good place for a man who needs a rest."

"Rest? That 'ouse ain't quiet at night, don't you believe it, sir. There's ghosties——"

"Only exist in your imagination, station master. Then you don't know him by sight?"

"Not me, sir."

Bremner reflected on the limitations of the local mind that could be fired by an itinerant curate, and remain serenely unaware of a name that had been discussed up and down the country for the past four years.

"You don't remember seeing me either, I expect?"

The station master after prolonged scrutiny shook his head. "I can't say I do, sir."

"Ah! I'm sorry about that. I hoped you might be able to win ten pounds for me."

"How's that, sir?"

"He suggested that I hadn't turned up after all, and I said I'd bet ten pounds the station master would remember me. I hadn't remembered how large the crowd was that day. Of course, it would be unreasonable to expect you to recall individual faces."

The station master's palm curved suggestively. "Now you come to speak of it, sir, I'm not 'arf sure I didn't see you. Come in the afternoon, didn't you?"

"That's it. About half-past three."

"Ah! The crowd was very bad then. You was going on to Four Corners?"

"That's right."

"And you took the train at five-forty? Of course I remember you, sir."

"You're sure you don't remember him, too? That would lose me the bet, you see."

"I don't rec'llect any other gentleman that afternoon, sir, though I couldn't say o' course for sartin sure he wasn't around. What was he like to look at?"

"Here he is." Bremner produced a photograph. The old man scanned it gravely, then returned it. "No, sir. I'm certain 'e warn't here. But you was. Bless my soul, I remember you quite well now."

"I shall make him come and hear you say so."

"I'll say it all right, sir. If I shouldn't 'appen to

be 'ere just the time you come I'll be in my little cottage over yonder."

"All right, station master, I shall remember. And you shall have half whatever I get out of him."

"That fellow's no dashed good as a witness," he decided. "Things are looking pretty black for Blount."

3

Bremner's last visit to Four Corners took place on the following day. The butler, looking preternaturally saturnine as though he suspected an ill wind, admitted grudgingly that Sir Gervase was at home and showed him into the dining-room. Here he was compelled to wait for some time. Sudden suspicion shot through him that Blount was preparing a getaway while the man with a warrant for his arrest was detained in another part of the house, but he dismissed that as ludicrous and began to glance idly through a copy of *The Field* that lay in a paper-rack by the book-case. The pages were folded back at a photograph of a tall, soldierly man labelled "The Duke of G—— who will unveil the new war memorial at Eversfield, Thebeshire, on Monday the 20th September." Bremner laid aside the periodical thoughtfully. Blount's story had gained such appearance of verisimilitude as it possessed from the casual mention of this incident. It had seemed unlikely that he would know about the unveiling ceremony unless he had been there. But here lay the information ready to his hand and Bremner remembered with a pang of foreboding that the man had said nothing of the substitute, as surely he must have done had he actually been on the spot. The detective turned sharply as he heard feet in the hall outside, and then

Sanders came in saying, "Sir Gervase will see you now, sir."

There was on this occasion no sign of Egerton or any other members of the party; the house was noticeably quiet and deserted. Blount was standing alone in the study with his back to the door. As it opened and without turning, he said sharply, "I wish, Sanders, you'd remember to change the date on my calendar every morning. It irritates me to see it standing a day behind."

Sanders said respectfully, "Yes, sir. Mr. Bremner, sir."

Blount swung round; he was haggard and worn, and the detective saw that there would be no necessity to explain his errand. Nevertheless, he gave his man every possible inch of rope.

"We have had a formal search made of your flat, Sir Gervase," he began, "and there are one or two things we must ask you to explain. First of all, you will identify this as your notepaper?"

"I certainly have some like it. My wife bought me some at a time when she also was ordering a box. Did this come from my flat?"

"It did. It also corresponds to the paper on which Charteris wrote the letter found on Miss Gell's table —that is, of course, Charteris' alleged letter."

"Then, presumably, he also had bought some."

"Men in his critical financial position don't spend their cash on fancy notepaper. You've no other explanation?"

"None. Anything else?"

"Can you offer any explanation as to why this scrap of paper should have been in your sitting-room?"

He watched Blount's face narrowly as the latter

glanced through the fragmentary draft. The man was holding himself in an iron control. His face was impossible to read. He merely said, handing the paper back, "I've never set eyes on that before. No, I can't explain it in the least."

"It's the original draft of the letter found on Miss Gell's table. Can you still give us no help?"

"None, I'm afraid. I'm completely bogged."

That last flimsy hope gone there was nothing left for Bremner but to carry out the task for which he had travelled down here. For a minute after he had spoken the formal words of arrest, and given the formal warning, Blount stood rigid; he had involuntarily shaken the other man's hand from his shoulder, but he made no other movement. The psychologist in Bremner rose again, and said, "I wouldn't like to meet that man when he's in a rage," and he wondered if he could conceivably be guilty. A nature so passionate and fierce would stop at nothing.

Then Blount spoke impersonally and coldly. "You wish me to accompany you now?"

"If you please."

"You have no objection to my giving my servant some orders?"

"Would you object to giving them in my presence?"

"Not at all." He summoned Sanders. Then, while they waited, a figure came strolling casually across the lawn. It was Scott Egerton, hatless, debonair, assured.

Blount went to the window to meet him. "I suppose you guessed this? Very smart of you. Or had you special information?"

Egerton shook his head. "Only the ability to put two and two together."

"And that's why you carried through the idea of a

picnic with such a high hand? Good of you. There's no need to break it to the others till the fun is over."

Typical that, thought Egerton. And Blount said nothing about breaking it to Pamela first of all and in private because he knew his man well enough to realise that he needed no such warning.

CHAPTER VI

"But I will wear my heart upon my sleeve
For daws to peck at."

—Othello.

THE arrest of Sir Gervase Blount for the murder of Raymond Charteris was a nine days' wonder. The fact that the prisoner was in Orders made it the more intriguing; a clerical dog-collar for some obscure reason invariably lends excitement to any criminal sensation. People went about saying, "It's what I've always told you; clergymen are just like everyone else"; as if hitherto they had expected them to be a separate sex. Or, "And to think that all this time he's been allowed to officiate with a murder on his soul," and then the reply, "They say he's been in hiding since that shocking book of his." Occasionally a whilom admirer would murmur half-heartedly, "He must have cared a lot for his wife," to be met with the inevitable rejoiner that he that hateth not wife and parents and brother and sister, etc., etc.

But on the whole Blount's real supporters were a small inarticulate crowd; they did not mingle with the gossip-loving majority, but they did meet a little shyly and ask one another what could be done.

Meanwhile, the House of Commons had re-opened and Egerton had gone back and was immediately immersed in correspondence, and various matters, political.

"Can we do nothing to help Sir Gervase?" asked

Rosemary impatiently; standing and waiting was a form of service to which she felt no call.

"Not unless we're invited," returned her husband imperturbably. "It would be sheer impertinence to offer. It isn't our trouble."

"Every one isn't like you," she pointed out. "Some people like to have help offered them."

"I don't, and nor do you, and nor does Blount. We'll wait." But they did not have to wait long. On the sixth day after the arrest Egerton received a letter at breakfast-time from Ambrose. It was brief but illuminating.

"DEAR EGERTON,—Lady Blount and I would be most grateful for the benefit of your advice and assistance in the matter of Blount's defence. I have seen him in the prison and he's given me the names of two possible men who might take the case on. But, as you know, I'm an Irishman, living mostly at home, and know nothing of English Law or English manners. Could you spare us half an hour to-morrow or the day after? Sorry to run it so fine but I've just had word that my father's pretty ill, and must cross as soon as this is fixed up. Perhaps you'd 'phone me here. All my time is at your disposal.

"T. N. AMBROSE."

Egerton passed the letter across the table. "I've got to go ahead and see Horne before I meet this other fellow at ten. Could you 'phone and ask him to come this afternoon about five? Better come here; we can't discuss such an intimate matter in a boarding-house or club. Explain that I'm sorry I can't make it earlier, but that'll enable Ambrose to catch the boat-train all right. Half an hour should see the job through. Can you be here when they arrive in case I'm detained?"

172

Rosemary, whose day had been very neatly mapped out for some weeks, said with cheerful mendacity, "Rather. I shall be free all the afternoon. Oh, Scott, what she must be feeling! And if you take all that cream in your coffee," she wound up without any change of tone, "you'll grow fat and I couldn't endure a fat husband."

"I would commend to your notice one Julius Cæsar whose predilection was for stout gentry," murmured Egerton politely. "I'll be back as near five as I can."

The visitors came a few minutes early, and Rosemary welcomed them and gave them tea, and talked of a new picture show at the Goupil Galleries that had attracted a great deal of attention, and at which she had bought two pictures for Egerton's study. Ambrose, understanding nothing of the ways of women, thought, "No heart at all," and relapsed into sullen silence, but Pamela was grateful to her for refusing to acknowledge any tension about the occasion, and she recalled some story whispered about the girl at the time of her first terrible marriage, that might account for her perfect handling of the case to-day.

Egerton was five minutes late, apologised a little absently and carried off the pair to his library.

Ambrose installed himself as spokesman. "I've been down to see Blount," he repeated. "He's given me these two names. Well, I don't know a lawyer when I see one, but you may have heard of 'em." He produced a slip of paper. "Waterlow." He looked up to see the effect of the name on his audience. Egerton was frowning a little doubtfully.

"He's a first-chop man, but I don't fancy this is quite in his line. You could get in touch with him, of course. I can't say I know him, but I've met him once or twice and could probably sound him for you, if you'd care for me to try. Who's the other fellow?"

"Chap called Harper. Know him?"

"By reputation. I've never met him personally. This is his line; he's specialised in criminal cases. He saved Armitage, and that unfortunate Mrs. Wheeler. If he'll take up the case——"

"Why shouldn't he take it?" demanded Ambrose belligerently.

"Too busy perhaps," was Egerton's nonchalant rejoinder.

"He may believe Gervase is guilty," put in Pamela Blount speaking for the first time. The wide, black hat she wore in defiance of fashion shaded her eyes; her whole face was more inscrutable than ever; the quiet, beautiful hands folded in her lap were clasped a little eagerly, but they alone betrayed the agony of fear that enveloped her.

"That's possible," Egerton agreed unemotionally. "As I say, I don't know him personally, but I dare say my man of law could help us. Did Blount say anything to indicate a preference?"

"I gather he knows Waterlow personally, or used to. He was a lawyer, you know."

"Yes. Well, we might get in touch with him. Or I might telephone Hammond and ask him if he knows whether there's chance." He lifted the receiver.

"Hallo! Hallo! . . . Yes, Temple 1890. That you, Hammond? . . . Egerton speaking. With reference to that Four Corners affair is there any likelihood of Waterlow undertaking the job? . . . What? . . . No, I didn't know. Poor chap! Well, that's that. What about Harper?" There was a long silence while Ham-

mond did the talking. Egerton's free right hand felt
in his waistcoat pocket, and he produced a pencil and
scribbled a note on a small pad lying on his desk.
"Right, then. . . . To-morrow. . . . Four o'clock.
. . . 'Bye," and he pushed back the telephone arm.

"Waterlow's been down with stone," he explained.
"Pretty bad, Hammond says. He's one of these big
men that Rosemary dislikes. So that he'll be on the
shelf for some time. Hammond thinks we could get
Harper, and I've arranged a provisional meeting at
Hammond's office to-morrow at four. Are you sailing
to-night or will you wait?"

"I'm sailing to-night," said the doctor promptly.
"I'm not such a conceited ass as to suppose that I
can do anything now. And Lady Blount agrees——"

"Dr. Ambrose's father has had a stroke," Pamela
explained.

"Then you——"

Her face hardened in a curious manner. "No. I
would prefer to remain outside this as far as possible.
I haven't been to see my husband in prison because
I should like to feel if—when he returns he won't have
to remember all this horror every time he sees me.
He understands that. He doesn't want me to go."
Egerton understood, too, though Ambrose didn't.
Blount would like to come back to one loved creature
who had played no part in his prison episode.

"I see. Then you'll let me write to you?"

"To me? But why not Gervase?"

"You'll want to know the result of our delibera-
tions?"

"Oh, yes. But I suppose this lawyer will go down
to the prison?"

"I dare say he'll have to go several times."

"But Blount can't go on inventing fresh stories," expostulated the doctor.

"No. But he'll have to go over every incident most minutely. Sometimes if you go thoroughly into the most insignificant details you discover the missing link. Possibly, if he has to recall the whole of the conversation between himself and Charteris he'll let drop some scrap of news that may be the key to the whole tangle." He paused and looked keenly yet deferentially at Pamela. "I'm afraid it'll mean all cards on the table," he warned her. "If your husband tries to keep any back from misguided motives——"

She leaned forward suddenly so that the light fell on her fine grave face. "I'll put them on the table for him, Mr. Egerton. You're quite right. He would try and keep some back. It's a long story and it goes back to the time just before the war, but it must be told because it explains how and where Raymond Charteris' life touched mine and Gervase's, so I'd better give you everything."

Egerton stood by the book-case with his hands locked behind him; the doctor stared at the fire and felt profoundly uncomfortable; the whole looked rather like a problem picture by Sir John Collier.

"I was about seventeen when I first met Raymond," Pamela began. "My father had died a year earlier, and we had to scatter and fend for ourselves as well as we could. I had an offer of work as a child's governess at twelve pounds a year, and a companionship, doing a great deal of uncongenial work in return for a roof and food. Then a friend said he thought he could find me an opening on the stage. Like most girls I had always believed I had only to appear to ravish actor-managers, and it took two years for me to recognise that the successful, the great actress needs some quality I don't possess. I think, perhaps, it is unselfconsciousness. I could never be quite sure that the woman on the stage was not Pamela Heath still, in spite of the wig and the grease-paint. And, of course, that was fatal. I had no sooner realised that all my life I should be fighting for small engagements than I was overwhelmed with terror. I had always known what it was to be extremely poor and to work, but at least I had always been sure of something to eat and a place to sleep. But two years on tour—third-rate tour at that—showed me that there was no security about this life at all, and never would be. A play might fail, or I individually might fail, and I should be helpless, without anywhere to turn. I might be ill—I tormented myself with such reflections as these, and meanwhile I played in stupid cheap comedies in seaside kursaals and north-country palladiums. Once I realised I should never be successful I became too nervous to do even my best. I had months when I was out of work and took anything that offered; and all the time I wanted security—not adventure or fire or battle, but to feel safe, to hear the storm on the other side of the window. I'm the type of woman, Mr. Egerton, for whom houses are built and locks are forged. Then Raymond and I met for the second time, and he asked me to marry him. He hadn't before, though I half expected him to. Afterwards I learned why. I refused at first; he wasn't quite the type. . . . He wasn't a first-class actor either, but he didn't know it, so he did a good deal better than I did. And he was better looking than a great many men, so he usually had work of a kind. That was before the scars; didn't the doctor say he had had them twelve years? That wasn't true; he got them in 1919 in an accident. I was with him and afterwards he grew a beard and found it harder to get engagements. After I had refused to marry him came four months when I used to watch desperately for the postman and pray that I might get something—anything—and count my shillings. I was half-crazy. I would have taken almost any way out, and when Raymond asked me for the second time I married him. We were married at the registry office at Cuxhaven, where we were on tour in a wretched little play that didn't even settle our salaries——" She paused, and Egerton realised that she was thinking of that hole-in-a-corner marriage that was so different from the ceremony she had expected in her more fortunate days. The quiet, dreadful voice continued, "And after all I found no security. I had married on the assumption that a husband implied a home, like thousands of other women, and like them I was wrong. We had been married in the spring of 1918. For a year we struggled painfully; up till the Armistice Raymond had work in a munition factory, and I had some clerical work offered me unexpectedly that summer. Three weeks at the factory had been too much for me. But both of us were dismissed before Christmas, and in 1919 we had to fight for every penny. On and off Raymond got a little work, but it was badly paid when it was paid at all, and sometimes without warning he would come back and say that it had stopped. It wasn't till I discovered why he had left the army that I began to understand certain perplexing things."

"Why did he leave the army?" asked Egerton. Ambrose shot him a furious look. No sense of decency, this long, conceited chap with a face like wood.

"It was a question of forging the name of a superior officer on a cheque. In peace time I suppose he'd have been prosecuted and imprisoned, but the war was on, and they just cashiered him and forgot him. Some man who had been in his regiment repeated the story; it went round everywhere and things grew harder than ever. In June my little daughter was born. She only lived four months, and just after the funeral Raymond had this accident and was terribly ill. Of course, the landlady wouldn't let him stay where we were, particularly as we didn't know where to turn for the rent, and I was fortunate to get a big, unfurnished room and nurse him myself. Sometimes I was working in the afternoon and evening, and nursing him whenever I could rush home. He was delirious when he dropped certain hints I couldn't ignore——" She stopped, her hands pressed together, her head lifted a little, eyes turned away from the men, as if something in her throat choked her.

Egerton waited a moment, then asked impassively, "Concerning the cheque?"

She shook her lovely head. "No. If it had been that I could have said nothing. It would be like taking advantage of information from a letter read inadvertently. But it was something I couldn't refuse to notice. When I taxed him he was quite callous and candid, and acknowledged that he had not asked me to marry him when I had first anticipated because at that time he had a wife living, and that he had certain knowledge that she was alive still. He had known, he said, at the time of our wedding, but made up his mind that he was free to do as he pleased, because he had only been nineteen when he married, and she had been a designing woman eleven years his senior. But, of course, whatever he persuaded himself to believe didn't make him free, any more than my longing to get away from him to the ends of the earth could make me free. He was ill still, and needed constant nursing; he was very, very poor; he had done what he could earlier on; for my baby was always very delicate and I couldn't work during the four months I had her. We must have been a drain on his slender resources. And it isn't as if he drank or gambled; he gave us all that he could. So I felt I must stay with him and nurse him till he was strong. That was nearly three months. Then I came to London and became a children's nurse, and presently a woman was very kind to me and got me work on the stage again and I was lucky and kept that until I met my husband when I was touring at Mannington. Even then"—for the first time her voice faltered—"I said that so long as Raymond Charteris was alive I would marry no man whose position or standing might be imperilled by the past. We waited eighteen months and then we believed we had definite proof of his death. I was married in 1924, and it was in April of this year that I was made to realise that Raymond was not dead, after all. I had a letter from him asking me to go and see him, and I went. I didn't dare stay away."

"And what did he want of you?"

"He was in bad health, he said, and couldn't get an engagement."

"Money," agreed Egerton. "Did you give him any?"

"Not very much." The rare flush came into her pure, oval face. Egerton, whose pride began where Ambrose's left off and was so great it could even stoop to humility, recognised that the hour when she learned she was not Charteris' wife had held less humiliation than this moment, when she unfolded her tragic story to her husband's friend, and the man who had promised to help them.

"Did you send it to him?"

"No. I took it."

"That's better. There's no proof that you gave it him. Was it cheque or cash?"

"Cash. I drew a personal cheque——"

"I see. And it didn't satisfy him?"

"It was not a great deal. I have a joint account with my husband, but I couldn't, of course, draw his money for Raymond. There was a little jewellery that was quite my own and my own money that Gervase gave me——" She seemed beyond humiliation now. All her thought was for the man lying in prison for her sake.

"Yes. I quite understand. By the way, where were you living when he discovered you under your married name?"

"We were up in the north, at Mannington."

"Perhaps he had been touring there recently?"

"No. He told me that he had not been in that neighbourhood for some years."

"Had you just been to London?"

"Not for several months as it happened. Why?"

"I was wondering how, if you never met, he contrived to discover you again. But please finish. He threatened—what?"

"To tell the story everywhere. Don't you see that I could never allow that? Gervase—my husband—is a man far too well known to be able to risk that sort of ugly scandal. Some men only matter to themselves and to those who love them. That's important, of course, but not of superlative importance. Gervase matters to thousands—literally thousands of men and women. He had to be saved for them."

"And so, when you'd come to the end of your resources——"

"He forged a cheque in my name for two hundred pounds." She spoke very slowly, and her eyes were quite empty like the eyes of a witless thing.

"How did you discover that?"

"My husband drew my attention to it. He asked if I were short of money for any particular reason."

"And you faced Charteris with the tale?"

"He laughed. He'd done it before, you see. There was the time in the army. There was, I know, at least one other occasion; there may have been more."

"He believed you wouldn't dare show him up, of course?"

"Yes."

"But Blount—your husband knew. Who told him?"

"I did. I had to. To keep silent and let Raymond, perhaps, forge a second cheque would be to put myself in his category, to become a thief. So I told him."

"Was this just before he went up to town?"

"I—think so. Does it matter?"

"It may. The prosecution will try to show that as soon as he heard the news he went on impulse to Charteris' rooms and murdered him before his blood had time to cool. If you could declare that he waited a week——"

"I couldn't. He only waited till the Monday. I told him on Saturday night when it became clear I had no choice. I promised him to have no more communication with Raymond, but to leave everything to him."

"I see." Egerton moved away from the book-case

where his face was in shadow, and lounged away to the window whence he spoke in the same efficient, impersonal voice. "There's one more point. Miss Martineau."

Lady Blount started so violently that Ambrose involuntarily rose, touched her arm and muttered something sympathetic. He thought this wooden-faced, political chap something more than callous. Egerton made no attempt to be either soothing or compassionate; his manner, cool, collected, detached, suggested that the story he had just heard was typical of most of his acquaintances and that each development was just what he had anticipated. He displayed neither curiosity nor surprise; the affair might have been a complicated but intriguing mathematical problem.

"Eloise?" repeated Pamela Blount.

"Yes. She comes in somewhere, I think. If she weren't in some measure in your confidence she would hardly have been among the company at Four Corners last week. Is she a friend of Mr. Charteris?"

"Y-yes. She was herself on the stage for a short time; then she left it and went in for millinery."

"Quite. And when she was on the stage she met him?"

"Yes. Oh, she isn't his wife or anything melodramatic like that. But she knows him very well, and she must have kept in touch with him all these years because—because——"

"It was she who put him on the track again after your marriage, in the spring of this year."

"How did you know that?" Pamela Blount's grey eyes were black in the ravaged pallor of her face.

"Who else could have done it? You say you hadn't been recently to London, and he hadn't travelled north.

Obviously Miss Martineau must have seen you—or heard of you."

"That's true, though I had never stopped to think how she found me again. The bare fact was sufficient. But I remember she did say she had been up north for some business reason. She must have watched my movements very carefully, for a little later when Gervase and I were spending a few days in town for some congress he was attending, I got a card marked 'Eloise' inviting me to some millinery mannequin parade. I didn't think very much about it, I so seldom go to such affairs, but a friend of mine said that she was going and was anxious for me to accompany her. And when we arrived it was Eloise Martineau whom we met. She was very, very discreet; not by a glance did she betray the fact that we had met before, but the next morning I heard from Raymond, a summons I did not, in Gervase's interest alone, dare to disregard. The day after I had gone to see him she came to call; she said she was so glad of this opportunity for re-union, and then she wound up by saying that it was unwise, to say the least, for me to visit the man I had —the man I once thought was my husband—now that I was married to so distinguished and public a man. I recognised then how hopelessly I was snared."

"Blackmail combine," growled Ambrose.

"It may be," agreed Egerton, all his dour national caution asserting itself. "Did she attempt to get money from you?"

"Yes. She said that many of her clients never settled their bills and she was perpetually in debt. I refused to give her anything; Raymond was a little different. I—perhaps—owed him something. I don't know. But not her, never her."

"Still, she blackmailed an invitation out of you."

"I dared not refuse that. Things were not going too well with Gervase as it was; there was a good deal of dissension in certain quarters about his book, I couldn't risk any further scandal. So I invited her to come down—to mark time."

"And played straight into her hands," commented Egerton drily. "That invitation was what she was scheming for. She wanted to get at your husband, or at all events, to be in a position to get at him, if necessary. If she hadn't been introduced her plans would have gone all agley. She couldn't write to him, a complete stranger, with stories of his wife's mysterious visits to a Bloomsbury lodging-house; he'd have destroyed any such letter half-read; if she had called and hinted at such things he would have had her shown out. She had to get to know him personally; your invitation paved the way for her. Then she could pose as your friend of many years' standing. Do you suppose she had told Sir Gervase anything before you spoke?"

"I don't know, but I don't think so. He said nothing to me. He wouldn't, of course. He would never try and add to any anxiety of mine."

"Still, she undoubtedly did say something that particularly upset him. My wife and I both chanced to notice her that night the doctor arrived, and you, Lady Blount, were playing the 'Moonlight Sonata.' She settled down by him and what she said we can only surmise. I hope he'll be persuaded to tell his counsel precisely what it was. No lawyer gets a chance if his client isn't candour incarnate. But the effect was instantaneous and dismaying."

"Dismaying!" repeated Ambrose explosively. "Why,

the fellow looked like a corpse, couldn't see, couldn't hear, couldn't speak. It was something pretty ghastly."

"You can add nothing more, Lady Blount?" asked Egerton thoughtfully. "You'd like to be kept in touch, of course. I'll let you know what Harper says."

"Damned fools these police are," muttered Ambrose, but Egerton took him up with fastidious care.

"They have no option really. On the evidence there was more than enough to convict Sir Gervase and not a scrap to implicate another living soul."

"Then how the devil is a lawyer going to invent evidence?"

"He won't have to do that. He'll have to disprove the Crown's case. Murders, as a rule, fall into three classes. There's murder for passion, impulsive, practically impossible to hide. Pretty often the murderer in these cases gives himself up, and it's seldom difficult to locate him. Then there's the murder for expediency; cases where a body is found and no apparent point in the crime at all. Often then you'll find that the murderer had committed some other crime and kills the second man to prevent his giving information. It's an axiom that one murder usually leads to a second to cover tracks. That's fairly common. And then there are murders like this one, where all the evidence points in one direction and it's been laid by some one else, the real criminal and his associates. That's the hardest kind of the three to solve, because you're up against the unknown quantity who may be feeding at the same board, who can watch your movements and circumvent them as you plan them, because he has the precious knowledge as to who did commit the murder, and so can head you off at every turn. This is clearly a case

of class C. What we have to do first of all is to establish some cause for sufficient hatred for murder on the
part of some one unknown. Undoubtedly a man like
Charteris would have a good many enemies; there's
something else to bear in mind; the man who killed
him knew a lot about Sir Gervase, at all events that
he had property in Thebeshire, that he was in residence
at the time of the murder, and that he was spending
that particular evening or week-end in London. Careful sifting should discover some one with all that information and a genuine grievance. But it'll take time.
There's only one thing more, Lady Blount. I expect
you realise that this will be an expensive affair? Life
is expensive. I should have to give Harper guarded
re-assurances as to fees, etc."

"That will be all right." For the first time it seemed
as though she would break down. "Anything——"

"Up to, say, a thousand pounds? I can't give you
any approximate figure, because I don't know what
fees Harper will expect. But they'll be pretty considerable, and this may be quite a long job."

"Double that, if necessary. Treble it. Is there anything else?"

Egerton thought. "Two points," he said at last.
"About the ear-ring. Your husband didn't know it
had been substituted?"

"No."

"And it hasn't yet been paid for?"

"Not yet. In fact, I had quite forgotten the ear-ring
in the general break-up. Messrs. Nettle and Beard are
very patient people. They wouldn't have bothered us
again for some time. They know Gervase quite well."

"And the other point—have you ever heard any

rumour as to Miss Martineau's relations with Charteris?"

"I think," said Pamela Blount, speaking with great difficulty, and so pale that it seemed as if she must faint, "that long ago, before I met Raymond, he and she——"

"Exactly. That may colour the situation a little."

"I don't mean to imply anything recent," she assured him, lifting her beautiful anguished face. "I don't know——"

"I should think most probably not," he agreed instantly. "He'd be no use to her now, of course."

While Pamela Blount was exchanging conventional farewells with Rosemary, Ambrose approached Egerton. He had been repelled by the young man's attitude throughout the conversation; he had appeared so unmoved, so unsympathetic, and he could not realise that this alone had kept Pamela from utter collapse. Spoken pity would have been intolerable to her; Egerton's coolness had allowed her to remain comparatively composed throughout the most difficult hour of her life.

"Are you going to see Blount?" the doctor murmured in an aside.

"Not unless he asks me. I'm not sufficiently intimate with him to invade his privacy without an invitation. I suppose you'll get back here as soon as you can?"

"I will." He sighed profoundly. "But you'll be a damned sight more use than I shall. 'Fraid all this will mean scrapping your political work *pro tem.*"

Egerton's light brows lifted. "Scrapping it? Oh, hardly. It's my job."

"And this?"

"You might call it personal inclination. At all events it isn't what I'm paid to do."

"Then if either is to suffer it's to be Blount?"

Egerton looked faintly bored. "Neither will suffer," he said politely, and went across to where his wife stood chatting with Pamela.

CHAPTER VII

"Altogether they puzzle me quite,
They all seem wrong and they all seem right."
—R. W. Buchanan.

EGERTON arrived at Hammond's office the following day fifteen minutes before the appointed time. He found the solicitor poring over various dividend certificates.

"Buying or selling?" he asked.

"Damned if I know. What ought I to do with these Bulgarian Oil Shares?"

"Sell. Any price you can get. They've touched their zenith. They'll drop to half their value in the next twenty-four hours."

Hammond reached for the telephone. "That you, Perring? Hammond here. Sell out my Bulgarian Oils, best price you can get. . . . What's that? . . . Market closes at four? . . . Damned easy life you beggars must have. . . . Well, of course. . . . Sell, to-morrow, first thing. . . . What will I buy instead? . . . How should I know? . . . What's a good thing, Egerton?"

"Why not ask your broker?" suggested the other drily. "It's his job."

"Oh, he ain't no good," was the confident rejoinder. "But he's married with six children." (The relevancy of this may not at first be apparent.) "What d'you advise?"

"Malay Developments will rise slow but sure if you can afford to wait for your profits."

"I'd better take those, you think? Right. Buy Malay Developments, Perring. . . . No, not till you've sold the others, of course. You won't know how much you've got." He snapped the receiver into place. "Well, this pal of yours seems to be in a pretty bad way. Harper's fairly keen. What d'you think yourself?"

"I don't think it's his work," said Egerton slowly. There was so much deliberation in voice and manner that Hammond looked up in amazement.

"Sounds as if you'd had your doubts," he observed shrewdly.

"I have, quite a number of them. If the man had been found shot through the head in his own rooms, I admit I might have yielded. It's the sort of thing Blount might conceivably have done in a white heat of rage. But this elaborate manner of concealing the body—no, that's not him."

"You talk as if murdering a man were part of the day's work."

"And your experience as a lawyer tells you that it isn't?"

"Well, you need a pretty hefty motive."

"Blount's married." His manner said that no more powerful motive could be conceived.

"You're married, but would you commit murder for your wife's peace of mind?"

"If there were no other way out. I'd have finished Bannister, if necessary, if he hadn't finished himself. And I'm a constitutionalist to the backbone. Blount's a born reactionary."

"H'm. Sounds cheerful. Hullo, here is our man."

Harper was short and dark, and looked ill-tempered. He walked with a slight limp, due to some accident in adolescence that had left its abiding mark on his mind as well as his body.

"And now," he observed, disregarding the finer courtesies and impatiently refusing offers of cigars and cigarettes, "let's get to work. Haven't much time. I've only read the newspaper account and that's not very hopeful. Let's hear the inside account."

"Mr. Egerton will give you the story. He's personally acquainted with Sir Gervase, and, was a guest at the house when the body was found, in fact, was one of the two guests who discovered it."

Harper turned to the young man expectantly.

"I can't tell you the whole story," said Egerton, "because I don't know it. There are certain parts, such as the part played by Miss Martineau, that only Blount can give you. Lady Blount has given us some very useful information that so far hasn't been offered to the press. It explains an excellent motive." He went into the story as briefly as his meticulous attention to detail would permit. Harper interrupted occasionally with a curt question, and then nodded to him to continue.

When at last Egerton had finished, he said, "We must deny the evidence, I suppose. It's pretty strong. The button, for instance, and the crumpled scrap of paper found in his rooms. Queer, too, that he can't find any one to answer for him in all that time. It isn't natural."

"Quite conceivable, sir," Egerton put in drily. "I was tried like that myself a good many years ago, and only a fluke pulled me out of a nasty hole. Now I make a point of telephoning some one every few hours if I'm alone."

"Your stock of caution, sir, appears to be excessive. Blount seems to have displayed less."

"Say, rather, that his experience has come later in life," suggested the young politician suavely. "Have you formed any alternative theory?"

"Where does the Martineau woman come in?"

"Blount could tell you more about her. As to her possible relations with Charteris, they're a matter for conjecture."

"She certainly seems to have something to lose if he dies, so it doesn't seem reasonable to suppose she's in it."

"It's conceivable, surely," argued Egerton, "that she might stand to lose something if he lives. Supposing there is some clandestine relationship between them —or has been at any time—and he holds it over her head? No, this is pure supposition. But she's made a certain place for herself; I admit that things are taken pretty casually these days, but supposing there's any question of a marriage, say? Well, Charteris, if he heard of it, might see his chance. It's impossible to see Miss Martineau marrying a poor man, and Charteris is one of those leeches, always on the make. He thinks that if Miss Martineau marries a wealthy man there's a perpetual source of income ready to his hand. Because even now a man might jib at such an incident in his wife's past. I only suggest this as a possible motive that he had to be got out of the way. Of course, investigation may show a very different state of affairs. Our trouble is that while there are innumerable people who might be glad to compass the fellow's death there isn't a scrap of evidence except a trail against Blount, laid down thickly enough to make one suspicious. It's against nature, after all. Nature isn't prodigal, and we are the products of nature. When we disregard her warnings or try to improve on them, we generally pay for it."

"Did that come out of one of your election speeches?" demanded Harper caustically. "Are you suggesting, sir, that a woman shot the fellow through the head and then lugged the body down all those stairs? It's a bit presumptuous."

"The whole case against Blount in that respect appears to me a bit presumptuous. It's true he's a tall man and strong in muscular power, but it's asking a good deal of any one's credulity to accept that explanation. Personally, I can't see any reason for supposing that the man was shot in his rooms at all. If there was going to be all this complicated concealment of the murder, why not entice him away with some yarn and shoot him in a lonely place where no one would be likely to hear the report?"

"You're riding in front of the hounds," Harper warned him grimly. "If you want to shoot a man you don't want to choose an empty place where every sound reverberates and attracts attention. London's the very place to choose, because it's full of racket. A fellow shot himself up in North Kensington the other day and the people who heard it thought it was a bicycle tyre exploding. And, besides, there's nothing to show that the elaborate concealment, as you call it, was planned. He took the revolver with him, I know, but he may have meant to force something out of the fellow at the point of the gun, and in the scrimmage the damned thing went off."

"And then he hastily arranged things and carried off the body, all on the spur of the moment?"

"A man's wits when he's in danger are twice as valuable as they are at any other time," snapped Harper, because he didn't like Egerton's gentle smile.

Hammond put in deprecatingly, "He was shot pretty neatly through the head. Doesn't somehow look like a scrimmage."

"May have been overcome by rage an' shot fair and square."

Egerton shook his head. He was serious enough again now. "I'm afraid not, sir. Whoever committed this murder planned it pretty carefully."

"How d'you make that out?"

"The scrap of paper in Blount's room. That was a draft of the letter he ultimately left in Miss Gell's hall. It's reasonable to suppose that it was written before the actual fair copy. A man doesn't draft letters after the event and then drop them in his rooms."

"Is this chap, Blount, a professional forger?" demanded Harper truculently.

"Not to my knowledge."

"Then d'you expect him to copy this fellow's fist first shot? Whoever did it must have had several shots before he finished something that might conceivably take the landlady in."

"You think they weren't made in his room?"

"Nothing to show, is there?"

"That scrap—I've seen it, because I'm fortunate enough to be on excellent terms with this man Bremner —is scrawled on cheap writing-paper, thin, ruled, of foreign make. No paper like it has been found in Blount's flat or in the offices of the C.P.O. I don't believe anything like it was found in his house at Four

Corners. So it seems fairly reasonable to conclude that it wasn't his."

"Might have scrawled it in Charteris' room and shoved the scrap into his pocket. His own story admits that he went back to his rooms that night."

"What precisely did he do with all the odds and ends of forgeries that he made? There's no trace of them among all the papers found on Charteris' table; they've all been pieced together by an expert, and there's absolutely nothing there to help you. Bremner and his men have searched the place millimetre by millimetre, and there's no trace of any ash in the fireplace or anywhere about the room to show that papers were burnt there. On the other hand, in Charteris' room was found an almost used pad of paper similar to that on which the scrap was written."

"And the paper on which the letter was written?"

"Was a half-sheet of notepaper exactly the same as that used by Blount."

"Pretty damning."

"I wouldn't go as far as that," murmured Egerton with maddening composure. "It seems pretty obvious that there's a discrepancy somewhere, in spite of the police. That scrap they found in Blount's flat must have been written in Charteris' room; I think we may take that for granted. Then it must have been written after the fellow's death. And that being the case, how did it get to Blount's flat?"

"Stuffed it carelessly into his pocket when he was clearing up the traces of his handiwork at Thermiloe Square, and afterwards dropped it out."

"Afterwards?"

"Yes. When he went back to the flat."

"But when did he go back to the flat?"

"After the murder presumably."

"But that upsets all the official theories. They say that having murdered Charteris he drove him straight down to Four Corners and pitched the body over the cliff. Why take him to his own flat at all and intensify the risk?"

"There was the question of changing the boots and shirt."

"You think he'd have kept the boots there?"

"It's possible."

"But how did he get them there?"

"Took them over himself earlier in the day."

Egerton shook his head. "I'm prepared to believe Blount's version that he went to King John's Mansions to sleep that night, and that no one saw him because he was both too late and too early to encounter the porter or the charwoman. But I can't believe that if he'd gone there at five o'clock or six, for you remember that he was at Thermiloe Square before seven, he'd have got in and out without attracting the slightest notice. Again, where did the boots come from?"

"The police suggest that he had a store of second-hand clothing at some place in Aldwych."

"And that he called there that night, changed the man's clothes and then drove on. Exactly. But if he changed them there he certainly wouldn't have taken any further risks by going to his flat, and if he didn't go to his flat he couldn't have dropped the scrap of paper there. Even supposing he could have fitted up Charteris with a vest and collar in his rooms (because he's always seen in lay attire and certainly wouldn't be wearing clerical get-up on that occasion) he wouldn't have such boots there, and though he might get the boots from the store he wouldn't get the other clothes. Stalemate?"

"Not at all. Why shouldn't he have clerical clothes at the store? Parsons are in a bad way often enough. I've had 'em among my clients."

"Of course he might have had them, but it so happened that he hadn't. I know that for certain because we happened to be discussing certain aspects of the organisation, and the type of men assisted and so forth, and he chanced to mention a young priest who had come to them utterly destitute and he wanted some clothes, and they had to fit him up in mufti *pro tem.* because nothing else was available. No, he isn't likely to have had any parson's second-hand garb there, and conversely, as I've remarked, he wouldn't have the boots anywhere else."

"Then your contention is that the whole affair's a plot?"

"If we allow Blount to be innocent it must be a plot. I don't think the letter is so hard to account for. The body was not found for some days and that would give ample time for the criminal to choose an hour when the flat at King John's Mansion was unoccupied, and drop the scrap of paper through the window. It's noticeable that it was found on the opposite side of the room from the waste-paper basket. A man standing in a room and anxious to get rid of a pellet of paper automatically takes a shy at the basket, if there is one, and even if he misses it it falls in that neighbourhood. But this bit of paper was found in the opposite corner, in the only corner, that is, where a window was open, a window, moreover, that is perpetually open, day and night."

"Having been dropped in from the outside?"

"Precisely."

"And what about the button?"

"That, I admit, presents a far worse difficulty. It's possible, of course, that during the struggle with Blount, that he's never attempted to deny—no, that won't work. He swears he wasn't wearing the coat. It's perfectly clear that whoever is guilty knew about Blount's position and presumably about his visit to Thermiloe Square that night. There can't be very many people situated like that."

"And so your proposition is that the murderer in some magical way possessed himself of Blount's button and fastened it into the dead man's hand? You'd find it a little difficult to get a jury to side with you." Harper was openly sceptical.

"It's going to be precious hard to get a jury to side with the prosecution when those facts have been brought to their notice. What really troubles me about the button is that the scrap of material attached to it has a smooth edge."

Hammond chipped in eagerly, "Showing that it was cut off?"

"Precisely. If this were one of those murders where the clues are perpetually being discovered it might be argued that the button was clipped off after Blount's return. But unfortunately it was found in the dead man's hand. So it must have been taken from the coat that night.

"And what's y'r deduction from that?" Harper had a manner of slurring the middles of his words so that only the beginning and last consonants were at all clear. It made argument with him a little difficult.

"That if it was cut off it was done before Blount entered Thermiloe Square. I can see no other explanation. That, of course, argues a premeditated murder. But we may find we have ample grounds for suspecting this murder to be premeditated."

"You mean that it was cut off by some one who knew he would be going to Thermiloe Square, presumably some one in London?"

"Not necessarily that."

"Where then?"

"Why not at Four Corners?"

"Before he left?"

"I think so."

"He'd have noticed it."

"Not necessarily. It was an idiosyncrasy of his to keep his coat unbuttoned. He would leave it so on the coldest day. I've met him myself."

"Has he no man to valet him?"

"If this were a put-up job, you may be sure that any one who could see so far ahead would have waited for an opportunity. The valet would probably have the coat ready some time in advance. Blount left immediately after an early lunch. While he was in the dining-room there was ample opportunity for any one to choose a moment when the hall was empty and nick off the button."

"Why that one particularly?"

"Because it's the only one that could be identified. Most coat buttons look exactly alike, but this one doesn't. Blount wouldn't notice the omission. In fact, he carried his coat over his arm because the day had turned out unexpectedly hot. I admit it's not an ideal explanation, but it will hold water, if a little precariously."

"It appears to me to leak all over the stage," commented Harper brutally. "You're pre-supposing the murderer to have been of the household at Four Corners."

"I don't say so, I only offer the suggestion. At the moment I can think of nothing more feasible. Of course, it may have been a question of an accomplice."

"And how did the button get into the dead man's hand if he was murdered at Thermiloe Square?"

"We've no evidence yet that he was murdered at Thermiloe Square. In fact, it seems to me there's a good deal against it. I don't much like the story of Blount or any one else carrying a man of that physique down the stairs and through the garden; I feel it's much more likely that he walked of his own accord."

"And how," asked Harper sardonically, "does one forcibly shave a man who's neither stunned (for there's no mark of bruising) nor an accomplice in his own murder? I take it you'll allow that much?"

"I don't see any reason why he shouldn't have shaved himself," rejoined the equitable Egerton with his customary imperturbability.

"Shaved himself?"

"Yes, it's a significant point that there was no sign of a shaving brush, a tumbler or soap, in the man's room. Nor a razor nor yet a strop. Now, it's possible that the murderer might have tipped the water out of doors, and even carried the razor and brush away with him, but he'd be practically certain to leave some trace. The tumbler, for instance. He'd leave that in case some officious policeman discovered its disappearance. Another point that struck me was the absence of water in the room. Charteris, you'll recall, made use of the bathroom and had no washing apparatus of any kind on the top floor. I especially ques-

tioned Bremner as to that, and also as to whether
there was a water-tap outside the door. But there
isn't, nothing nearer, in fact, than the bathroom two
floors lower. Now, a stranger wouldn't know the lie
of the land, wouldn't know where to find the bathroom, and certainly wouldn't take the risk of lugging
a lifeless body down there and shaving him in a room
that's common to the whole house. It's true he'd just
been told it was empty and no one would be back
until ten o'clock, but there's always the chance that
some one will be taken ill, some plan will be abandoned,
and take it all round, the idea is far too dangerous
to be entertained. So that the shaving, if done after
death, would be done in the man's own room."

"And you're satisfied in y'r own mind it wasn't?"

"Where's the tumbler? Where's the brush? Where's
the soap? Even the towels were found folded neatly
over the rail at the foot of the bed. But supposing
Charteris to have shaved himself he would naturally
go down to the bathroom; even if he were interrupted
he could say cheerily that he wouldn't be long, and
wait for the other to vanish. People don't sit in rows
outside bathrooms at that hour of the evening. There'd
be plenty of opportunity for him to evade the new-
comer and get back to his room without any one realising that he had shaved."

"And the hair found in the fire-place burned to a
brittle ash?"

"Manifestly he couldn't leave it in the bathroom,
where it would certainly have betrayed him. It's very
unfortunate that the crime wasn't discovered until so
much later; the bathroom, of course, would have been
cleared and washed several times in the interim, so
that it's impossible at this stage to establish the evi-

dence of possible black hairs on the bathroom floor. Once up in his room Charteris burns the hair and scatters it on the hearth in the hopes that it won't be noticed."

"But what's his motive?"

"I fancy it's a question of his personal liberty. Lady Blount has said that he forged a cheque in her name shortly before his death; one if not two similar affairs are known to have taken place, and there is nothing to show that there are not others. Possibly in one instance the police had been informed and were on his tracks. Charteris' one chance was to disguise himself. He was one of those men whose faces change greatly when they shave a beard. He destroys all his letters that may implicate him and scrawls a note to say that he's gone north after a job in the hopes that this may throw sand in the eyes of his pursuers, while he himself actually goes south."

"Having planned his own disguise?"

"Most probably."

"Where does he get it from?"

"You know the neighbourhood of Thermiloe Square?"

"I could find it on the map."

"But you've never actually been there?"

"I can't say I have."

"Then you don't realise that it stands in a welter of cheapjack shops where you buy cheap, foreign meat, and Jewish delicacies, and all the second-hand clothes conceivable. The boots might quite easily come from there; the stall would be chock-a-block with them. As for the vest, I feel it's more than probable that he had this. You remember he told his landlady that it was sometimes useful to be an actor, because you could use your properties. That's why he wore the black suit, clearly part of his professional wardrobe. Men in the ordinary course of events don't go about in black suits unless they're parsons. But even supposing he hadn't got it I fancy he'd find little difficulty in buying one from the stalls. You can get the dress of most nations and I should think all professions there."

"You think that, having shaved, he went out and bought the things?"

"Yes."

"After shaving?"

"I think so. Who was the man who spoke to the policeman at twenty minutes to nine? The man who wore his coat turned up round the ears—that was to conceal the scarred chin, of course—and wouldn't let any one see his face? It isn't easy to trace these stall-holders, either. And there's no use hoping any one will come forward; these folks will sit tight and watch the policeman patrolling up and down, but they won't lift a finger. So that if a fellow buys a pair of boots or a clergyman's vest and is shortly afterwards found at the bottom of a ravine, what is that to them so long as they've been paid for the goods?"

"All the same, we might send a man down there to inquire. Have to be tactful, of course. Don't want to get 'em suspicious. In any case I s'pose the fellers all hold together?"

Egerton nodded. "They have to; they never know when their own day of wrath will come upon them. Still, you can but try."

Hammond, who had been frowning for some time, now broke in, "But I must say I can't see why there should be all this hurry? Of course, I recognise that it was a divine opportunity—house empty and so forth—but it was running things pretty fine. Why not have the diguise on the premises?"

"Oh, as to that," returned Egerton, "there are two alternatives. I think we may take it that Charteris had only just been warned of his danger. There was no post that night, so it can't have come that way. There's the telephone, of course. But it seems reasonable to suppose that whoever warned him came in person. There's the clot of mud that shows some one came in after the rain started——"

"May have been the man himself, if y'r theory about his going out to buy boots is true."

"One for you, sir. It may quite well have been."

"Nothing to show any one else went near the house that night. Warning probably came by telephone."

"There's the light."

"The light?"

"Yes. He left it on. Now most people turn out a light by instinct when they leave a room, particularly people who are as poor as Charteris was. He'd learned through years of cheese-paring to be careful for other people's lights. Yet this night of all nights he left it on. Why? Because there was some one else in the room, some one waiting to help Charteris to get away. That was the ostensible reason, of course. It's possible that Charteris was in no immediate danger, but that the murderer, knowing of Blount's visit to the house and anxious to fix the crime on to him, came round with fictitious warnings and persuaded Charteris to fall in with his plans."

"Which included murder?" Harper roused himself and snatched a cigar. "Let's get it down straight. Y'r scheme is this. Charteris has landed himself in some criminal mess, and some one we'll call A comes up to his room to warn him, and offers, to help him to get away disguised. Charteris agrees and proceeds to shave. Then he burns the hair—why doesn't he scatter the ash out of the window?"

"Because it would make his hands black and leave possible clues; he wouldn't dare run the risk of going to the bathroom a second time now the beard's off. There are no facilities in his room. Secondly, there's a balcony belonging to some one else just below his window and he's taking no risks, no matter how trivial."

Harper grunted. "We'll pass that for the moment. Then, having shaved, he leaves his accomplice in the room, probably shredding letters and anything else that may betray him; while he goes out in a blind hurry and gets the disguise. He talks to the policeman a minute to give. him the impression that Raymond Charteris is gone north, and then discovers what his beat is. Then, once out of sight, he doubles on his tracks, gets what he needs and comes back again. As the policeman's been told that the house is empty he makes a point of leaving the light on when he goes. Then he scrawls the necessary letter. . . . Does the accomplice bring up some of Blount's paper? I thought he only kept it at his flat?"

"Did you notice the sheet? One edge was rough, while the other three were deckled. See what that implies? That it wasn't a single sheet of paper at all, but had been torn from a double sheet. Lady Blount had given her husband a box of single sheets while she herself had double ones. Most probably she had written to Charteris on this paper, and when he wrote his note for the benefit of the public he tore off half a sheet and scribbled on that."

"Why go to so much trouble when he had a sheet of his own notepaper in the cupboard?"

"Remember this was a planned murder. Probably the second man—A—suggested the paper. Charteris would be in too much of a hurry to trouble about a small point like that. Of course, the original scheme was to pitch the body overboard so that it would never be discovered. But if by some mysterious chance it did come to light then all the evidence was to point to Gervase Blount. Incidentally, if he were guilty it's not very likely that he'd attempt to dispose of the body on his own property, or take so long a journey when there was suitable sea-coast so much nearer town."

"He was playing for safety," put in Hammond soberly. "He knew his own place, knew that it would be little short of a miracle if the body were cast up again. The coast there is unapproachable. He'd rely on the quicksand and the tide between them to swallow up the body."

"And yet, knowing his own coast, he pitched it just on the one spot for more than a mile where there was a ledge where it might conceivably fall."

"The mills of God," murmured Hammond with a smile that was half apologetic.

Egerton looked sceptical. Harper rushed on, "I suppose he discards his luggage because he's afraid of being traced by it. But doesn't he know the sort of fool he'll appear when it's realised that he's gone without it?"

"I fancy he's in such a hurry. In any case the schemer doesn't want anything else to dispose of. A body is quite sufficient."

"So he leaves the papers—no time to burn them

presumably—and they go down—why doesn't the policeman see them?"

"Car parked in the cul-de-sac, I should think. Anyway, the bobby's been told the house is empty; he wouldn't be expecting them. To say nothing of the fact that they probably watched their chance."

Hammond made another point. "What time are you supposing this to be? The fog cleared about a quarter to ten, but up till that time it would have been mighty hard to steer a car."

"The car must have been in the alleyway. No, why should it though? Bremner's allowing that the fellow was dead when he was taken out. But if he was alive they might have slipped out of the back and walked. Then where would they pick up the car? Depends on who the murderer is, I suppose."

"And as he gets into the car he's shot? That your theory?"

"Not precisely. I should think he was shot at the last possible moment."

"Why sh'd you suppose that?"

"The attitude. The journey to Four Corners from London would be on such a night approximately five hours. If he had been shot as soon as they got into the car *rigor mortis* would have set in to too great an extent for him to have fallen in the position that he did on the cliff; the arms from being compressed in the car would have remained either closely at the sides or folded on the knees. In any case one couldn't have lain loosely as it did overhanging the sea. And the same, of course, applies to the legs; they'd have been bent. But if he hadn't been shot until he began to get apprehensive, until he began to suspect a ruse, then it wouldn't be so hard to roll the body over the cliff and trust to luck that it would splash down out of sight, and never be heard of again. Four Corners in the nature of things was the last place where any one would look for it; the connection with Lady Blount was known to no one——"

"Miss Martineau."

"With Charteris dead her fangs were drawn."

The lawyer drew his shaggy brows together and thundered, "Do you realise that that is tantamount to accusing Miss Martineau of a hand in the murder?"

Egerton remained cool. "Not at all, sir. Merely that now Charteris is dead the weapon is wrested out of her hand. What's the good of resurrecting that story? Who's going to listen? There's no Charteris to back her up."

"H'm. A fantastic affair anyway. Why people can't commit crimes like gentlemen. . . . Well, well, I suppose I better go and see this fellow. Wanted to meet him for a long time. Read his absurd book. Flogging a dead horse. Should like to tell him so. 'Afternoon."

He stamped to the door, then turned and flung an abrupt question over his shoulder.

"Forget your name. Egerton? What? Chap who was mixed up in the Freyne affair? Well, well. Wanted to meet you, too. What d'you want to go round taking the bread out of our mouths for? Understand y'r method is to get hold of a first-chop lawyer and then show him up. Well, show me up, if you can. Bet you my new hat you don't do it."

"Well?" Hammond asked his friend as the handsome Buick glided down the road.

"I very much question," returned Egerton thoughtfully, "whether we should take the same size in hats."

CHAPTER VIII

"If your governor don't prove a allebyi, he'll be what the Italians call reg'larly flummoxed."—MR. WELLER, SR.

I

THE next morning, immediately after breakfast, Harper went to interview his new client. He found Blount haggard and pale from lack of sleep and a perpetual gnawing anxiety, less on his own behalf than his wife's, since he was still unable to comprehend his own danger, being at this juncture in ignorance of the more astounding clues discovered by the police. His manner was courteous but discouraging. Harper had visited many men in prison for a capital charge and believed that he had run the gamut of all possible attitudes—sullen, jovial, passionate, dignified, numbed almost to resignation, terrified, pleading, fierce—but in Blount he discovered a new type. "Really," reflected Harper with a concealed grin, "feller might be welcoming—no, not welcoming, admitting—me to Buck-'n'm Palace on sufferance."

He shook hands automatically, recognised the other man's immense muscular strength, and began, "Read your book. Didn't like it. Read this case in the papers, too. Didn't like that, either. Fishy. Let's hear your version."

Then, as Blount hesitated as if uncertain where to begin and what was the least he could possibly admit to give his supporters a fair chance, the lawyer continued, "No need to go over old ground. Read the police version; heard Egerton's version; heard Lady Blount's story."

Pamela's husband stiffened like a man suddenly struck by alarm; his eyes changed like the eyes of a cat, the pupils shrank to pin-points. "Dangerous fellow," thought Harper irritably. "What's he want to give himself away like that for?"

Blount spoke. "What precisely do you want me to tell you?" he asked. "I don't want to take up more of your time than necessary."

Harper smiled unexpectedly, and a grim, sardonic affair his smile was. "You're buying my time just now," he pointed out. "And paying for it, full measure, pressed down and running over. I see to that. Ha ha! What I want to know is—when did you first hear of Raymond Charteris?"

"In 1922."

"Who mentioned his name to you?"

"My wife, then Miss Pamela Heath."

"Why?"

"I had asked her to become my wife and she told me——" He hesitated, as if unsure how much the other man knew. Harper speedily relieved his doubts.

"We know all about Lady Blount and Charteris—marriage, sickness, separation and blackmail, the whole story. Carry on."

"She told me the story that she appears to have told you, and she added that she would marry no man whom she was pleased to suppose would be injured by its repetition so long as there was any likelihood of its being told, that is so long as Charteris was alive. We had reason to believe that he was abroad at that time; I had inquiries set on foot and in the spring of 1924 I was assured that he had been killed in a train accident in 1922. Three months more we waited, at my wife's request, and then we were married, and the name of Charteris has never been ·spoken between us till quite recently."

"Had you heard the name from any one else?"

"Not until I was staying at Four Corners three weeks ago."

"Who first mentioned it there? Lady Blount or yourself?"

"Neither. In point of fact, it was one of my guests."

"Miss Martineau? Thought as much. Never been mixed up in criminal proceedings before, I take it? Y'rself, I mean?.Thought not. No good being squeamish, plank all your cards on the table; got to fight like the devil and all his angels to win this rubber. Where d'you meet the lady?"

"For the first time, early in the summer, at some reception I attended with my wife. Miss Martineau came up and greeted her, my wife, I mean, and Lady Blount introduced her to me. We didn't exchange more than a dozen words, and I didn't expect to see her again."

"So that when Lady Blount suggested inviting her to Four Corners you were considerably surprised?"

"I was."

"Ever hear Lady Blount speak of her before?"

"Never. I understood later that they had met years earlier."

"On the stage? H'm, quite so. Not a lady to be encouraged I should suppose. Well? She spoke of Raymond Charteris?"

"Yes. On the third day of her visit. I had noticed her very deep in conversation with my wife the day before, but thought nothing of it, but the following evening she joined me in the garden and asked me if I were aware that Charteris was still alive. At the moment it seemed to me of the greatest importance to keep that information from my wife, lest she should be distressed, and Miss Martineau assured me that she was still in ignorance of the fact. I believed her—foolishly, as it turns out—and asked for her connivance in keeping the truth from Lady Blount. Miss Martineau was discretion itself, on the surface; she promised not to breathe a hint and left me. The next day she asked me—that is to say, she dropped hints as to the price of her silence, with precisely the same discretion as she had employed when she mentioned Charteris' name. It appeared that her business affairs were less prosperous than she could wish—a little financial assistance would be most welcome. I brushed the matter aside and spoke of other things. A day later she spoke outright; she was willing to befriend me, and keep Lady Blount in ignorance, if I for my part would help her."

"Blackmail, in fact?"

"Precisely."

"And you said?"

"That I was afraid it was impossible."

"What did she do?"

"She told me, candidly, what would happen unless I could fall in with her plans, and when I still refused she told me that she proposed writing to Charteris that night and explaining the position."

"Didn't occur to you, of course, that she might be fazing you first to last?"

Blount turned quickly. "It hadn't."

"Wouldn't, of course. Women like that are wasted

ANTHONY GILBERT

in private life; ought to be company promoters, makin'
dividends with no capital. D'you give way?"

"No. That was out of the question."

"She was still y'r guest? You let her stay in y'r
house?"

"She was my wife's guest."

Harper groaned; he hated these fellows who made
a fetish of the conventions and were courteous to the
point of suicide.

"D'you know if she did write?"

"There was no necessity. That had been a bolt
drawn at a venture. When she saw that I shouldn't
give way she changed suddenly, and smiled and said
that it would be superfluous, since my wife knew quite
well that Charteris was alive and had been visiting
him clandestinely for some months. In fact, that she
was with him that very day. It so happened that my
wife had spent the day in London; I asked no questions when she returned and she said nothing, but a
couple of days later she told me that Charteris had
been striking at her through me for the sake of money,
that she had done what she could with money that
she could strictly regard as her own, but that he had
added one more forgery to his list and had signed her
name to a cheque for two hundred pounds. The cheque
had apparently been cashed, and at the moment I
determined to raise no question about it with my
bankers since it gave me a weapon with which to de-
fend myself."

Harper looked irritated. "Don't see what all this
fuss was about. Storm in a tea-cup. Suppose this feller
had told his story, how he misled a woman ten years
ago, who'd have suffered?"

"My wife."

"No decent man or woman could have thought or said——"

Blount interrupted him to ask, "Are you married, Mr. Harper?"

"Yes."

"And would you care to hear that story going round London about your wife?"

"That sort of thing," returned Harper gloomily, "would never have happened to my wife." His tone, at once grim and melancholy, subtly conveyed a compliment to Pamela Blount. "Well? You went up to see the chap?"

"Yes. I realised, of course, that matters were far worse than they would have been had my wife not attempted to spare me. Now if Miss Martineau unleashed her poisonous tongue she could add that Lady Blount had been surreptitiously visiting the man while her husband was in the country. Can you see them licking their lips over that?"

"If there were no fools there'd be no lawyers," snapped Harper curtly. "You can't expect me to decry the very crowd who give me a living. When did you go and see the fellow?"

"Lady Blount told me late in the evening of Saturday, the eighteenth. It was manifestly impossible for me to travel up and interview Charteris on the Sunday, and in point of fact I was assisting the local vicar for a curate who was sick. But I went up on Monday, taking the two-ten train from Little Kirbey."

"Did you give any one any reason for coming up?"

"My wife knew, of course, and very probably Miss Martineau guessed. To my guests I merely said that business of a very urgent nature called me to town, but that I hoped to be back that night."

"And you reached town?"

"At four fifty-five. The train was late owing to the fog that lay over the outskirts of London all the afternoon. I wanted to be sure of catching my man in so I telephoned his house and was told that he was out. I had used a public telephone at a post-office quite close to Thermiloe Square, and as soon as I had hung up the receiver I slipped into the square itself and began parading up and down, a not very difficult thing to do on account of the fog that was becoming momentarily denser. I had got a fairly accurate description of him from my wife—I had never met him, as you will realise—and just after six I saw him cross the road and let himself in. I settled myself to wait for the next arrival, for my plan was to slip in behind him as though as I was another occupant, thankful to be saved the trouble of searching for a latch-key. My one fear was that Charteris might go out before I had an opportunity of bearding him. It was impossible for me to ring the bell and ask for him, as that would be to court the very publicity I dreaded. I was anxious not to be observed, so I waited until about six-thirty when a young man loomed out of the fog and ran up the steps. I was at his heels in an instant, my hat pulled well over my eyes. My idea was to avoid being seen by a soul. I reached his room without any encounter and found him at his table——"

"Were there at that time any scraps of paper scattered upon it?"

"No, nothing of that kind. He had been writing, I think; at all events he leaped up in evident surprise and even fear as I shut the door. He didn't know me as we had never met before, but as soon as I mentioned my name his whole manner changed, became even composed. I imagine he thought he held all the aces. I told him I knew that he had been threatening my wife, and that if he ever addressed her by word of mouth or by letter again I should hand over to the police the cheque he had forged."

"Doing a bit of blackmailing on your own, eh?"

Blount's expression, relaxing for an instant from that set composure, said that he would go very much further than that to protect Pamela Blount. But he made no comment on the lawyer's remark, continuing inflexibly. "He laughed at that and said that I was in a cleft stick, that if I moved to bring a case against him he would immediately release the story of his own—infamous conduct"—Harper thought he had never heard so much concentrated hatred put into a simple word before—"for the benefit of the world. I told him that his first murmur meant prison and not merely for a month or so. I have reason to believe— I speak, of course, in complete confidence—that this cheque is not the only occasion on which he has embezzled money. I personally know of two other occasions and presumably there would be others, as opportunity occurred. He swore I could never face the racket——" He paused, and Harper said sharply, shooting out his heavy underlip:

"Which was quite true. You wouldn't until you were driven."

"I wouldn't," agreed Blount colourlessly. "But at the same time I'd have kept my word. The money that Charteris had embezzled from other men was no concern of mine. I was aware, of course, that at any moment he might be arrested on another charge, and in that case it would be next door to impossible to avoid all mention of this affair. Then the whole thing would have obtained the most repulsive publicity. But that was out of my hands. Charteris was clever enough to recognise the position and he suggested that I should supply him with funds to 'smooth down' the gentlemen in question, should occasion arise."

"And what did you give him?"

"Nothing. He'd have sworn, naturally, that it was hush-money."

"And the position when you left him was?"

"Stalemate. Neither of us could move. I dared not expose him, and he dared not blackmail us any further, because I should have been as good as my word and he knew it."

"And the time when you left him?"

"About seven-thirty."

"And after that?"

"As I told the detective, I went to an inexpensive restaurant and had a meal; the place was crowded and I fail to see why I should be remembered more than any one else. After that I went to the C.P.O. headquarters and worked there till a little after eleven."

"In which room?"

"The library."

"Back or front?"

"Back."

"And then?"

"I went to my flat, where I slept. I was exceedingly tired and neither touched any papers nor even sat down in my arm-chair. I was up early the next morning, had breakfast out and caught the eight fifty-five train. Owing to the fog on the line we missed the connection, as I've already explained, and I had to wait at Eversfield. I don't think I can add anything else that would assist you."

Harper seemed profoundly dissatisfied with the trend of events. He grunted and coughed and swore, and then said, "Want you to answer some questions. You undressed in your flat that night?"

"Oh, yes. I had a small despatch-case with me containing clothes for the night."

"You intended, then, to sleep in your flat?"

"I thought it extremely probable that it would be necessary. The trains to Little Kirbey are very few and even to Tenbeigh it is often difficult to catch the connection. The last decent train gets back to Eversfield at nine thirty-four, though I believe it is actually possible to manage it later, but the trains are so poor it scarcely seems to me worth the candle. So it seemed better to me to spend the night in town and travel down the next morning."

"But if you left Charteris as early as seven-thirty that 'ud give you abundant time to catch the last train, if not the one earlier. Well?" He shot out the question pugnaciously.

Blount hesitated and appeared extremely embarrassed. "I could, of course——" he admitted and stopped.

"But y' thought you'd rather not. Why?"

He was made aware of a startling change in his client's face; that iron self-control that he had preserved up till this moment was yielding; he was struggling with some extraordinarily powerful emotion to keep himself taut and reserved; but beneath that his fury lashed and stormed like the waves of an angry sea. The force of that rage was a revelation to Harper; a man in such a mood would, he felt, be capable of killing a man with his bare hands—and if he had a revolver in his pocket. . . . But when he had granted that possibility Harper felt doubtful as to the subsequent proceedings. Still, the fellow had been a lawyer, he had a cool head and an uncommon quality of clearsightedness. Also his wife, regarding whom he was fanatical, was involved. He might for her sake plan even this elaborate complication. His story was woefully unsatisfactory. He asked again, "Why?"

"To be candid, I wasn't in a mood when I cared to face my wife or my guests."

That admission costs you a devil of a lot, my friend, thought the lawyer caustically. Pride, dear Lucifer. By that sin fell the angels, etc., etc. And by that sin falls also, unless I'm pretty well mistaken, Sir Gervase Blount, Bt.

"You mean you felt like hell?"

Blount rejoined very slowly, "The interview had been a difficult one. Neither Charteris nor myself was disposed to take the affair lightly. I hadn't been aware of my own capacity for hatred until I met him face to face, and it was equally amazing to me to discover that his feeling for me was tantamount to mine for him."

"Meaning he hated you? Why?"

Blount made no attempt to answer that. The lawyer did it for him. "Because of Lady Blount, you mean? Because you got what he——"

His companion wheeled sharply. "That's enough," he commanded. "I don't want to bring Lady Blount's name into this more than we can help."

"Case is saturated with her name already," growled Harper uncivilly. "I'll finish what I was saying. More than your good fortune and your position—that type of chap always hates any one better off than himself— he envied you for Lady Blount. I dare say in his own way he cared for her. Otherwise he'd probably have forgotten. What precisely did he say?"

"Is this necessary?" The words were almost a cry.

"'Fraid so. Pretty tough case, this. Everything counts. What did——?"

"As soon as my wife's name was mentioned he became frenzied. I can think of no other word. He kept saying, 'You stole her from me; she was mine first. At least I can remember that, that she was mine first. If ever I can get back at you for that, I will.' He was savage. Then he came back to the question of money——"

"You parted on the understanding that you would give him none. Sure he understood that?"

"If he did not it was not for want of my assuring him on the point," returned Blount grimly.

"Ah! You were explaining why you couldn't return to Four Corners that night. Felt too much upset? Did you s'pose study would cool your blood?"

"Work is the panacea—you know the rest. There's a great deal in it."

"And you're going to ask a jury to believe that after an impassioned scene like that you went calmly to y'r office and wrote on the higher criticism?" Harper's tone was sceptical, his smile openly jeering.

"I reached my office about eight-twenty," answered Blount in measured tones. "I took down a certain volume of an ecclesiastical encyclopædia; at nine-thirty I discovered myself reading the same column. I shook off my pre-occupation after that and contrived to lose myself in the work. When I came back to the flat I was too much tired for thought. I don't believe I even entered the sitting-room."

"Did you undress?"

Blount seemed surprised. "Certainly,"

"You had a change in your bag?"

"A change? D'you mean pyjamas?"

"I mean collars, socks, handkerchiefs. The police have searched your flat and can't find a thing to show you've been there during the past month."

"No," agreed Blount thoughtfully. "I suppose they wouldn't. I did take a change as it happens, but I brought the soiled collar and socks back with me."

"Did your servant unpack your bag?"

"By an odd chance I did it myself. It was quite a small affair, not a week-end case at all, but originally intended for papers and so forth. I had, in fact, tipped out some papers in order to take it up to town, the one I generally use for a night's absence being at the repairer's with a faulty lock. As soon as I returned I saw the papers lying on my table and, as I was going upstairs, I took the opportunity to empty the bag and bring it down with me. I see your point, of course, about a servant giving evidence, but I'm afraid it's sterile."

Harper looked increasingly glum. "You say you didn't go near the sitting-room that night. Did you go in in the morning?"

"I really couldn't tell you that. It's quite probable."

"You c'n think of nothing that 'ud be proof positive?"

"Nothing, I'm afraid."

With melancholy aspect Harper let that go also. "Another point. Did you take a revolver with you? I'm not asking if you showed it to Charteris, or if you threatened him with it. All I want t' know is did you take the thing up from Four Corners?"

"I did not. The idea never went through my mind."

"Not usin' it as a threat?"

"No."

"When you went to the cabinet to look for it you were genuinely amazed to find it had gone?"

"I certainly was."

"Couldn't think of any reason why it should?"

"I was completely mystified."

"You know now, I s'pose, that Lady Blount admits she hid it to prevent your takin' it up with you?"

"I've already explained that no one but myself possessed a key to that cupboard and that I always carried the key about with me."

"Lady Blount swears she took the key when you were in the bathroom and collared the pistol."

Blount's face flushed a terrible scarlet; the blood ebbed unevenly in a kind of passionate shame under the pale skin. He seemed to have nothing to say.

"That," the lawyer warned him bluntly, "is a piece of information we'll do well to keep out o' court if we can. Even if it could be proved that Lady Blount did actually hide the revolver before your departure it 'ud prejudice the most charitable jury to be told that your wife was so uncertain of the lengths to which you'd go that she didn't dare leave you in possession of fire-arms. They'd say with the banality of juries (and of most men and women for that matter), 'Ah, his wife must know!' as if wives necessarily knew more about their husbands than any one else. Then you're prepared to swear on oath that when you went to Charteris' room you had no weapon of any sort with you?"

"None whatsoever."

"Ah! Another point. Can you explain why the police found in the living-room of y'r flat a scrap of paper obviously torn from a sheet of which a pad was found in Charteris' room, and on the scrap the identical words of the letter left in Thermiloe Square—the draft, in fact?"

Blount was silenced utterly by that unexpected blow.

"You found that in my room?"

"The detectives did."

The other began walking rapidly up and down the cell, hands locked behind his back. "Who bears me such a grudge as this?" he demanded.

Harper observed in dry tones, "Dare say y'r state of mind and body ain't troubling the murderer at all. All he wants to do is preserve his own precious skin, and you're a convenient whipping-boy. Probably you're the one person with a thoroughly powerful motive for wantin' Charteris out of the way. You don't matter in the scheme of things more'n that. This chap is thinking of himself first, last, and all the time." He paused watching the effect of his words on his companion, but Blount's expression did not alter. "Now," continued the barrister, "as to the other damning piece of evidence—the button. D'you remember noticing anything missing on your journey up from Four Corners?"

"No. I wasn't, as a matter of fact, wearing the coat. It was a warm afternoon and I was late for my train."

"And when you did put it on?"

"I didn't close it. I seldom do. So I should scarcely notice."

"You're absolutely sure—oath and so forth—it couldn't have been torn off in the row with Charteris?"

"Absolutely. As I've explained several times I never wore the coat in his rooms. I didn't even put it on till

I stood on the step and realised how foggy and cold it was."

"Incidentally, this row—how did it arise?"

Blount returned in forbidding tones, "I took exception to an expression he applied to my wife."

"Glad it wasn't I applying the expression," reflected Harper. "Looks as if he'd gouge your eyes out first and hear what you had to say afterwards." And aloud he added, "Did Charteris damage you at all?"

"He had no chance. I threatened to break his arm if he didn't instantly withdraw the offensive phrase, and when he realised that I should keep my word he did withdraw. As to the precise wording that doesn't matter. In any case I should never repeat it and as Charteris is dead it need never be bandied about from one newspaper reporter to another." His thin, finely-cut lips curved into a line that was less rage than agony.

"And when did you first notice that the button was missing?"

"I didn't notice it at all. My man didn't point it out to me, merely substituted one. The detective was the first to draw attention to it."

"H'm. When you left Charteris' rooms you're positive that you met no one, didn't leave the coat anywhere it could be tampered with?"

"Quite sure."

"Now, think carefully, did you take up your own coat in the hall at Four Corners, or did your man do it for you?"

"I took it up myself. I'd just sent my man upstairs on an errand."

"Where did you get it from?"

"A stand in the hall."

"Where your man had put it?"

"Yes, when he brushed it. He couldn't give me his undivided attention since neither Egerton nor Ambrose—no, Ambrose wasn't there at that time—Egerton hadn't brought a man with him and Paull was valeting him, too."

"You don't know precisely when he put it ready?"

"I couldn't tell you."

"Ah, well, don't matter. He'll remember, I expect. What's his name, d'you say?"

"Paull."

"Right. Must get in touch with him. Anything else you can think of that might help us?"

Blount looked puzzled and distressed. "It sounds as if you're trying to trace the criminal back to some one in my own household," he observed. "Why all these questions concerning the coat?"

"Want to find out how the button parted from it. If it didn't come off in Charteris' rooms must have come off your end. I'll come and see you again when there's any progress to report."

2

Leaving the prison, Harper visited an agency that had worked for him on various occasions in the past. Here, as soon as he sent in his name, he was shown into a very comfortable room where a small, energetic man was standing waiting for him by a writing-table of light oak.

" 'Morning, Mr. Harper. What is it to-day?"

"This fellow, Blount."

Blackie, the private detective, head of the famous agency bearing his name, became more alert than ever.

"Another of your cases? Good, very good. Profoundly interesting. Any suspicions?"

"I've just seen the fellow; swears he knows nothing of Charteris' death."

"Of course. Does he swear he knew nothing of Charteris in life either?"

"No. He admits he visited him surreptitiously—thief in the night sort of business—on the day of his death, and that there was a row. After that he's got a long yarn that may be true, but unfortunately there's no hope of proving his alibi. Our only chance is to disprove the evidence. It's a pretty tall order. On the assumption that one equals one, it's obvious that if he didn't kill the fellow some one did. And it's occurred to me that we may all be working on the wrong line. The chief points are the gun and the button. If Blount's innocent it's hard to see how anyone else could have killed him up in that room and pushed the button into his hand. But supposing he wasn't killed up there, that he was killed making his escape——"

"From——?"

"Justice, I should say. Fellow was a bad hat. No question of that. Nothing to show the police weren't after him for some other forgery. Suppose he was trying to get away disguised and was shot before he escaped? It's the button I'm thinking about. Seems to me it must have been clawed off at Four Corners. It's the only chance." He explained his idea in greater detail. "You'll have to send a man down there to see the man-servant who looks after Blount's clothes, and then he'll have to trace the movements of the rest of the party that afternoon and evening. I sh'd say they were all more or less on the *tapis*, as otherwise immediate suspicion would fasten on the absent member.

But no one probably would think much of an absence lasting an hour or so. But that 'ud be long enough to get the job accomplished."

Blackie smiled. "I see, Mr. Harper, you've got something up your sleeve, some well-crystallised notion as to how the job was done."

"You've read the case, of course. Any suspicions of y'r own?"

"I've only seen the police reports. I haven't heard anything private, as you presumably have. It's impossible to fix the shadow of a suspicion on a soul, barring Blount, on the knowledge I have."

Harper settled comfortably into his chair. "Say, you've read the police view? Then you'll realise they s'pose the murder to have been committed at Therm'-loe Square. They've framed a programme that answers that supposition, but it's got some bad gaps in it. I've discussed the affair with one or two other men, one of whom knows Blount personally, and we're of opinion that the actual murder was committed after he'd left the square. The police find it hard t' fit in the man who talked to the policeman at eight forty-five; they think it was the murderer, but we're by no means sure it wasn't Charteris himself. We haven't spot cash f'r anything, but we're s'posing him to have received sudden warning—real or faked to get him away from the square—that it wasn't altogether a healthy neighbourhood for him. Either he himself or the other fellow, called A, suggests a disguise. It's true there are one 'r two points that can't be explained away, but it's a reasonable explanation of his tie left on his dressin'-table. 'Course, he may have been decoyed into a car and shot then and there, and the boots hidden in a convenient ditch, but the medical evidence shows he must have been killed quite close to the place where he was found, as otherwise the body'd have been too stiff to fall in the position it did. Now, s'pose he came by arrangement to this place on Blount's estate and was met there, ostensibly by a friend who was, perhaps, goin' to supply him with money; you'll remember they found next to nothing on the corpse. He'd probably be vamped fairly easily; these blackmailing fellers get the idea they're God A'mighty's elder brother and no one dares to stand against 'em. The notion that he might be asked there treacherously wouldn't enter his mind. Well, here he is disguised, all except the boots, because the boots were missin' from his room; and, anyway, he'd find it next door to impossible to walk in the boots they found on his feet; so we can suppose that when he left Thermiloe Square it was in his own boots, and he carried the others. Or he might have bought 'em as he went along and not gone back at all."

"That's very feasible," the other admitted energetically. "I'm not *quite* sure about the boots, though. He might think the changes he'd already made were sufficient. If you're looking for an out-of-work actor with a black beard and you run upon a clean-shaved parson with two noticeable scars on his chin you're not likely to connect the two."

"On the other hand the police are devilish fly. Suppose they did trace the fellow, the fact that he was wearing specially made boots—every one testified to the care he paid to his boots, always cleaning 'em himself, and keeping 'em on trees, never wearing 'em indoors, only some low-class down-at-heel pumps—might give them his name. These made-to-measure boot manufacturers always know their own wares and most of their time they can fit a name to a shoe of theirs without turning up the index. There's no doubt those boots would betray him."

"Well, Mr. Harper, you may be right. Then he takes the train to the nearest station—to Little Kirbey, presumably. Might be possible to trace him down there? No, I suppose not, as it was a foggy night and he'd be sure to keep his collar turned over his chin. Perhaps we could trace a man without an overcoat, though. Then he goes up to meet the murderer, is shot, stumbles over the cliff—half a minute though, there's the button. No, he doesn't stumble over the cliff, but is dressed for the part, complete with button, and then shoved overboard. Now we have to find A, the unknown quantity. As you say, a man might be able to ascertain which of the company was out that evening. It was a misty night and damp, up here at all events, so it's possible some servant will remember."

"We can rule out several of the household—most of 'em in fact—without going down to Four Corners," rejoined Harper with some asperity. "Egerton and his wife for example—it isn't likely to be either of them. Ambrose wasn't there at the time. The servants —well, it's unsafe to rule 'em out without inquiry, but it's only in the novelettes of the nineties that a devoted servant risks an uncommonly unpleasant death for the sake of a beloved master or mistress. That leaves Lady Blount and Miss Martineau, both of whom admit to knowing the dead man, both of whom had been recently in touch with him, both of whom probably had cause to be glad he was out of the way. How far that's true in Miss Martineau's case will be your job to ascertain. Her relations with him in the past are a bit of a mystery. That'll have to be sifted too, unless you can discover any recent correspondence that'll give you a key to the puzzle. Let's take Lady Blount first. On sight there seems to be a pretty strong suit against her. It's known that she has more reason than any one, except her husband, for wishing Charteris out of the way; she knows he's going to visit him; she can't stand the thought that Blount's career may be smashed up by some past misfortune of hers; she may have evidence of other forgeries; anyway, she has evidence of this one; she telephones or wires—for all we know he has another address in London—or even writes— Blount didn't go up till Monday; she may have written Saturday night, and she undertakes to give him money if he'll come to a specified spot. *En passant,* I should say the fellow changed his boots after he left the station, hiding the others in some pool or marsh along the roadside; there are scores to choose from. The place is deserted and it's a hundred to one against their ever being found, but he wouldn't want to leave distinctive foot-marks that might get the police on his track. The night was damp, remember, and he wouldn't be keen to take risks; foot-marks would show clearly in that marshy soil. The land from the station to the house is wild and desolate; so is the place where he was found. He wouldn't be likely to meet a soul, and nor would she. She's wise enough to recognise that Charteris with the police after him, or believing that they are, is a person much less to be feared than Charteris with a secret of hers he's prepared to sell to the highest bidder. They meet and she shoots him, tips him over the cliff, gets back to the house and hides the gun, and probably rejoins her guests. She admits that she had the gun and the bullets tally to a hair. Well, what d'you make of that?"

"Blount will hardly thank you for exonerating him at his wife's expense," he suggested urbanely.

"Don't want his confounded thanks; his fee's good enough for me."

"And there are one or two details I confess I don't understand. Are you suggesting that Lady Blount's anxious to free herself in one stroke by getting Charteris and Blount permanently out of her way? It's a tall story. You have a lady, a hostess, planning out this complicated scheme, making some excuse to her guests for leaving them, going out on a wet and miry night through a wood and a cliff-path, murdering a man and then rejoining her guests as if nothing had happened. Don't you agree it's a little far-fetched?"

"Not for a woman," growled Harper, who didn't like them. "But I'm not laying down the law. I'm simply tryin' to discover, by the process of elimination, who c'd conceivably have murdered Raymond Charteris. It's bound to be more or less guesswork, but at least that might give us a theory to build on."

"Only if you allow that Lady Blount is anxious to become a widow, and what would she gain? There's no question, I understand, of friction between them. Blount's known to be infatuated, and I believe the lady is in a similar case. That isn't evidence, of course, and if you can point to a single thing she'd gain——"

"She'd have his money——"

"You call that strong enough? But even granted all that, what about the scrap of paper in his rooms? That presupposes an accomplice."

Harper thought for some time. "She may have shoved the scrap in his pocket and he tossed it out without noticing it."

Blackie shook his head. "Too thin. There's no trace at Four Corners of any paper exactly like that. And how would she know the precise words Charteris would use? She'd hardly dictate his letter to him. No, no, Mr. Harper, I'm sure you're on the wrong track there. Even if Lady Blount had shot Charteris she wouldn't have hung about the hall, sneaked the button from her husband's coat, and then put it in the dead man's hand. There's no motive. In any case——" He paused, deep in thought.

Harper looked up suddenly. "Has Lady Blount not been in town since that date? If so she'd have ample opportunity—it's practically established that the paper was dropped in through the window, since it was found *behind* the curtain."

Blackie stubbornly opposed him. "Not a workable theory at all, Mr. Harper. I'd be more inclined to suspect the other lady. Of course, our chief difficulty is that we know so little of any of the parties concerned. So we must build up a suppositious case against the lady—Miss Martineau. It's possible, I think, that she also is being blackmailed by Charteris; she's a woman of some influence in her own sphere and she has a certain personal appeal; it may be that she's contemplating developments with which Charteris may very materially interfere. She's got to get him out of the way; she evolves the plan of luring him down to Four Corners, follows, in fact, precisely the same procedure as we have presumed in Lady Blount's case. She may quite likely know about the revolver, have seen it hidden. . . . Supposing she contrives to lay hands on the weapon——?"

"I understand it's concealed in a secret drawer," snapped Harper.

Blackie's thoughts were turned for a moment in a new direction. "I take it it's hardly likely the ladies would be working in conjunction? If so, you're going to have a job to get at the truth because they'll cover one another's tracks and be each other's alibis. If that were true, we might suppose that Lady Blount knew nothing of the plot to cast the guilt upon her husband. It's no end of a tangle." He rose impatiently and went over to the window. "Well, Mr. Harper, this is all supposition and doesn't get us much forrader. We can't do much till we've had the reports of the woman I shall send to discover Miss Martineau's past, present and future, and the man who'll elicit facts for us at Four Corners. By the way, are you working with Egerton in this?" His manner was an odd mixture of eagerness and reserve.

"No," snorted Harper, "I'm not. I'm not denying that he's been precious lucky in spotting two murderers——"

"Hardly lucky," deprecated Blackie, "the man's an artist at his job. I'm always sorry he dropped the secret service or at all events didn't carry on with that type of work afterwards."

"Was that what he did? H'm. Do well?"

"Brilliantly. Of course, it's a thankless job, no decorations and fanfare of trumpets, but its value is inestimable."

"Very likely," assented Harper testily, "very true, no doubt. But if so, all the more reason for avoiding Mr. Egerton's company. The actual murderer will recognise that any one seen in his neighbourhood is out for blood and will act accordingly. Let Egerton work on his own lines and if he attracts the quarry's attention so much the better. Give us a chance to stalk the fellow from behind."

CHAPTER IX

"The statement was interesting but tough."
    —The Adventures of Huckleberry Finn.

THAT afternoon a man called Anstruther went down to Tenbeigh where he booked a room for the night. Early the following morning he presented himself at Four Corners and was met by the butler.

"Good-morning," said the stranger. "I am acting on behalf of Sir Gervase's defence. Are you Sanders?"

The butler, who had appeared antagonistic at first, seemed mollified by this information.

"That's my name," he admitted.

"Then, Sanders, perhaps you can spare me a few minutes. I want to get your help to unravel this tangle."

The butler took him into a small, plainly furnished room at the back of the house.

"We shall be safe here. You don't believe, of course, that Sir Gervase had anything to do with this?"

"No. But unhappily appearances are against him. Do you remember the night in question?"

"Yes, as a matter of fact, I do. I'd been going out that night. I was going down to 'The Case is Altered' to meet a chap I knew there, a good chap, in service with Mr. Atherley of the manse. We used to meet now and again—I met him in London oddly enough—and we'd play draughts and have a drink together, and chat a bit, you know. Well, when I saw the fog that afternoon I felt a bit doubtful, and then when the mist blew away—it wasn't very dark down here really, not like it was in town—and the rain come down, I thought, 'Ramsey won't be there to-night, and even if he is I shan't be,' so I sat tight."

"I should suppose most men would in the circumstances. I imagine all the household would be indoors that night?"

"Most of them, yes."

"H'm." Anstruther produced a cigar-case. "Try one. I think you'll find they're good. It's unfortunate that no one was out, who might have heard any sounds."

"What sort of sounds?"

"A revolver shot, for example."

The man started. "Do they think he was killed here, not in his rooms at all?"

"If we're to prove Sir Gervase innocent I think we shall have to show that the shot was fired this end, not in town. Now, can you tell me, first of all, whether it was you who put Sir Gervase's coat ready on the day he went up to London?"

"Yes. I brushed it and hung it in the hall so that I could give it him when he asked for it. He was going up directly after lunch and I knew he'd want it in a hurry."

"Can you remember exactly when you put it ready?"

"Before lunch, about half-past twelve, I remember."

"You left it in the hall?"

"Yes. Just on the stand."

"Was any one in the hall at the time?"

"I don't think so, but of course I couldn't be sure. I wouldn't notice particularly."

"Did you see any one lingering in the hall afterwards?"

"To tell you the truth I wasn't in the hall much. But, of course, anyone could have been there if they'd liked, and very likely no one have known."

"And when Sir Gervase went, did you give him the coat?"

"He said he was late and he mustn't miss his train, and he just pulled down the coat himself and threw it over his arm."

"So you didn't really get any clear view of it at all?"

"No. He sent me up to his room to fetch him a paper he'd forgotten, and while I was getting that he took down his own coat off the stand."

"Ah! That may be useful. Now, can you remember whether any one in the house was out on that evening?"

"None of the servants-hall was out; 'tisn't like London where you can go into a cinema or an empire if it rains; there's nothing to do here but walk down to the pub or pick daisies. We all thought we was better off indoors."

"And were any of the guests out?"

"Miss Martineau was out that evening at a concert given at Tenbeigh, a charity concert I think it was. She wouldn't be back till about eleven-thirty."

"And she left at what hour?"

"About eight, sir. Took a cab, though the roads are so shocking. Said she couldn't go by train because she couldn't walk on a night like that."

"Of course, it was foggy, wasn't it?"

"Well, not so foggy then; but it was drizzly and dark."

"Would you know the driver again?"

"I might. But there isn't so many cabs round here that the man himself wouldn't remember coming."

"That's true. And she came back in a cab?"

"No, by train and walked the last part. The rain had stopped by then, stopped about ten-thirty. Blossomed out about eleven into quite a nice night, moon and all."

"H'm," murmured Anstruther drily. "You were more fortunate than we were. We didn't get a glimpse of the moon in London. It's a bit odd, isn't it, though, walking at that hour of the night?"

"Not for Miss Martineau, sir. She walks a lot, she does, and often at night—mostly alone, too."

"I see. The trouble is we don't know precisely what hour this man was shot. If we did we should know whether there was any possibility of her hearing any sound. But, of course, it may not have been till much later. Has Miss Martineau her own maid here?"

"No. She said she was going to 'rusticate' and would live the simple life." He laughed. "You should have heard Rogers on that when she saw the lady's frocks. Nothing fit for country wear at all, nothing but a beautiful fawn, woollen suit that 'ud mark with the first spot of rain."

"Then does Rogers look after her while she's here?"

"Yes. That's her ladyship's maid, you understand."

"I suppose I can see her presently?"

"Oh, yes. She might be able to tell you something I wouldn't know."

"You've told me a great deal I was anxious to hear. Just one more thing. Do you know if any one else was out that night?"

Sanders hesitated. "Well, not exactly out——"

Anstruther pounced on the unskilful admission. "What does that mean? Either you're out or you're not, surely?"

"It was her ladyship," confessed Sanders with a

twinge of dismay. "She seemed rather poorly all day, we thought, not like herself at all. We'd none of us seen her really bad before, but she said she had a headache and she lay down a bit in the afternoon, and in the evening she just sat and watched Mr. and Mrs. Egerton play chess. Sir Gervase and Miss Martineau was away, you see, and the doctor hadn't come then. Mr. Egerton plays chess a lot they say, a regular dab. Won a prize or something——" He would, reflected Anstruther silently.

"You say Lady Blount had seemed strange all day. What precisely does that mean?"

"Well, it was Rogers spoke of it. She said she'd gone up to her ladyship's room with a little table-cloth that comes from there; she'd had an accident that morning, upset some water over it, and it had been drying downstairs. And her ladyship was there, standing by a bureau she has in her room, turning a key, and Rogers heard her say, 'No, not that way, my dear, never that way. Better I——" or something just like that. And then Rogers said, 'I beg your pardon, my lady,' and she turned round and said, 'Come in, Rogers. What is it?'"

"I suppose Rogers is sure of her words?"

"She came straight down and told us. Very odd she thought it."

"And after that did Lady Blount go out?"

"It was a bit after ten. She said her head was that bad she couldn't stand a lighted room, and Mr. Egerton, he took his wife to go and play billiards, and her ladyship said to Rogers, 'I can't sleep to-night; it's too hot,' though it wasn't hot at all. And she put on a cloak and said she'd sit on the balcony. Well, Rogers didn't like it, but she wrapped her up and made her put on some thicker shoes, because the airs are treacherous this time of the year, and her ladyship's none too strong, and then Rogers comes down and says, 'I'm worried about her ladyship; I've never see her like this before.' Well, we didn't think too much about it, because sometimes ladies have fancies, and about an hour later Rogers goes upstairs before going to bed to see if there's anything she can do, and the next minute she runs down again, looking as if she'd seen a ghost, and she calls, 'My lady, my lady,' and then she stands on the stairs and says, 'Her ladyship's gone out in all this wet. She must be ill.' Then Mr. Egerton comes out of the billiard-room and Mrs. Egerton follows him, and she says, 'Well, I'm not surprised. The house is too stuffy for words. I should like a breath of air myself.' Then while we were all talking, about a quarter past eleven in comes her ladyship, her face white like a sheet, her shoes thick with mud, her coat shining with the rain."

"I thought you said the rain stopped at ten?"

"Well, so it did. Her ladyship seemed surprised to see us all there, and she said in a nervous, quick sort of voice, 'It stopped raining, so I went for a little stroll.' Mrs. Egerton says, 'I wish I'd come with you. But how wet your coat is!' and her ladyship says that the trees are dripping something awful, and they dripped all over her."

"And Miss Martineau didn't return till later still?"

"About a quarter of an hour later, or maybe a little more. She said she'd tried walking across the fields, as it had turned into such a nice, moonlight night. But the mud was too thick so she had had to come back and walk by the road, after all. She's a queer one, she is."

Anstruther allowed him to ponder Eloise Martineau's queerness for thirty seconds and then said, "And after that?"

"Well, sir, I locked up after that, seeing as Sir Gervase couldn't be coming back. He'd have been in before if he'd been coming. But he told me he expected he'd stay in London."

"Ah! He said that before he went? Of course. And he took a change of clothes with him. Who packed the bag?"

"You couldn't hardly call it a change of clothes," deprecated Sanders. "It was no more than an attaché case really. Paull packed it, I expect."

"I must see him later. Now, one more point. This is of the utmost importance. Has any member of the household been away from the house since that night?"

"Do you mean left altogether?"

"No, no. I mean, for the day. Gone up to London, for instance?"

"Oh, no."

"You're sure? Quite sure? Swear it on oath?"

"On oath, sir."

Anstruther frowned. He liked nice, straightforward murders. These complicated cases offered immeasurable loopholes for the criminal. If Sanders was right it stood to reason that the murderer had a London accomplice, and that made matters more difficult than ever, for there would be two men (or women) covering tracks and tangling evidence.

Anstruther next interviewed Paull whose evidence practically was nil.

"You packed Sir Gervase's case for him on the twentieth?"

"I did, sir. He didn't take much, saying he'd only be away one night."

"Did you unpack it on his return?"

"He was wanting the case for some papers, I think, so he tipped out the things himself."

"Leaving them for you to sort?"

"No. Sir Gervase was never like that. Like a new pin he was. He'd everything straight by the time I got up to his room. Well, he's like that." His tone generously conceded a similar weakness in the majority of men.

"Would you be able to tell, for instance, whether he'd actually changed the collar he was wearing when he went up to town? Could you see by looking in the soiled linen basket, or counting the clean ones in the drawer?"

Paull stiffened. "It isn't to be expected that Sir Gervase would wear a collar two days," he said coldly.

"But could you prove it? I'm trying to get some fact that'll help to save his life." Anstruther spoke forcibly and with some impatience.

Paull looked slightly ashamed. "Well, sir, if I'd been asked at the time, I might. I couldn't swear even then it would ha' been any good, but I might ha' known. But the soiled linen basket's been emptied since then. Laundry goes out on Wednesday here."

"You don't, of course, know the precise number of collars Sir Gervase possesses?"

"No, sir." Paull sounded curt again. He could add nothing that was of any use to the private detective, who shortly dismissed him and asked for Rogers instead.

Rogers confirmed the butler's story.

"You cleaned Miss Martineau's shoes, didn't you, on the morning of Tuesday, the twenty-first?"

"The day after the concert party, sir? That I did,

and a rare mess they were in, too. Of course, in London there'd have been Albert, but Sir Gervase says that in Rome he does what Rome does." It was clear that the meaning of the phrase had entirely escaped her.

"Muddy, were they? It's clay round here, isn't it?"

"Thick, yellow mud, all baked hard by the morning. I never did have such a job."

"And were her ladyship's as bad?"

"Not near. Mud all right, but not that thick, yellow mud. She told me she'd been walking in the wood; it was such a nice night! Nice night, indeed! And a moon wild and tossed that any one would have known meant a storm next day."

"I see. That's very useful. Well, there's no reason on earth why Lady Blount shouldn't walk in the wood at night if she pleased. I'm very fond of night walking myself."

On the stairs, as he left the butler's sitting-room, where Rogers had come to him, Anstruther saw Lady Blount. She was composed and aloof as always, and even paler than usual. She said, trailing gracefully down the stairs with the lovely elegance that habitually clung to her smallest movement, "You're employed by Sir Gervase's lawyer, are you not? So? Will you come in here a moment? Have you discovered anything from the servants that will help you?"

"I hope their evidence may help to exculpate Sir Gervase. Lady Blount, there is just one point on which you may be able to throw some light. The question of the revolver. You say that you removed this from Sir Gervase's desk on the morning of his departure?"

She was pale as death; her eyes burned like smoky fires in her ravaged face. "Yes; at about eight o'clock."

"And you concealed it in your room?"

"In a secret drawer in my bureau."

"Does any one else in the house know the secret of that drawer?"

"Not a soul, to my knowledge."

"Not Sir Gervase himself?"

Her head was lifted in proud displeasure. "He would know, of course."

Anstruther recognised that instant change in her mood and exerted·himself to placate her. "The prosecution, you see, will make every endeavour to show that Sir Gervase was in possession of his revolver at the time of the murder. You checkmate them if you say that it was concealed in a secret drawer, but the question I have just put as to whether Sir Gervase knew of that secret cubby-hole is one you will certainly be asked in court."

"Sir Gervase could not have taken the revolver to London, for during his absence I opened the drawer and contemplated disposing of it altogether. There are," she added, blushing faintly, "many pools on the estate where it might lie undiscovered until the sea gives up its dead. However, my maid interrupted me so I decided to leave it in the drawer—the safest place I could devise."

Anstruther bowed, but circumstances forbade his pointing out that all her evidence was really very frail, since a jury would not hesitate to imagine collusion between husband and wife; if Blount came back, admitting that he had shot Charteris and had concealed the body, Pamela would doubtless back him up and concoct with him a story to defeat justice, in the historic phrase; she would probably do this in any case, but if there were any strong tie of affection be-

tween them she would have no compunction in perjuring herself, and she could produce no witness to
prove that the revolver was actually at Four Corners
while Blount was at Thermiloe Square.

"And when you went out later, into the woods, you
heard nothing that might have been a revolver shot?"

"I should not be near enough to hear. I only lingered on the outskirts of the woods."

That was the end of her evidence, and then Anstruther had to set about verifying the various scraps of
information he had been given during the morning.
First of all he went to the wood where Pamela Blount
admitted she had lingered and examined the soil there.
It was rich and black. "Good for the trees," reflected
Anstruther. "Blount's lucky to get a patch like this in
such country." Thence he walked on to the cliff-path
where the body had been found. The soil here was
heavy with clay, thick and wet. "I wonder," he reflected, gingerly peering over the edge, "whether the
road-path is as bad as this? I shall have to see." Then
it struck him that the distance between this cliff-side
and the wood he had recently left was not so great
that a sound as sharp as a revolver shot could not be
heard, especially by night when there would be no
other noise to distract the attention. He decided to
test this, and for the purpose walked by the short-cut
down to Little Kirbey, where he commandeered the
services of a police constable, and a pistol with a round
of blank cartridges. The man he placed on the cliff-
side, himself taking up his station at the furthest outskirts of the wood, so as to give Lady Blount the
benefit of the doubt. He had timed his walk from one
spot to the other, and he had not been in position
more than a minute before he heard, clear and dis-

tinctive, the sound of a revolver shot; after a moment there came another. So it appeared to him that either Lady Blount was perjuring herself, when she said that she heard nothing, or else the shot had been fired after eleven-fifteen. To make doubly sure he insisted on the constable changing places with him and himself firing a third shot, in case it might merely be a case of particularly good hearing. But the constable declared that the sound would awake a thousand sleepers.

"Now, we shall have to go through the same process by the road, I'm afraid," said Anstruther as they walked back. "What's the nearest spot to this place if you're coming from Little Kirbey?"

The constable told him.

"And is that the only way you can come?"

"Unless you come across the fields."

"What's the road like there?"

"Pretty bad, stony, but passable."

"Muddy?"

"N-no, not like it is here. Just slush maybe."

"But not yellow mud?"

"Oh, no, nothing like that." And so it proved. Nevertheless, it seemed to Anstruther improbable that he would be able to refute Eloise Martineau's contention that she had tried walking back by the fields and had been forced to desist.

His next visit was to the small station of Little Kirbey where he asked for the station master.

"Can you remember the night of the twentieth, a damp, foggy sort of night?"

"Yes, sir. A rare dirty night up till half-past ten or thereabouts, and after that, bless me if a moon didn't come sailing out like Noah's dove."

"Do you know if any passengers from London

alighted here that night? There's a connection through from Eversfield, isn't there?"

"That's right, sir. But none came here."

That was a distinct check. "None? You're sure?"

"Absolutely, sir. There isn't as a rule many folk coming here from London, and that night I remember passing the remark to Wilkes, our porter, that if there was any London passengers I reckoned they must ha' got left behind at Eversfield."

Anstruther frowned. "What time does the London train stop here?"

"Due at ten-fifteen, sir. 'Course, she's a bit late mostly, but that's the time on the table."

"And that night?"

"Must ha' been about half-past."

"Not later? Not in all that fog?"

"Well, sir, she only comes from Naughton, ye see. She ain't the London train; London passengers take her at Eversfield. She don't start till ten past nine, and the fog was gone by then, and a bit of rain don't trouble an engine. Why, I orfen say to my missus, I wish you was as reasonable about a bit of damp as an engine is. She don't mope and say 'er best feather's gone outer curl. She just runs through it. But it beent no good argufying with women, sir. They ain't got no sense, women ain't. "

"And you'll swear no one alighted here?"

"Certain I will. What's more the driver of the train'll swear it, too. Mate of mine, he is. I asks him what he stops here for, seeing there's hardly ever any one getting out and never any one getting in."

"H'm. That train runs through Tenbeigh."

The station master looked dignified. "Stops at Tenbeigh. Stops four minutes."

"What time does it get there?"

"Due ten-five; gets there about ten-ten mostly. Dessay it was"—he calculated an instant—"say, ten-eighteen that night."

"I see. Thanks very much. By the way, that's not the last train that calls here at night, is it?"

"Oh, no, sir. Last train comes in from Tenbeigh, local train that is, arrives about a quarter to eleven. That's pretty punctual, that is."

(Could Eloise Martineau have walked from the station to the house in three-quarters of an hour, coming by road? The distance was between two and three miles. She probably walked about four miles an hour; she was renowned as a swift walker. But could she have tried the field-way and discarded that route and then met Charteris and disposed of him, and still have got back by half-past eleven? If she hadn't come by road, though, but across the fields she might just do it.)

He turned to the porter again. "Many people get off that night on the local train?"

"A goodish few; been in to a concert at Tenbeigh, they had."

"Oh, yes, I believe Miss Martineau, one of the guests at Four Corners, said something about it. Do you know the lady by sight?"

The station master nodded lugubriously. "Oh, yes, sir."

"I dare say she was on the train that evening."

"Might ha' been. I didn't see her, but then I didn't see any of the faces. I got something better to be doing at that hour than trying to guess who folks are in their best clothes."

"Oh, well, perhaps she wasn't here. But she did

say she'd been to the concert and came back to this station."

"Very likely she did. Can't say I remember seeing her all the evening, but then that don't amount to much." It didn't, of course. Anstruther had an uncomfortable feeling that he hadn't got much further in his quest. Passing the station master a florin, he walked on trying to dovetail together the information he had received. His next inquiry must obviously be made at Tenbeigh. He asked the quickest way thither, only to be informed that neither train nor omnibus (a ramshackle, broken-springed vehicle dignified by the name) left for more than an hour.

"Quicker to walk," he decided gloomily, since Little Kirbey was only three miles out on a sideline. As he left the village, however, he espied a Ford motor van, half-filled with vegetables, driving into Tenbeigh to dispose of these, and the driver proved an affable person ready enough to give the gentleman a lift, particularly with a shilling at the end of it.

"Quiet little place, this," observed Anstruther conversationally as the van turned into the main road that was rutty and poor but negotiable.

"It is, that. O' course, things goes on at Tenbeigh a bit." He spoke with the broad, slow enunciation of his county.

"Yes. So I've heard. Had a concert of sorts there the other day, they tell me. In aid of the blind, was it?"

"That's so. Not that I was there myself."

"Do well? I hope so. It's a good charity."

The driver smiled and did some rather pretty road-stealing past a horse and cart. "Better than the concert, folks are hoping."

"Rotten, they thought?"

"Oh, aye. All this slow music that means naught so far as us can see. A-many people went out afore the end."

That set up a new train of thought in Anstruther's mind, as suggesting a new hypothesis. It might easily be possible for Eloise Martineau to prove that she had actually gone to the concert, but in the general exodus might unobtrusively have disappeared in good time to meet her whilom lover on the cliff-side. He must endeavour to obtain evidence—though the hope was forlorn enough—to show that she was in fact in the concert hall at the close of the programme. If it could be shown that she had left earlier, then she would have had ample time to carry through the plot by which Charteris had met his death.

Arrived in Tenbeigh he went to the Victoria Hall, where the charity entertainment had been held, and discovered the identity of the young man who had acted as box-office clerk on the night in question.

"Have you any idea what they'd ask for the use of this hall for charitable purposes for one night?" he asked confidentially.

The clerk shook his head. "Couldn't say, sir. If you was to ask at Mr. Wick's office——"

"Where's that?"

The youth came out of his place to point the road. "Straight down there, door at the end."

"Right. You've no idea, I suppose? When you're getting up a charity show you don't want to fritter away too much on expenses. But they tell me there's a good chance of getting a really first-class audience in a place like this. Didn't the Association for War-Blinded men give a concert recently?"

"That's right, sir."

"Takings pretty good? The hall was none too full, I thought. Perhaps they chose a bad night. Pretty foggy, I remember."

"Chose a bad concert more like it. These swells won't cotton to the idea that every place isn't London. Folk down here want something to chuck 'em up a bit, something jazzy and bright, and they bring 'em a new funeral march and slow music, and shadows, and violins making a noise like cats looking for their kittens. 'Tain't good enough. Folk has to earn their money here, and they're precious careful how they spend it."

"That's perfectly true. I noticed a lot of people leaving the hall before the end of the show. And I can't say I was surprised."

"You didn't like it, sir?"

Anstruther smiled. "Well, to be perfectly candid, I didn't. I'm not a musical genius, and I, too, like something that chucks you up. As a matter of fact, it was a great nuisance. You remember what a dirty sort of evening it was? Well, my car missed the road in the dark and came down very late. I had engaged to meet a lady here, but at the end of the show she'd vanished. At least, I hunted for her without any luck."

"There was a goodish few left, even then," said the clerk.

"Well, she's pretty noticeable. Staying down here, in fact. I should think you'd recognise her if you saw her. Tall, with wonderful hair. Look here, this is a photograph of her. D'you remember her by any chance?"

The clerk took the photograph. "That's Miss Martineau, staying at Four Corners. Yes, she was here that night, though she went out in the middle. London lady, isn't she? I thought so. Funny, you know, you'd have thought coming from London she'd guess that folks put on their best clothes for a show like this. But she just came in a high dress, thin and all that, but as if she was going out to tea. Rare put out Lady Marks was. Said she supposed the lady didn't think it worth while dressing for such a small affair. Very touchy woman, she is."

Anstruther remembered that Miss Martineau was supposed to be a friend of his, so he asked haughtily, "Did you say she left before the end?"

The clerk, recalling that vaunted friendship too late, answered in quick, abashed tones, "Yes, soon after the middle. About ten to ten, I should think. Looked as if all the hall belonged to her."

"Really?" said Anstruther so coldly that the clerk blushed. "Now, I think I ought to go and see Mr. Wicks. I'm much obliged to you."

Having seen Mr. Wicks and earnestly discussed with him fictitious plans for renting the hall for a night six weeks ahead, Anstruther turned towards the railway station, where he pursued the tactics that had been so successful at Little Kirbey.

Here, however, the station master had his own small office, and on presentation of his card Anstruther was admitted there.

"It's in connection with this man who was found shot at Four Corners," he explained. "There's a new theory on foot that he was not killed in his rooms, as was at first suggested, but that he came down here to meet some one and was murdered after his arrival. It's been proved that he didn't alight at Little Kirbey, and it is thought that he may have got out here and walked across the fields to Four Corners. Now, were you on duty on the night in question?"

"Certainly I was. But there were a good many people alighted here that night. There was a charity concert on and folk came in from all round about."

"But surely you can discover whether there were any London passengers on the train? Do you have many in the ordinary way?"

"Well, none that comes and goes daily; it's too far from town for that. But often enough there's several comes. I dessay some of the folk playing in the concert would come by train."

"Ah, but he'd be later than that. He'd probably arrive on the train that's due here just after ten."

"Oh? Well, if you'll wait a minute, sir, I'll find it out for you."

While he was gone Anstruther busied himself by mental calculations. As the crow flies it was about four miles from Tenbeigh to Four Corners, but that meant a road crossing various fields that would be veiled by the darkness, and would necessitate a good working knowledge of stiles and breaks in hedges, a road, in short, that only a man thoroughly familiar with the landscape would care to tackle.

"So far as we know Charteris was never in this neighbourhood," reflected Anstruther. "All the same, it's just as well to be sure. I must find out from Lady Blount if he ever did track her down here. That would put the fear of the devil into her heart, in case he encountered Blount. But even if he had come, could he have found his way over just from seeing the place once?" He knew that in these circumstances it is impossible to dogmatise since a sense of locality is, like a sense of humour, a gift of God and not to be acquired by gold. Following up the other road of supposition, he decided that supposing the fellow had taken the carriage-path (as it was grandiloquently called locally), a man would have to tramp slightly over five miles, which meant on such a night, at least an hour and a quarter's walk. Then it would be practically half-past eleven before he reached the cliff-path near the house, and at the half-hour Eloise Martineau was said to have returned! Turn where he would Anstruther could find no explanation that fitted all the facts. Then a new thought occurred to him. He had not waited to ask the servants whether Miss Martineau had entered the house by the back or the front door. There was no way of reaching the front save by the carriage-path; but supposing she had come, as Egerton and Ambrose had come on that fatal evening, by the back entrance, then it was just conceivable that he could make the times tally. For she would probably have shot Charteris on sight rather than take any risk, and the whole business would be over in less than five minutes. It was also probable that she had been a little later than Sanders had first declared; it would be almost impossible for the man to be accurate within five minutes or so.

Here the station master returned with the information that six tickets from London had been passed on that evening on the nine-thirty from Eversfield, but that no one remembered Charteris in particular. Before leaving the station Anstruther insisted on examining personally every employee or official on the premises, without, however, getting any nearer his objective. Leaving the station he entered the post-office where he telephoned Four Corners. Sanders answered him.

"Can you remember whether Miss Martineau came in by the front door or the back on the night of the concert?" Anstruther demanded.

"The front, sir."

That smote his latest version of the crime to ruins. "You're certain?"

"Dead certain Mr. Egerton could say the same or Mrs. Egerton and there's Rogers, too—not to say her ladyship."

"Ah! Do you think her ladyship would speak to me a moment?" He waited while Sanders switched the call through to Pamela Blount's private sitting-room.

"Lady Blount, this is Anstruther speaking. Will you tell me if Mr. Charteris ever came down to Four Corners, within your knowledge?"

He heard the swift gasp of fear over the wires. "Yes, once. He had threatened to do so before."

"And you saw him?"

"He insisted on it."

"But not at the house?"

"Oh, no. A little beyond the woods."

"Near the place where the body was found?"

"Yes, quite near."

"Did any one else know of his coming?"

"Not unless he told Miss Martineau."

"Had he a good sense of locality? Do you think that having been there once he could find his way there again?"

"I think so. He would say that any road he had tramped or any book he had read remained stamped on his mind for ever."

"Do you know which way he came—from Tenbeigh or Little Kirbey?"

"From Tenbeigh. He said he didn't want to be conspicuous."

"Thank you. One more question, if I may. I understand you were in the hall when Miss Martineau returned that night."

"I was."

"Could you with any accuracy tell me the time?"

"Half-past eleven. The clock struck as she came in, and she commented on the fact, saying, 'I'd no idea it was so late. The most wearisome evening I have ever spent.'"

That seemed to Anstruther slightly ominous. For why should Eloise Martineau specifically call attention to the hour of her return?

Reviewing the case in all its unsatisfactory entirety it seemed to him that the only person who could help him now was Eloise Martineau herself, and being of those who believe in grasping the nettle boldly he returned next morning to town to report to Harper on the case as he saw it at present, and to outline a possible plan of action for the immediate future.

Arrived at the lawyer's he found Blackie there also, and at once commenced to put his view.

"I'm convinced in my own mind," he said, "that the murder was committed at Four Corners. The original notion is too difficult. If the man had been shot in his room, even allowing that the body could have been carried to the car, at that time of night when the fog was still thick it would have been impossible for the car to have passed through Thermiloe Square without being seen by a constable or a passer-by. Its lights make a car conspicuous in a fog, particularly in a quiet neighbourhood like that. Now, the public loves a thrill, and most of the public loves a chance of taking a hand in a thrill. So that if there was any one who recalled hearing the car—and the head-lights in the fog would have been particularly noticeable, as I've just observed—he or she would almost certainly have come forward. Again, if the body had been taken either to King John's Mansions or to Aldwych, as the police suggest, it's probable that some one would have noticed it. Then there's the question of Blount's car having been used at all. The garage proprietor and his assistants declare that Blount hadn't been near the place that afternoon, and in the evening he couldn't have got it—after the murder, that is, assuming he's the man who spoke to the bobby—without every one being aware of it. We haven't, so far, been able to unearth any evidence that would implicate any one else, any one, that is, beyond Blount and his wife and Miss Martineau, all of whom admit knowing the dead man. The fact that the body was found on Blount's private property shows that it was put there by some one who knew the lie of the land. There aren't many people who do that. The place was practically shut down in Caryl Blount's time. No one was allowed to go over the house or the grounds, and the right of way was scarcely ever used. So that people with a knowledge of the route are precious few. I'm inclined to limit the crime to that triangle. So far we can prove nothing against Miss Martineau beyond the fact that she was virtually blackmailing the Blounts; as far as the murder's concerned her alibi appears irreproachable. For if Blount's yarn is true, and he did actually leave Charteris at seven-thirty, then at the earliest the man couldn't reach Tenbeigh before ten or a little after. It's reasonable to assume that he alighted there and walked. It's open to question whether he was met on the road by Miss Martineau, who had left the concert hall before ten, but if so it seems likely she'd have shot him at the first opportunity. However that's guesswork. It was an ideal opportunity of ridding herself of the man. He'd left his own fictitious letter, no one knew his destination or whereabouts. She must have seen that such a chance would never come again. As for motive, he may have been blackmailing her; we don't yet know enough of her past with certainty to swear to that. My chief difficulty is that I can't for the life of me see how she could get Charteris to the place where he was found, shoot him, and get round to the front entrance by eleven-thirty. There's a hitch somewhere."

"And you," snapped Harper, who was in his most disagreeable mood, "are employed to discover what it is."

Anstruther bowed.

"We haven't been wasting time either," Blackie interposed, "I've put Mlle. Duclaux on to the job, and she's discovered this much about Miss Martineau. She was originally an actress—I fancy Lady Blount had already told the police that—and she played at one time opposite Charteris in a musical comedy called *The Musk Rose Girl*. It never came to London, but it toured the northern provinces, a week at a time, you know the sort of thing. We've been very fortunate in discovering some one who remembers the company who was, in fact, one of its members, and he says it was open gossip that the two were living together quite openly at the time. I asked him about Lady Blount but he was quite definite that she joined afterwards.

It should be quite easy to verify that from Lady Blount's own statement. Afterwards Miss Martineau, who was known as Ellen Martin in those days, was set up in the millinery business by some man who was prepared to pay a good price for security. I can't give you the exact details but he was a married man and anxious to preserve secrecy. For years it's been rumoured, even among her assistants, that it isn't only hats that pay the rent of the premises in Bond Street. Now, we come to the crux of the affair. Miss Martineau, we learn, is at present engaged to Sir Samuel Sotherby, the shipping man. The announcement is to be made public shortly. He's a Scot, with all the Lowland prejudice where morality is concerned, and if he had any notion of irregularities in her past the engagement would probably be called off. Now, the fact of her engagement has made it imperative for her to sack most of her whilom admirers and helpers, with the result that she's got no one but this chap to turn to when times are bad, and she literally can't afford to lose him. So you see how important it is that he shall hear nothing whatsoever of a possible scandal. Now, allowing that Charteris had proof of—indiscretion—it's obviously in her interest to keep on good terms with him as long as she can. But, better still, she'd like to have him out of the way. So long as he lives he's a persistent danger and drag to her. I don't say any of that's proof. It isn't. But, at least, it gives us an excellent motive for murder on the lady's part. The next thing is to try and substantiate the story. And that, Anstruther, as Mr. Harper has just pointed out, is your department."

CHAPTER X

"The shroud is done," he muttered, "toe to chin."
He snapped the ends, and tucked his needles in.
—The Widow in the Bye Street.

MADAME ELOISE'S premises in Bond Street were sufficiently imposing without being ostentatious. The windows were like masks, backed with tightly pleated net curtains that changed their colour with the seasons. In spring they were daffodil yellow, in summer, leaf-green, and in autumn, russet-gold. In one window a grotesque, wooden figure held aloft a single hat, while a scarf was draped artistically over a second stand; in the other was a frock and an opera cloak, flanked by magnificent flowers in a Chinese jar. On the day after Anstruther's return to town some one rang up shortly after lunch, asking for Madame Eloise.

"Name, please?" asked an assistant primly.

A low, beautiful voice answered, "Lady Hope-Potter. It is very urgent."

Madame Eloise swept to the telephone. "Madame speaking."

"Oh, Madame Eloise, I have to arrange for a trousseau at very short notice, and I am told that you will be able to fit me up with one or two hats and gowns. Very short notice, indeed, I'm afraid. Perhaps you will be in this afternoon about four? . . . Yes—Lady Hope-Potter. . . . Certainly. I will bring my maid, and should like to arrange for a fitting-room to be reserved for me."

"I think," said Mlle. Duclaux to Anstruther as she laid aside the receiver, "she will probably wait until a quarter to five. If you get to her flat about four you will get quite three-quarters of an hour. That ought to be sufficient."

"I must be certain of getting admitted," observed Anstruther. "Have you ever heard Miss Martineau speak?"

"I bought a hat there yesterday."

"Do you suppose you could imitate her well enough to ring up her flat, and tell her maid that a gentleman will be calling about four and he is to wait?"

"I think I could." Mlle. Duclaux picked up the receiver again. "Park 11111. Is that you?" Another voice, very obseqiously took up the conversation before Mlle. Duclaux could say anything further. "This is Parks. Is that madame?"

"Yes. I'm expecting a gentleman this afternoon, soon after four. I should be back by then, but by no means let him go if I am late. His name is Mr. Giles Bruce."

The pseudo-Mr. Bruce reached the flat in Kensington Mansions at five minutes past four. The maid, a stolid, elderly woman, admitted him sullenly.

"Miss Martineau is expecting me, I think. She is in?"

"She will be back any minute, sir."

"Oh." Anstruther frowned. "She did say four."

"Yes, sir, but she telephoned she might be delayed a few minutes. Will you wait in here, sir?"

She showed him into a room furnished as a sitting-room. Anstruther sat down in a tall Elizabethan chair and became interested in a Rabelaisian print of quite unusual excellence and wit. The maid stayed in the room for a few minutes, setting ornaments crooked, and re-adjusting the blinds. Anstruther, outwardly composed, was secretly examining with his eyes every nook and cranny of the room. He had no very clear plan in his head except to get rid of this tiresome woman. As it became evident, however, that she proposed to linger in the room until Miss Martineau's return, Anstruther grasped his nettle boldly. Standing on the writing-table was a lapis-lazuli hand-blotter; this he casually picked up.

"Pretty thing," he observed. "The marking is exquisite." He drew it a little closer and glanced rapidly at the under-side. The paper was unsullied.

The woman continued to watch him loweringly. "Useful, aren't they?" murmured Anstruther setting it back on the table. "Provided the blotting-paper's changed often enough? Otherwise it's apt to blur the writing."

"Madame's is changed every day," returned Parks in austere tones. She looked with disfavour on all men just now. A chance slip and farewell to Sir Samuel. And Parks had had enough of insecurity.

"No hope of imprints there," Anstruther was gloomily reflecting, while from his chair he continued to examine the handsome room. He waited wearily; the maid might have been a stone. The clock stood at twenty-past four and so far he had discovered nothing. It was impossible to inveigle Parks into conversation. It seemed to him highly unlikely that he would learn anything at all from this visit. Eloise Martineau was no fool; if there had been any letters or other documents linking her up with the dead man she would have destroyed them before now. Suddenly, however, this duel of patience closed in his victory. Parks left him to complete duties elsewhere, and as soon as the door closed Anstruther was on his feet. The bureau on which the hand-blotter lay contained four drawers, but a single touch on each convinced him that they were securely locked. On the desk itself, however, was an extremely handsome blotting-book bound in Russia leather, with gold initials—E.M.—intertwined in one corner. Anstruther opened it and commenced hastily to flick through the pages. It was clear the book was either a very recent acquisition or that a new blotter had just been slipped into the silk binding, for there was nothing to show on most of the pages. Suddenly, however, he stopped. On a page in front of him was a looking-glass impression of a letter in Eloise's dashing hand-writing, written so firmly and blotted so quickly that it was no hard task to make out its purport. Resisting the temptation to hold a pocket-mirror over the sheet Anstruther carefully cut both it and its companion at the other end of the book with the pen-knife, and folding these carefully slipped them into the capacious pocket of his coat just as the telephone began to ring.

The maid answered it in the hall; Anstruther saw that there was a second instrument on Eloise's desk. The door opened and Parks came in to find the visitor sitting patiently on the same chair as before.

"Mr. Boots?" she asked. "Oh, Mr. Bruce? I think it's a call for you." She waited sternly while he answered.

At the other end of the wire Mlle. Duclaux said clearly. "She's just left the shop in a towering temper.

She's coming back in a taxi. She'll be home in about twelve minutes."

Anstruther put down the telephone, passed one hand over his forehead and said in a jerky voice, "I will come at once. I had no idea——" Then he hung up the receiver and the face he turned to the woman was startled, and his voice stammered.

"I have had—had bad news, very bad. I must go at once. You will explain to Miss Martineau——" He groped for his hat. Parks, who knew her employer only too thoroughly, asked tonelessly, "Another appointment, sir?"

Anstruther was already at the door. "I—it may not be necessary—now," he gulped and vanished.

Eloise Martineau returned fifteen minutes later. "That damned woman never turned up after all," she cried stormily. "She needn't think, though, that I'm going to wait there all day for her." The fierceness of her mood explained the necessity for her financial backers. No business man allows himself to feel insulted during business hours.

The maid shivered. She knew these black moods of old. "The gentleman was very sorry, madam, but he had a telephone message, and couldn't wait."

Eloise spun round, raging. "The gentleman? What gentleman?"

"The gentleman you rang up about."

"I? You're drunk, Parks, that's what it is. I always did think you were too fond of your glass. I never rang you up all day."

"It was just like your voice," reiterated Parks steadily, and she smiled as she saw Eloise shudder. "It said a Mr. Giles Bruce was coming about four, and you might be a little late but be certain to keep him. But he was telephoned ten minutes ago with bad news, and he said that now it mightn't matter; he mightn't want anything, I mean."

Eloise laughed harshly. "No. I suppose he's got it already, whatever it was. And you mean to say you let him in?"

"Well, madam, I thought it was you. . . . And you've sometimes told me that before. . . .

In Eloise Martineau rage died suddenly and fear took its place. She turned towards the uncurtained window that framed the lovely, dim autumnal dusk stretching over the Kensington Gardens. And she shivered for the second time.

"Parks, do you think ghosts walk? Sometimes I wonder. I can hear their feet come so close, so horribly close. And I'm afraid."

2

Anstruther took a taxi from Miss Martineau's flat to Mr. Blackie's agency, where he met Mlle. Duclaux, and together they examined the sheet torn from the blotting-book. So fierce had been Eloise's mood when the words were written that they had little difficulty in reconstructing the threat they contained.

"I . . . Soth . .y lear . . . . he . rut . . . . . out . . s . . t . o th . t da . . th . . . . tte . . . rom . . Ala . . . ir Wy . . . m go . . . . . o the . . . ice . . . . . know . . . . t . . . t means.—five ye . . . . . t somet . . . g . . orse . . to . . ou . . . n dea . . An . . . o . dec . . . . an . . ul . . ever spe . . . . ou ag . . . .—"E. M."

"First of all let's try and place the name," said Anstruther, his professional excitement rising. "Fortunately there aren't many names beginning with Wy and ending in 'm.' A short name I should say, five or six letters. You take the telephone directory, will you, and I'll take *Who's Who*. And if that's no good we'll try the country directories and all reference books. We're bound to get it somehow, if only through the voters' lists in the hand of the town clerks."

In point of fact, *Who's Who* told them all they needed to know, for the only name that fitted their requirements was that of Lord Wytham of Park Place, London.

"Christian name, Aubrey," reflected the man. "Presumably this would be a son. Half a minute though. Would he also be Wytham? Yes. The fellow's one of those courtesy peers; a second son apparently, and his children take their father's name after the manner of commoners. Hallo, here's proof. One son, Alastair. How's that? I should say the next thing is for us to see Mr. Alastair Wytham."

He had gleaned this last piece of information from a list of members of the peerage that gave more details than *Who's Who*.

"Boy appears to be in the early twenties," he went on. "God help him if he got in Charteris' hands."

Mlle. Duclaux nodded. Her face was sad. In her professional life she had seen so many tragedies of youth and inexperience. While Anstruther had been hunting through books of reference she had occupied herself in puzzling out the message and they soon were able to put it into a coherent form, so that it ran thus:

"If Sotheby learns the truth about us two, that day the letter from Alastair Wytham goes to the police. You know what that means—five years of something worse to you than death. And no decent man would ever speak to you again.—"E. M."

"We must act on the supposition that this letter was, in fact, addressed to Charteris," observed the detective. "I think I'd better go along and see Lord Wytham now."

Lord Wytham was in when Anstruther arrived, though not disposed to see him.

"Please say it is in connection with Mr. Alastair Wytham," said Anstruther sending in his name a second time, and as if the word had magical properties he was instantly admitted. Lord Wytham interviewed him in his smoking-room. He was a thin, handsome, austere man in the early sixties. He had married when he was nearly forty, and his only son at this date was about twenty-two. He had been a widower for some years, and his unmarried sister kept house for him.

He rose haughtily when Anstruther entered. "Please sit down. I understand you have something to say to me concerning my son."

"Is Mr. Alastair Wytham in the house?" asked Anstruther.

The effect of that on his host was startling. The older man's face hardened, his hands clasped themselves over a black ruler that he turned softly round and round; his jaw was like a vice. His reply was as surprising as his expression.

"You are evidently not aware that my son was drowned in a boating accident several weeks ago?"

Anstruther's distress was so spontaneous that it was obviously genuine. "I beg your pardon. I am indeed

sorry. As a matter of fact, I had no notion——"
(For these reference books were drawn up once a year
and that was in the spring.)

"Then why did you wish to see me?" inquired the
dry inflexible voice.

Anstruther paused a moment before replying. "I'm
afraid, my lord, this is bound to be a painful interview for you, but in the interests of a man at present lying under suspicion of murder it must be proceeded with. I believe it is true that Mr. Wytham was
acquainted with this man, Charteris, whose body was
found on Sir Gervase Blount's estate a short time
ago?"

Lord Wytham rose; his hand moved towards the
bell. Anstruther warned him drily, "If you do that, my
lord, you will be pressing the matter into the glare
of publicity. That we are anxious to avoid. Certain
facts have come to our knowledge that make this inquiry necessary. I need hardly say how much I personally deplore my own position."

Lord Wytham re-seated himself. "Very well," he
agreed icily. "Pray be as brief as possible. If what
you say is true, which speaking for myself, I find extremely difficult to believe, then I can only assure
you that I had no knowledge of such an acquaintance."

"I'm afraid it is true. A letter has come into our
hands—I should, perhaps, explain that I am acting
for Sir Gervase Blount's defence—appearing to
threaten the late Mr. Charteris with a certain letter
written by your son to him, a letter that had fallen
into dangerous hands. I can give you the actual text,
which is that in the event of certain information leak-
ing out in a detrimental manner to the writer of this

second letter—whom we will call X—that from Mr. Wytham will be placed in the hands of the police. X adds, 'You know what that means—five years of something worse than death. And no decent man would ever speak to you again.' In the circumstances, we are inclined to believe that the 'something worse than death' refers to penal servitude. It seems likely from that to suppose that your son's letter contains information regarding some criminal offence."

In Lord Wytham's stark, white face the dark eyes blazed dangerously. "Have you the temerity, sir, to suggest that my son was a criminal?"

"Certainly not, my lord. But that he had information regarding certain criminal proceedings enacted by Mr. Charteris seems inevitable. It is known to the officials that Charteris had more than once committed forgery, and it occurs to us that it is remotely possible he has once more done so by using your name. Have you, perhaps, your pass-book at hand?"

Wytham's indignation was so great that it momentarily choked him. He was on his feet again, hands resting heavily on the table, mouth working spasmodically. At last he brought out, "If this Charteris did forge my name it is tantamount to saying that my son was his accomplice. It is a charge no man but a blackguard would bring against a living man. It is doubly infamous to bring it against the dead."

Anstruther retained his seat; he had witnessed so many domestic tragedies, so many high hopes burn out into grey drifting ash. He said again, "My lord, to complete a painful business as rapidly as may be, may I ask you to examine both your pass-book and cheque-book and, if possible, reassure us on this point?"

There was nothing but contemptuous disgust in the

older man's bearing as he unlocked a desk and drew out a long, grey book and the pass-book of his bank. It was the latter that he opened.

"It is a practice of mine," he observed, "to examine most meticulously this book every three months. It is about eight weeks since I did this. It will not, therefore, be necessary for me to go further back than the last two months."

Methodically he commenced checking up each outward payment against the counterfoils of two empty and one partially-used cheque-books. For some time there was silence. Then Wytham paused obviously troubled. He looked back at the last counterfoil, then beyond it. He opened a drawer and drew out a bundle of honoured cheques, and sifted rapidly through it. After an instant he withdrew one from the elastic that bound them, and laid it on the desk in front of him. Then he lifted his eyes and Anstruther saw that the proud, worn face was grey with apprehension.

"There is a note here of a withdrawal of one hundred pounds for which I cannot account," he acknowledged with so fine a dignity that the detective longed to crawl under the door and leave the old aristocrat to his own bewilderment and grief. "All the counterfoils in this book, however, tally with the other entries in my pass-book."

"Possibly a cheque has been taken from the new book; I see that you have one in reserve in your drawer."

"That I have received since my son's death. And I have never bought or borrowed a cheque."

"It's possible that a cheque has been abstracted from that book you are now using," suggested Anstruther slowly.

Lord Wytham did not move. "It would be infinitely simpler for the criminal to buy a cheque from the bank."

"Quite. But there are other considerations. If, as we think probable, Mr. Charteris forged your name to a cheque, he would certainly wish to avoid attention. May I remind your lordship that he was a figure whom the average clerk would remember? In any case he would find the risk too high."

Wytham slowly turned the leaves of his cheque-book, and stopped at the penultimate page; and Anstruther saw here a counterfoil only.

"A cheque *has* been abstracted," agreed the old man, "and its number corresponds with the one before me."

"Would you say, my lord, that that signature is your own?"

Wytham bent over it for a long time. At last he looked up. "I can say that I am practically certain it is not. There are quite trifling discrepancies that possibly no one but myself would recognise. You will understand that I should be delighted to say that the signature is mine and that I had forgotten drawing the cheque. But I fear only too deeply that your suspicions are well founded. It is an excellent copy." Then he straightened himself. "And now?"

"I think my next step must be to see the owner of your son's letter and discover precisely what it contains. I should say without doubt a reference to this affair. Possibly you, my lord, can recollect whether at the time Mr. Wytham seemed at all pressed for money."

"He had been spending a little recklessly, but I paid up his debts and started him straight again."

Anstruther looked out of the window. "It not in-

272

frequently happens that a young man has debts he scarcely likes to acknowledge. *Nil nisi bonum*—and so forth, but Charteris was hardly a desirable acquaintance for a youngster, and it's possible that he was pressing him too hard and drove him to desperation."

A terrible look blinded Wytham for the moment; despair, horror, self-condemnation, all were there. Anstruther thought, "He's blaming himself for being too stern. I wonder if it was an accident after all," and as soon as he had thought that he became certain that it had not been an accident, and that Wytham recognised this also.

"You promise me to do your utmost to keep this terrible affair out of the press?" The old man's voice was like a ghost, weak, wavering, shocked out of its normal vitality.

"Everything possible. It is hardly likely that X will be anxious for publicity."

"And you will let me know what you learn—in confidence, of course."

"Yes," said Anstruther slowly, "I think I may promise that. And, now, there is one other thing. Could you get in touch with your bank and discover if anything is remembered about the cheque, who cashed it and so forth?"

It was too late that night to prosecute inquiries, but Wytham went in person to the bank at an early hour the following morning, and interviewed the manager. It was not difficult to establish the facts.

"Why, Mr. Alastair himself cashed it. We remember because he asked specifically for small notes—five pounds."

Wytham nodded. "So that they shouldn't be traced.

273

May I ask you, Merriless, to keep this matter quite secret? It's inexpressibly painful to me."

"Of course, of course. I will tell the clerks that if I hear the matter so much as discussed in the outer office that man shall be dismissed on the spot. Nothing counts for so much in a bank as discretion."

Reaching Park Place, Wytham telephoned to Anstruther who immediately on receiving the news went round to Bond Street to see Miss Martineau. She seemed perplexed and a little distraught. The mysterious occurrence of last night had shaken her nerve.

Anstruther came straight to the point. "Miss Martineau, we are inquiring into a certain cheque forged in the name of Lord Wytham and cashed by his son, Mr. Alastair Wytham, early in August, the eleventh to be precise. We have information that you were aware of the facts of the case——"

"I'm not interested," interposed Eloise Martineau languidly, "I know neither the Wythams nor yourself——"

"My name you have on the card before you. This cheque is believed to have been drawn by Mr. Raymond Charteris whom, of course, you knew intimately. A letter from you to him threatening him with exposure should he be the cause of your engagement being dissolved, tells us all we need to know, and incidentally makes you an accessory after the act at all events. That, as you are aware, is an offence punishable by law. We are not anxious, as you will realise for yourself, to court publicity, and we shall, therefore, be glad if you will give us the history of this cheque so far as you know it."

Eloise Martineau looked at him incredulously. "You coolly suggest that I shall tell you——"

"We have your letter," Anstruther reminded her.

She flared up suddenly. "It's destroyed. I know it."

Anstruther was on to her like a flash. "How do you know it?"

"I saw him do it."

He eyed her narrowly. "Are you sure?"

"Perfectly."

"You would recognise your own signature?"

"Of course."

"Lord Wytham's bank believed they could recognise his signature, yet they cashed the cheque Raymond Charteris drew."

Eloise gasped. "D'you mean to suggest that that —skunk—forged a copy of my letter to him and that that was the one he burnt, and he kept the other to throw up against me? But it wouldn't have helped him. He wouldn't dare bring it forward."

"If he had been arrested for forgery——"

She interrupted passionately, "As he would have been. He's better dead. It was a good turn the—murderer—did him."

"I'm not sure of that."

"I am. He was terrified of prison. It hung over him like a black curtain of dread. I've often heard him say—often and often—he'd rather be in the grave. And so would I. So would I."

"What do you mean when you say he would have been arrested?" demanded Anstruther, disregarding all this fandango of emotion.

She relapsed into sullenness. "This Blount affair. No use trying to conceal that, is it? Gervase Blount would never have the sense to keep his mouth shut."

"And you were aware of that? By word of mouth through Charteris himself?"

"Yes."

"So you had seen him quite recently before his death?"

"I chanced to meet him a few days earlier—the day before I went to Four Corners."

"He told you that Lady Blount had informed her husband?"

"Yes. He said, 'That little fool, Pamela, has given the show away, and Blount's one of these strong, righteous men.'"

"Still, he didn't believe that Blount would act."

"He thought it probable. Anyway, he knew his hands were tied."

"So that he could forge no more with impunity? Quite. But considering the sums for which he forged, he seems to have had remarkably little out of it."

"There were always the others behind him, on his back. Big fleas and little fleas, you know. Plenty of people could have sworn him into gaol and he had to fight like a demon to hold them all off."

"And how did he contrive to snare young Alastair Wytham?"

She laughed shrilly. "You don't expect me to tell you that?"

"I think you'd be wise." Anstruther's voice was very grave. "As I've pointed out already you stand to be arrested as accessory after the act. If you'll be utterly candid we shall do what we can to prevent publicity. Lord Wytham is anxious to avoid that."

She laughed again. "He would be, of course. How he'd hate people to know his only son committed suicide to prevent a scandal."

Anstruther pulled her up sharply. "Why do you say that?"

"Because it's true. Do you think a boy who knew as much about boats as Alastair Wytham could have had an accident on an afternoon when the river was like a mill pond, and there wasn't a breath of wind? Besides, he could swim like a fish. Why didn't he? No, no, he killed himself because he knew that sooner or later some one would find out, and he couldn't bear to face his father."

"Supposing you tell me all the facts? Believe me, it's your only chance of avoiding arrest. How did Charteris meet young Wytham?"

"I don't know. But he had a manner that succeeded in impressing wealthy young men and women. That and his unusual appearance. He had a good voice, too, and had cultivated it. I fancy the boy wanted to dabble in life like most of them these days, and Charteris got hold of him and offered to show him London after dark. Gaming-hells, illicit drinking-dens—he knew 'em all. He got the boy thoroughly soaked one night and then frightened him, said that the police had got hold of his name as frequenting some house under their surveillance and he had to buy them off. The boy raised every penny he could, and still Charteris wasn't satisfied. At last he persuaded him to steal a blank cheque that he himself filled in, and made the boy cash. A week later he tried to blackmail him on that account, and the boy, rather than let his father know he was a thief, killed himself. But he wrote to Charteris first, telling him what he was going to do. A horrible letter, a vitriolic letter——"

"And Charteris? How did he take it?"

"I think he was relieved. He had felt that the youngster might in desperation confide in his father, and then he'd be finished. Then he made the mistake of believing he could frighten Pamela Blount like that, and he was horribly stymied when he realised she'd told her husband. He hadn't thought of her doing that. He'd meant to go from money to—other things, with her," she finished deliberately.

Anstruther, without change of expression, said, "You'll take your affidavit that he knew what this would mean for him?"

"Of course. He knew he'd be caught." And if he was caught, said her white, furious face, he'd have spit on me, too, and roped me in on the Wytham cheque.

Anstruther asked a sudden question. "You bank at City and Mortons, don't you? Ah, I thought so."

"What's that got to do with it?"

"It's Blount's bank also. I was wondering where he'd got his blank cheque. Of course, you lent him one—for a share of the proceeds."

Eloise Martineau preserved a tight-lipped silence. Anstruther with an eye always on the main chance, went on movingly, "Hadn't she had a sufficiently bad time without your handing her over to such a man? She'd earned a little peace."

Eloise's face suddenly flamed into a rage so white, so pitiless, so searing that even the private detective recoiled. "Her!" she cried fiercely. "What did I care about her? She'd wronged me as it isn't in my power to wrong her. And badly treated! Why, didn't Charteris *marry* her?"

"I don't think so."

"At the time of the marriage he believed his wife was dead. Afterwards she found out and blackmailed him. At that time he worshipped the ground the little fool trod on. And as soon as he was able to stand she threw him over!"

In that passionate speech she revealed the whole position. Beyond doubt, decided Anstruther, there had been intimate relations between her and Charteris before Pamela's appearance on the scene; and then Charteris had basely deserted her for the new and rarer beauty that had dawned in his sky. Possibly he had even cared for her afterwards. Anstruther couldn't guess. The love of men for women manifests itself in many and incomprehensible ways. As he came away from Bond Street he thought he could read Eloise Martineau's motive for murder clearly enough. If, as he said, Charteris expected to be momentarily arrested for forgery, he would probably be arraigned in due course for the Wytham cheque also, since there must be witnesses above ground who could testify to his intimacy with the hapless young man. In that case the name of Eloise must inevitably be mentioned and she would possibly be included in the charge. No wonder she was so anxious to be rid of Charteris, in view of the sordid and wealthy marriage she herself contemplated.

Feeling sick with disgust, yet elated at the way in which the plot was unrolling itself, he went to report to Harper. The latter, that same afternoon at about two o'clock, finding himself in the neighbourhood of Hammond's office, dropped in to find a handsome car by the kerb and Scott Egerton in bridal finery on the point of taking his leave.

Harper surveyed the young man with disapprobation. "Well?" he barked, "found your man yet?"

The imperturbable Egerton shook his head. "Not yet. I'm not one of the magicians who can make bricks without straw."

"And what straw do you want at this stage?"

"Two things. Firstly—the rest of the envelope. And secondly, proof that Charteris had been in communication with Blount."

"What difference does that make?"

"If he hadn't it seems to me inconceivable that Blount could have murdered him as the police contest. By the bye, I've just proved to my own satisfaction that he was at his flat on the twenty-first."

"Brilliant," mocked Harper. "And how?"

"I went round there this morning."

"Why?"

"It occurred to me that he might have a calendar there."

"Very likely. What of it?"

"A tear-off calendar," pursued Egerton.

"And he had?"

"Yes. Standing at the date of September twenty-first."

"What does that prove?"

"That he was there on the twenty-first. You don't know Blount so well as I do. The greatest men have their foibles and his is never to tolerate a calendar a day behind time. I've heard him rebuke Sanders; so, I believe, has Bremner. He tore off that leaf on the twenty-first. Therefore, he was in the flat on that day. I don't say the police will accept that as evidence —they may think I tore it off myself—but it's good enough for me to go on."

"Won't do much to indict the actual murderer. You may be interested to know that affairs have moved on a good deal. We fancy we're in sight of our quarry."

Egerton picked up his silk hat and stroked it negligently. "Miss Martineau? Ah! Have you brought off the crumpled scrap of paper in Blount's rooms to her yet?"

"An accomplice, one presumes."

Egerton smiled and collected his stick, a slight, handsome affair of polished snake-wood and clouded amber. "Oh, but you'll find that very complicated," he murmured gently. "And if you only realise it, the affair is much simpler than that. You'll excuse me now? I'm due at a wedding in ten minutes and I'm keeping my wife waiting all this time." He lifted the stick in salutation to Hammond and vanished.

"Detestable young cockscomb!" growled Harper. "Hope to God he comes an unholy mucker soon. Now, listen!"

3

The wedding, that was as tedious as such ceremonies normally are, was not strictly speaking over until four o'clock. Egerton, looking unwontedly pale, came out of the hotel where the reception had been held, with harassed brows, and sighed with relief that it was over at last.

"I'm inclined to think the attractiveness of all weddings except one's own are over-estimated," he observed to Rosemary, as they approached their car. "Do you mind going home alone? I have to see Blount now."

He was turning away when some one grasped him with more strength than care by the shoulder. Egerton gently disengaged his faultless tail-coat from the intruder's hand and turned to find Ambrose at his elbow.

"I've been trying to get you all day," panted the

latter. "They told me I'd find you here. Tell me, what's happening?"

"I've just been to a wedding, and now I'm going to see Blount. Will you come along?"

"What, now? Can I do anything?"

"No," said Egerton thoughtfully. "I don't suppose you can. Well, will you come down to Four Corners early to-morrow morning? Rosemary and Hammond will be there, too. We meet at the house at midday."

"Why Four Corners?"

"I have to drag that water in the Mermaid Rocks," was Egerton's staggering reply.

"The water——?"

"The rocks just under the ledge where the body was found.

"What for?"

"I think the missing boots may be there."

"But why should they be? Why should he or any one else carry them so far?"

"That's what I hope to prove. Also, I want to discover what they're weighted with."

"That all?"

"No," answered his companion in a peculiar manner. "It isn't. I believe that in that pool we shall discover the crux of the whole situation; it will be something that will explain all the puzzling features of the case, including the pen-knife and the empty match-box. I fancy this is the last lap."

"Tell me," said Ambrose abruptly, "do you know who killed Charteris?"

"I think so."

"Who's that?"

"I don't want to sound a surly brute," said Egerton candidly, "and I don't want to appear to take an excessive size in hats, but in my profession, and probably in yours, too, we're forced to recognise that mere suspicions without definite foundations are fruitful of nothing but danger. I swear that by this time to-morrow you shall know as much as I do. And in saying that I've told you as much as I've told any human soul. Even Rosemary knows no more. Even the most hardened criminals should have the benefit of the doubt."

"All right. Look here, I'll drive as far as the prison with you. I'm sick of my own company. Do you seriously suppose you'll find any one to drag that pestilential pool?"

"I expect so," returned Egerton coolly, hailing a taxi.

The doctor seemed sceptical. "Why should they? It's taking their lives in their hands. What do they get out of it?"

"Cold cash," returned Egerton indifferently. "Men are doing that every day of the week—miners, drivers, railwaymen, airmen, sailors, factory hands. The majority of men do. There are always the few—who go in for danger for love of the adventure, and the fewer yet who're artists. But danger's one of the concomitants of life. In the last strait I'd take over the job myself. Here we are. I shan't be more than five minutes if you care to wait."

At the prison he was taken at once to see Blount, whose trial was timed to commence the following week.

"I apologise in advance," said Egerton crossing the cell. "I haven't really any right to butt in on you here, but I'm afraid it's inevitable. I shan't take up much of your time. I only want to show you this, and to ask one other question. Perhaps we'd better have the question first. After the row with Charteris, did you leave at once?"

"No. Oh, no. I was there another half-hour, I should suppose."

"Talking to him?"

"Most of the time."

"Watching him?"

"Not all the time. I remember wondering once if he'd put a knife in my back, but he was too goose-livered for that."

"Quite. Thanks for that information. And, now; this." He passed the older man a sheet of thick, parchment paper covered with writing in a thin Italian hand.

"By the way, were you ever in correspondence with Charteris?"

"Never."

"Ever see any of his letters?"

"No."

"Well, this appears to be, from the paper, a letter written by him to some friend or other and discovered among his effects rather late in the day. Or of course it might be mere journalism."

Blount, having read it, was inclined to believe it was the latter. It ran:

". . . and that's how matters stand at present. This government will ruin the country; I've always as you know been opposed to democracy, and this perpetual succouring of those who are contributing nothing to the common sack sickens me. Emigration, I think, is the only cure, and if the powers that be would spend their dole millions in shipping unemployed youths to the Colonies. . . ."

here it broke off abruptly.

Blount turned over the sheet and frowned. "Why doesn't he write on the other side? And what does it mean anyway?"

"It's an expression of views on the conduct of the present government."

Blount looked sterner than ever. "I can see that. But what has it to do with this case or with me?"

Egerton put the sheet back in his pocket. "A good deal, I think, sir, though you'll have to take my word for that for the moment. You see, I happened to write it myself a couple of hours ago."

CHAPTER XI

"The wheel is come full circle."—*King Lear*.

I

EGERTON, having set his affairs in order thus expeditiously, decided to save time by travelling down to Four Corners that night by car, leaving the others to come down on the morning train.

"Be at the house at twelve," he told them. "I don't expect to be through before then."

The day dawned cheerless and cruel; the atmosphere, inded, was sufficiently menacing to damp the most ardent heart. The sky hung low and grim, with great banks of dark cloud rolling perpetually towards a stormy horizon; the tide was going out in sullen rage, dashing up the sand and receding with a growl of frustrated desire; over the cliffs hung a ground mist, and not a sail was visible from sky to sky. The air was dank and chill and the cold ate into the bone. On the journey from London to Little Kirbey Rosemary sat quiet and composed by a window, facing the two men; no one spoke much, but Hammond guessed, while Ambrose did not, since he was of the type that can only fathom suffering where he himself experiences love, as in the case of Blount, that her heart was troubled and tormented by the perpetual inward vision of Egerton, frail and dauntless, against those pitiless rocks, hunting inexorably for the evidence that would save his friend.

"Wouldn't like to be in his shoes," confessed the solicitor to himself, with a shiver of relief. "Or in his wife's. Sinking sand they tell me. A chance step would spell death."

Pamela Blount was waiting for them at the house, having been apprised by letter the night before. She wore black, with a touch of rose colour at the throat and wrists, and a single crimson blossom flaunting at her breast. After the gloom and despair of out-of-doors that vivid patch of colour was like a lantern. It filled the room with life, with vigour, with enchantment; it was like a fire burning lustily in a chill castle. It cheered while it delighted.

"We're rather early," said Rosemary gravely. "Scott says he won't be here till twelve."

"That's half an hour. Are you in his confidence, Mrs. Egerton?"

"Not a word. He never speaks till he's sure and can prove it."

She sat down and the men followed her example, talking desultorily. Hammond's mind was thronged by possible fantastic solutions to the puzzle, each more daring than the last; Ambrose thought of that lonely silent man in prison; Pamela's thoughts were tinged with dread; Rosemary was like a rock.

The minutes passed until the clock struck the hour, and Scott did not come. The house had fallen from a cheerful busy-ness to a terrible silence from which all four instinctively shrank. It was uncanny, this deathly stillness wrapping them about. The house, like the women's hearts, was tipetoe with apprehension. It was passionate and restless like themselves, speechless as death, fearful as death, sinister, incomprehensible. Like creatures enfolded in some strange spell they waited, unable to move, waited, straining ears perpetually, for feet that did not come. Rosemary's horror increased; she wished she had over-ruled her young husband's injunctions to stay away from the scene of inquiry; and in her mind she saw him alternately battered to pieces, that splendid, finely knit young body ground upon the rocks, or sucked slowly down by the relentless sand. At half-past twelve without warning the storm broke. The rain tore down, hurling itself with terrible ferocity against the windows, shaking the sashes with futile rage, battering on the doors, hissing down the chimneys; great hail-stones clattered against the glass, thunder shouted from one end of the sky to the other; lightning zig-zagged across the heavens; the house suddenly flashed into a sombre, creeping life; whispers muttered in the shadowy corners and the corridors echoed to the unquiet shuffle of the forgotten, unresting dead. If the silence had been maddening, this was worse; a numb horror enveloped them all. Ambrose remembered it had been said that the cliffs on which the house was built were dangerous in the extreme, and he momentarily anticipated the tilt and sway of the foundations of the building. The wind at an ill-fitting door screamed and moaned, and in the sudden silence that followed they strained, hearing their own hearts beat.

It was Ambrose who broke the silence. "At home when we have a storm like this we say the devil's dancing on the roof trying to find some cranny where he can come in."

No sooner had he spoken than there came a resounding knock on the front door. The doctor started.

"What's that?"

Rosemary answered him. "Scott, at last." The long suspense had driven every vestige of colour from her cheeks, and now she rubbed them vigorously and without shame, lest her husband should plumb the depths of her alarm.

Sanders opened the door and they could hear the young man's voice. "You'd better put this where it won't damage any carpets. No, I want that bag. What? A whisky and water presently, when I'm through."

Then the door opened and he came in. A burberry had preserved him from the worst of the storm, and he had discarded heavy rubber boots in the hall. In one hand he carried a shabby gladstone-bag that he set carefully on a mat.

"I'm a little late. It was a longer job than I'd allowed. I apologise. The bottom of the pool is sand and mud, and what I wanted was buried in it."

"But you got it?"

"Oh, yes, I got it. I came down here to get it. I've brought it up here to show you. It explains the penknife, always a difficult feature to understand." He snapped open the bag and produced a pair of boots, beautifully cut, but still showing marks of the thick, clayey mud of the district, despite their immersion of many days. They were filled with chalky stones, now softened by the action of the water. Attached to each was a long piece of stout string.

"That accounts for the missing ball," he said superfluously as he returned them to the case. "But this is what I really went to get."

He opened his hand and showed them something small and heavy, and cold, something already rusted by the effect of the water.

"What's that?" demanded Ambrose sharply, and Egerton replied:

"The revolver with which Charteris was killed."

2

"The crisis in this case," he said presently, setting down the whisky and water and leaning over the fire to get warm, "was the crumpled scrap of paper they found in Sir Gervase's room. The trouble that the police experienced existed in precisely the same degree for the defence. If he hadn't left it there, who had? The button didn't present nearly so many difficulties. I dare say you noticed that the edges of the scrap of cloth adhering to it were quite smooth. If the button had been clutched off in a struggle there'd have been a tattered shred only. So that clearly it had been deliberately clipped off. As the police showed, various people might have done that. It might have been done this end. That, in fact, is what the defence originally tried to prove. In that case it had to be cut off before Sir Gervase's departure, which means it must be done by some member of the household. You will forgive me if I am frank," he bowed to Pamela, "and remember that I am merely putting the case as it appears to the legal mind. Of the household only two members can reasonably be suspected of any interest in Charteris' death; they are yourself and Miss Martineau. It would suit the interests of both parties if Charteris were safely out of the way. So far the suspicion of the umpires was fairly evenly divided. Both suspects had been out at approximately the time of the death (he had got into his stride now, and spoke like a machine), and in neither case was there a really sound alibi. Then came the question of the button, and it was argued that it was inconceivable that Lady Blount should wish to rid herself simultaneously of her husband and of Charteris. Yet, whoever had killed him had deliberately fastened the button in his hand. The case, therefore, against Lady Blount was virtually dropped, but it continued against Miss Martineau and progressed favourably enough until the question of the scrap of paper was raised. It was suggested she had an accomplice; a clumsy way of working a murder, by the bye, and in this case quite unsupported by any facts the prosecution could elicit. All manner of theories were put forward but they all crashed against this one piece of conflicting evidence, because it was shown that no member of the household had been to London since the murder. There was, therefore (if we disregard the hypothetical and to my mind fantastic theory of a nameless accomplice), only one person who could have left that scrap of paper in Sir Gervase's flat. And that was Charteris himself."

"D'you mean," broke out the doctor incredulous and half-scornful, "the feller did it himself? The whole bag o' tricks?"

Rosemary's hand closed fiercely on his arm, silencing him. "Oh, be quiet," she breathed. "Go on, Scott."

"Starting with that idea I tried to see if the various other clues could be made to fit in with it. First of all, motive, because it was obvious that the affair was schemed to look like murder and the blame to rest upon Sir Gervase. Now, the motive was abundantly clear. I suppose it's fairly common knowledge that Charteris had involved himself on various occasions in proceedings that were actively criminal, the last known being the forging of Lady Blount's name. Miss Martineau is prepared to testify that he said on more than one occasion that he preferred death to imprisonment. We have proof of that ourselves, since Sir Gervase also heard him say it, and his word is corroborated by a maid employed at the house at that time, on the night of his visit. Moreover, he—Charteris—said something else that is profoundly illuminating. 'If I die I shall take you with me.' There are only two possible constructions to be put on such a statement. One is that he proposed to commit murder and suicide that night in his rooms. But this, we know, did not occur; he doesn't even appear to have threatened Sir Gervase with any weapon. The alternative is that he meant he would see to it that his own ruin (or death) involved his enemy. (I take it that is how he would phrase it.) And he did very nearly succeed in that. There's no doubt—if I may speak plainly, Lady Blount—that his primary cause for hating your husband was the fact that he was your husband. I'll be as impersonal as I can here, but it's delicate ground. You'll acquit me, I am sure, of deliberate offensiveness."

Pamela Blount leaned forward to say quietly, "That's quite true. That was his first reason. He could have forgiven Gervase his success and his popularity. He spoke of the matter several times, always most bitterly."

"Thank you. That was very kind. Of course, we can't dismiss the cheque as something of no importance. Obviously, it's of the first importance as decisively bringing matters to a head. Charteris believed, whether truly or not I cannot say, that Sir Gervase would get him committed to gaol and in the circumstances, and taking into consideration his own destitute position, decided on suicide."

"Guesswork?" questioned Hammond with lifted brows.

"No. You remember the matter of the envelope they couldn't find? That is to say, they found a scrap or two with a few letters on each: 'The . . .' 'Fo . . .' 'Cor . . .' 'ner,' and they took for granted that this was part of an address, this address, Four Corners, Thebeshire. But there was something else. The police agreed that the torn fragments containing the letters, 'Cor' and 'ner' roughly approximated. But only roughly, and they put this down to the torn edges of the sheet. But that wasn't thick cartridge paper that is apt to 'fray' when torn; it was smooth cream-laid paper that tears quite cleanly. And it seemed to me probable that the pieces didn't actually fit because there had been another letter between them, a letter occupying a very small space, certainly, but likely to alter the complete trend of the message."

Hammond snapped his fingers. "The letter 'O.' How infernally clever of you!"

Egerton merely nodded. "You see the effect of that, Lady Blount? By inserting an 'O' the word 'Corner' becomes 'Coroner.' The 'Th' and 'Fo' are obviously parts of 'For The . . .' The police couldn't find the rest of the address for the simple reason that there was no more address to find. Before Blount's arrival Charteris had determined to take his own life. Then his mortal enemy appears. No doubt there was a good deal of bitterness between them, and Charteris, who's acted many parts and has the dramatic instinct strongly developed, suddenly sees his chance of taking a fine revenge on both the people whom he is pleased to consider have wronged him. I especially asked Sir Gervase how long he remained in the room after the struggle that resulted in the strained wrist, and he said, 'Quite half an hour.' That was sufficient time for the plot to materialise. Charteris' quick brain—and in revenge, and particularly at the end of life, provided the mental faculties are not atrophied by sickness or disease, the brain moves with abnormal celerity—recognised that if he could apparently prove the struggle with Blount his work was half done. All the way through I've been puzzled by those small sharp scissors they found on the table. The police accounted for them by the cropped beard, but a beard of several years' growth doesn't yield so tamely. But they were precisely what a man would use if he wished to snip a button from a coat and this, I'm convinced, is what Charteris used them for. It wouldn't be hard to choose a moment when his self-imposed guest was looking the other way; in fact, Sir Gervase confessed that there were moments when his back was turned when he wondered if Charteris would try and slip a knife through his ribs. That was the foundation of the fellow's plot; the rest he could work out at leisure when his visitor was gone. He didn't run the risk of putting papers in Blount's pocket; for he knew he was dealing with a man quick enough to scent danger. But he did hide the baffling clue in a place where Blount would probably not discover it. I dare say there had been some mention of the flat in town where Sir Gervase proposed to spend the night. At all events, by striving to be ultra-intelligent, Charteris gave himself away. Had he omitted that feature he might have carried through his detestable plot. As soon as Blount left him he sheared off the beard, disposed of the ash, and began to destroy any letters that might mar his scheme. The majority were from women; any others he presumably carried away with him, as he must have carried off the letter to the coroner, and disposed of elsewhere. Then he put the confession in the hall. When I saw you yesterday"—here he turned to Hammond—"I said that if Sir Gervase had not been in communication with Charteris and had none of the fellow's letters to Lady Blount in his possession, then I thought the forgery charge against Sir Gervase would collapse. For it's significant that, except for those few letters on the torn envelope, not a scrap of Charteris' hand-writing was found in the room. So the question naturally arose as to how it's possible to forge hand-writing you've never seen. I proved the point yesterday evening, by producing some stuff in a hand as unlike Charteris' as I could contrive and showing it to Sir Gervase as another paper found among Charteris' effects, and said to be in his writing. Now, if Sir Gervase had seen Charteris hand only once he must have exclaimed, 'But that isn't his. It's utterly dissimilar.' But he didn't say a word.

"Two other small points. First, the light. It's not reasonable to suppose that Charteris inadvertently left the light on on two occasions that evening. It was done deliberately in order to attract attention to the room, first, the policeman's attention and secondly, Miss Gell's. The other point is the ring. He meant the police to take up the stand that, in fact, they did, that the body had been carried in a more or less horizontal position through the garden. That's why there were stains on the handkerchief—stains of rust from the bolts on the long disused doors. And he left the ring in an obvious position to attract further attention. No doubt he himself brought back the scrap of mud."

"From the garden, of course. I wondered why it was so thickly plastered with leaves," broke in Hammond.

"Exactly. There were two other features that had perplexed me from the outset—taken separately, that is—and they were the ball of string and the penknife. Now, it was easy enough to picture the murderer taking the string if he had occasion to bind his victim's feet or anything of that sort, but the only signs of string were the tied cuffs, and that was very fine twine. But following up my thesis of Charteris as his own murderer then I put two and two together—that is, the string and the knife—and found they made as clear a four as ever I came upon. That collection of rubbish in his pocket struck me as odd; a man who carefully destroys the tabs of his clothing, his letters and any papers by which he might be identified is not likely to burden himself by useless lumber. The matchbox could be explained by his need for a light. He'd been down here once before, taking much the same route, but all the same he'd need some sort of illumination to make his way down that cliff. It seemed clear that Charteris had taken nothing with him that he would not expressly want, and the only *raison d'être* of the knife that I could see was the string. Then I thought of the boots. He didn't change these until he was actually on the ledge; he couldn't even have managed the descent in those found on his feet. There was a large nail in one boot that must have raised an ugly sore on the sole of the foot, but there wasn't a mark on the body. So I concluded that having crawled down as Ambrose and I did he carefully lowered the boots by the string in to the water beneath. You'll remember, Ambrose, the ledge was scattered with stones, but there were none on the cliff-top so the boots couldn't have been weighted there. It was a moonlight night, so he could see to some extent what he was doing; but even if they'd missed the water they'd probably have been taken by the sand. However, he didn't want to run any risks. You'll see that one piece of string is much longer than the other, because he didn't dare keep a scrap of string in his pockets lest his deception be unmasked and his revenge denied him. He would have been wiser to pitch the knife after the boots, but apparently that didn't occur to him. A re-examination of the cliff-side confirmed me in my view. You'll remember, Ambrose, my pointing out to you a certain shrub that had been practically uprooted by some weight quite recently. Your suggestion was that the body had struck it in its fall, but had it done that it would have missed the ledge altogether, deflecting its course and pitching clear on to the rocks. The only other explanation was that it had been used as a step by some one climbing down the face of the cliff. Then there was the noteworthy fact that in spite of the fall and the thorny nature of the surroundings, the face and body showed no marks of bruising, which must have been inevitable if he had fallen there by his own weight. The last part of the affair was the most ticklish. Charteris knew, of course, that when a man shoots himself the weapon drops automatically out of his hand. How often have you heard of the gun being found in the dead man's hold? Never, probably. So he arranged himself in that extraordinary attitude, lying on his face with one arm stretched over the abyss. So that as soon as the shot was fired the revolver would drop by its own weight into the pool below. It was all very neatly done and was nearly successful. But it fell just short of genius."

"An infinite capacity for taking pains? Seems to me he took a deuce of a lot of pains. Where did he go wrong?"

"In taking the string; in not concealing the knife; in forgetting to allow for the bruises and cuts; in leaving the paper in the flat and the ring in the garden; in choosing a night when Sir Gervase was in town. It would have been simpler to hang about the place waiting for some evening when he was out and about on his property. It's well known that he often goes for long walks in the evening, walks when he probably meets no one. The soundest part of his scheme was the button. But I suppose he could hardly be expected to foresee everything. It was less a question of his making mistakes than of the other side displaying sufficient imagination to view the matter from his criminally distorted angle. In the end it's simply another of those crimes of passion to which there is no end."

As he stopped speaking there was a long silence that no one dared break. Rosemary still stared into the fire. She knew that anything in the nature of sympathy or pity would be intolerable. Pamela Blount was rigid and pale; Ambrose fidgeted; Hammond looked meaningly at Egerton.

The young man rose.

"I have to support an amendment on this new Agricultural Bill at five-thirty," he said, "and I think we should be getting back now. Rosemary'll drive me. Can we give you a lift, Hammond? I've promised to leave

this evidence"—he touched the bag with his foot—
"with the local authorities, who will get into touch
with Scotland Yard."

Pamela Blount rose and gave him her hand. He took
it and for that instant she divined that he also knew
the agony of suspense, the terror, the self-accusation,
the wild beauty of love that stormed so eagerly through
her passionate blood. The instant of mutual betrayal
passed and they were once more cool, detached, remote.

For some time after leaving the house the Egertons
travelled in silence.

"Well?" demanded Rosemary suddenly, "what are
you thinking of? Lady Blount and Sir Gervase?"

Egerton shook his head. "No need. People who
care for one another like that can stand on their own
feet. No, I was wondering whether the Opposition
realise that if they defeat this amendment of ours
they'll bring chaos crashing down on the agricultural
industry."

Rosemary sighed. "Oh, Scott, are you never tired?"

He laughed oddly. "Your insatiable energy would
shame any mere fatigue of mine," he answered.
"Tired? Of course I'm not. You can never be tired of
people. In politics or in crime they're too madly interesting."

>>> If you've enjoyed this book and would like to discover more great vintage crime and thriller titles, as well as the most exciting crime and thriller authors writing today, visit: >>>

The Murder Room
Where Criminal Minds Meet

themurderroom.com